FIELD OF FIRE

A Jackson Payne Thriller

JEREMY WALDRON

ALSO BY JEREMY WALDRON

The Samantha Bell Mystery Series

Dead and Gone to Bell

Bell Hath No Fury

Bloody Bell

Bell to Pay

Burn in Bell

Mad as Bell

All Bell Breaks Loose

To Bell and Back

Never miss a new release. Sign up for Jeremy Waldron's New
Releases Newsletter at JeremyWaldron.com

CHAPTER ONE

IT WAS FIVE MINUTES BEFORE MIDNIGHT ON A COOL January night, and Viper was nearly out of cigarettes.

The white contrails of smoke slithered up and around his fingers as Viper sat debating whether to kill himself or the two women who lived up the street. Each choice had its merits, but only one of them would end things tonight.

Tucked beneath his left arm was a Sig Sauer semi-automatic 9MM pistol and, with it, a desire to protect and defend everything he held dear to his heart. But death by bullet was so cliché. If he went down tonight, it would not be because he swallowed his own gun.

Viper grinned at the thought as he checked his mirrors.

Though the streets were quiet—the weather too cold for people to want to be outside—he was a little paranoid about the neighborhood watch. If he sat too much longer, he would certainly make someone a little more than suspicious.

Holding his cigarette near the window, Viper cast his gaze forward and was once again thinking about the mother and child he was here to murder.

It wasn't like the two women deserved to die. Not like

him, at least. They'd done nothing to earn an early exit, but he certainly had. That was what had Viper most angry. He was here, debating his future, not because it was his choice, but because others had forced his hand.

He was running out of options, and Viper wasn't sure he was ready to give it all up. Though he had little to look forward to after some recent life-changing news, Viper also wasn't one to go down without a fight. He just never imagined this would be how it ended.

He closed his eyes and brought his hand to his face, thinking about his tremendous loss and how this hadn't been his year. If only things had worked out differently. If only his decisions had worked out in his favor. *If only...*

At some point in the last sixteen months, the world had turned on him and, because of that, he had spent most of the year going against the current. Now, it was his chance to correct course and ride his white horse to a new and brighter horizon.

He pulled the last drag from his smoke into his lungs and flicked the cigarette butt out the window. As soon as it hit the pavement, sparks flew in all directions. Viper watched until the last ember burned out, then lit a single match and watched the flame flicker until he knew exactly what he had to do.

CHAPTER TWO

I GENTLY CLOSED THE CAR DOOR AND LOOKED OVER MY shoulder. The air was still, besides a few neighbor dogs barking. I headed for my front door, determined to get this visit over with. As I walked along the hedge, the motion sensor light flicked on and I lowered my eyes away from the glare.

At the front door, I checked the time on my digital wristwatch. Ten minutes after midnight; the reason I suspected all the house lights were off inside. I used my key to open the front door, thankful my wife hadn't yet taken that away from me too, and hurried to the opposite wall to punch in the security code before waking up my wife and daughter.

It wasn't like I wanted to sneak into my own home, but I also didn't want either of them—or anyone else, for that matter—to know I was here. As badly as it hurt, I didn't have the heart to tell Selina how bad things had gotten between me and her mom, though something told me Ilene had already broken the news to our daughter.

I passed through the kitchen, smelling tonight's dinner still lingering in the air, and made my way to my old work study, trying my best to ignore all the familiar scents of home.

It proved to be impossible and, as hard as it was for me to push down the pain of knowing it was all over, I stepped inside the small home office and closed the door behind me, before flicking on the overhead light.

The study had always been my refuge—the one place in the house I could come to escape. Whether it be to watch a football game alone, or to quietly review case files, it had always been my space.

But not anymore.

Ilene had moved things around and the desk no longer looked like mine. That too had hurt, but again, I ignored everything I was feeling as I grabbed a few important items from the drawer, stuffing bank statements and personal documents into a manila folder, when I discovered Ilene's notes on our divorce.

I stopped to read them and felt my heart break—again. But mostly I was just angry.

Did she know I would come for my papers? It wouldn't surprise me in the least.

Ilene was my high school sweetheart and the mother of my child, and now the person calling it quits on our marriage. It was her idea; one of the few I wholeheartedly disagreed with. Though she was one of the smartest people I knew, this decision wasn't.

How could she? I thought, unable to keep myself from reading over her notes.

As much as I wanted to pass the blame, I knew it was mostly my fault. I was a tough sonofabitch, but when it came to fighting my wife, Ilene always won. I didn't want to have to fight her. Not on this. And certainly not with our daughter watching.

I left the study and made my way up the stairs to my daughter's bedroom door. I just needed to see her one last time before it all went to shit. Gently, I opened it. Selina was sound asleep. I smiled. Her breaths were as harmless as the day she was born. Seventeen years had gone by in a flash, and it broke my heart to know it all came down to this.

Feeling like I had let her down too, I walked to the edge of her bed and bent down to kiss my baby's head, whispering, "I'm sorry for what I'm about to do, sweetheart—" Tears welled up in my eyes as I clamped down on my knuckles with my teeth, attempting to hold it together but knowing there was nothing I could do to stop myself. "But Daddy doesn't have a choice. It's over."

CHAPTER THREE

IT HAD BEEN NEARLY THIRTY MINUTES SINCE VIPER HAD made his decision. Now that the first gallon of gasoline had been poured and the gas stove knobs turned on, he was on his way to Ilene's bedroom to finish the job.

He set the gasoline can down on the wooden floor outside the door and peeked his head inside the master bedroom. Ilene lay on her side, hand tucked beneath her ear, sound asleep. Viper glanced at her bedside table and noticed the sleep meds at her side.

There was nothing waking her now.

He made his way to the bed—the opposite side from where Ilene slept—and opened the top drawer of the bedside table. Inside was a carved wooden box and, when Viper opened the lid, his eyes landed on an extremely rare hand gun. The 1847 Walker Colt.

He took the gun into his gloved hand and marveled at the weight. Over four pounds of muscle—an old weapon that packed a serious punch.

Was she planning to sell this?

Viper knew, if sold correctly, it would fetch a pretty penny.

With little time to spare, he put the gun back into its box, closed the lid, and tucked it under his arm. He fetched the gasoline can from the hallway and continued pouring the remaining gasoline around Ilene's bed, down the hallway, and past Selina's room. There was just enough to take him outside —to the backyard—where he could light it at a safe distance, knowing the explosion would come fast.

Viper took one last look at the house before he lit a match and tossed it onto the accelerant. The flames caught quickly and, in a flash, a bright red dragon's tail slithered into the house. Then he ran to his car, still holding onto the Walker Colt, and left the scene as bright orange flames licked up the outside walls and black smoke rose into the night sky. Then, the entire house was engulfed in an orange ball of fire.

CHAPTER FOUR

THE NEXT MORNING, I WOKE TO THE SOUND OF SOMEONE beating on my front door. It took me a moment to realize what it was. I had little choice but to get up.

The leather couch stuck to my bare back as I rolled onto my side and reached for my cellphone to check the time. Twenty minutes past nine a.m. and two missed calls. I was having my doubts I'd be able to take the day off.

Another rap on the door, the pounding certainly getting more aggressive. I turned and looked around, attempting to recall the night before. Then I remembered what I had done as I rubbed my face and swung my feet to the floor.

"Jackson, wake up. I know you're home," the voice called from outside.

I knew who it was, and suspected why he was here. What frustrated me most was that he wouldn't go away until he got what he came for.

Standing, I hiked up my jeans and lazily walked beneath the low ceilings of the basement apartment I was currently renting and opened the door with little thought. Wyatt Blackwell stood there with a quirked brow.

"Jesus, you look like shit," he said.

I pushed my fingers through my thick black hair and caught remnants of a scent that had me pausing to smell the tips of my fingers.

Wyatt, who I knew simply as Tex, leaned forward and sniffed my right shoulder. "Smell like it, too."

I stared down at my bare chest and thought about taking a shower. Instead, I turned around and went back to sitting on the couch. Tex closed the door and followed me into the small living room I called home. There was only one couch, and it wasn't big enough for both of us. Taking a cigarette from the pack, I stuck it between my lips and sparked it up. Tossing the lighter into my Stetson, I leaned back and closed my eyes.

Tex said, "I thought you quit."

I kept my eyes as closed as my ears, enjoying the light-headedness the nicotine offered, when I heard Tex pick up my unsigned divorce papers. I didn't have to look to know the reaction on his face.

"Did you talk to her?"

"It's too late," I said.

Tex set the papers down onto the messy coffee table and said, "I hate to be the bearer of more bad news, but I thought you'd like to know."

I opened one eye and raised the same eyebrow as I inhaled a deep pull.

"The jury acquitted Raymond Frank."

My other eye opened and I leaned forward. Today was the day Raymond Frank should have been going to prison —the reason I requested the day off. Accused of murdering his wife to be with his much younger girlfriend, I knew from the beginning the case relied too heavily on eyewitnesses instead of scientific evidence. Now I knew I was right. The state prosecutor convinced me — convinced us all — otherwise, and I was certain to receive the blowback.

"Frank's guilty," I said. "He knows it. I know it. Hell, we all know it."

Tex knew it too. He smoothed his hand down his silk tie, and said, "Out-bought. Out-thought. I'm sorry, partner. It's just the way it is."

CHAPTER FIVE

I T MIGHT HAVE BEEN THE WAY IT WAS, BUT IT WASN'T HOW
it was meant to work. Raymond Frank murdered his wife, and
the only reason he was a free man was because he was worth a
fortune. I told Tex all about how Frank had inherited a trea-
sure from his oil tycoon grandfather, and Tex nodded and
listened, like he didn't already know the story. I was preaching
to the choir. Tex knew it as well—if not better—than I did. I
was just glad Tex didn't represent Frank himself—then we'd
really have something to talk about.

"Would you like me to talk to Ilene?" Tex asked, staring at
my divorce papers.

"What's there to talk about?"

"Maybe I can convince her to sit on this just a little while
longer?"

"You know Ilene as well as I do; when she makes up her
mind, there's no changing it."

My cellphone rang. When I saw who was calling, I questioned whether I should answer. All I needed was this one
day, twenty-four hours away from the job to clear my head—if

there ever was such an opportunity as a deputy sheriff in the Travis County Homicide Bureau.

Tex said, "You want me to answer that?"

I reached for my phone. Not because I wanted to see what the call was about, but because I knew Tex wouldn't shut up until I did.

"Payne," I answered.

"Jackson, where are you?"

I lifted my gaze to Tex. It was my Sergeant, Ty Hart, and it sounded urgent.

"What can I do for you, Sergeant?"

"It's your wife." Hart paused between breaths and I knew he was making the call he didn't want to have to make. "Is she with you?"

I felt every muscle inside me flex, but I remained quiet. I reached for my smoke and avoided Tex's judgmental gaze. "What about my wife?"

Hart said, "There's been a fire. A big one. I'm here now. It's your house, Jackson. Everything is gone."

CHAPTER SIX

TEX ASKED ME WHAT HAPPENED, BUT I DIDN'T HAVE TIME to explain. I gathered my things, tossing everything inside my hat, and picked up a shirt off the floor on my way to the door. I jammed my feet into my boots and ran to my car.

"Jackson, what is it? What happened?" Tex chased after me.

I told him to get inside. He climbed into the passenger seat of my '87 Toyota Land Cruiser and barely had the door shut by the time I sped off.

I kept one hand on the steering wheel and palmed my cellphone with the other. I dialed the home line and, when it went straight to voicemail, I called Ilene's cell. Again, it went to voicemail. I punched the steering wheel as hard as I could and stomped on the gas pedal, lurching my old engine forward.

Tex clung to the grab handle when he said, "Jackson, talk to me. What happened to Ilene?"

I took the turn a little too wide and nearly collided with a compact sedan. The tires squealed and Tex cursed. I knew I could drive fast, but wasn't sure if the old car would hold up in the race to my house.

When I didn't answer Tex's question, he assumed it was bad. "What about Selina; is she all right?"

I glanced out the corner of my eye and felt my chest swell with angered worry. With my cellphone in hand, I tried Selina's number. She didn't answer either, but that didn't stop me from trying again. And again.

"Jackson, watch out!" Tex grabbed the wheel and yanked hard to the right, saving us from another near collision.

My heart was knocking hard in my chest, my mind on my family. It was a miracle we arrived at my house in one piece. Neither of us could believe our eyes.

There was a giant gap in the trees where my house once stood, and the destruction was incredible. Tex muttered his disbelief as I skidded to a stop.

Fire trucks and emergency personnel were on the scene, but nothing seemed urgent. Their work—and the show—appeared to be over.

I kicked open my door and ran to the house, flipping over smoldering timber and hot metal. There was nothing left. I looked to where the garage had once stood and saw only the remnants of Ilene's car. It, too, had been caught in the inferno.

Then I caught sight of something Selina would never leave behind. Walking over hot ash, I moved toward it, wondering how in the world I had seen it at all. Covered in black soot, a metal corner shined in the daylight. When I crouched to pick it up, I felt my throat close.

It was the compass rose pendant necklace I had gifted Selina on her sixteenth birthday, the one Selina hadn't taken off since. She wore it everywhere. Had things changed? With the prospect of divorce, anything was possible. Even worse was knowing that surviving a fire like this was damn near impossible.

CHAPTER SEVEN

I WAS STILL CROUCHED WITH MY HEAD HANGING TO MY chest when Tex came up alongside me and set his big hand between my shoulders.

"I'm sorry, Jackson," he said. "This is just terrible."

I tightened my grip around Selina's pendant, determined to forge my sadness into anger. It wasn't hard for me to do. In a matter of hours, it seemed like I had lost everything, but I never expected this.

"Jackson, I hate to even ask, but is it possible Ilene set this fire herself?"

I watched the smoke rise from the ashes as I mulled over Tex's question. Ilene could be as hot headed as anybody, but she wasn't the vindictive type.

I said, "No. This fire was meant for me."

I turned my head and looked into Tex's dark eyes. He knew what I was thinking. That Raymond Frank could be responsible for sending an obvious message that he couldn't be touched.

"It's possible, right?" I said.

Tex said, "Why take the risk? He's a free man."

I stood and caught Sergeant Hart across the street, speaking to my neighbor, Pam Johnston. He nodded his head as Pam made wide gestures with her hands.

Pam was a wild card, someone who had made it clear on several occasions, that she didn't like me. I wondered what she had to say about all this, and what, if anything, she might have seen last night.

Pam was the only one on the street who had an unobstructed view of our house, but I wasn't about to speak to her myself. She'd made herself perfectly clear, long ago, that I wasn't someone who could be trusted to keep our neighborhood safe. Maybe she was right, but I wasn't about to admit that to her now.

Hart turned his head and, when we locked eyes, I met him halfway to see what else he knew. Hart asked again if Ilene and Selina were home last night. I knew Selina was home just past midnight, but they could have left before the fire. Hart sighed. "Christ, Jackson. I'm so sorry."

I turned back to the rubble and squeezed Selina's pendant a little tighter. I didn't know what to do, but I swore my revenge upon whoever was responsible.

"We're working on collecting statements from neighbors, though many were sleeping at the time the fire began."

I nodded, still assessing the damage myself.

"There is a chance your neighbor's home security system picked up how it started. Though we might have to get a warrant before she decides to hand it over."

Home security system? That surprised me. I didn't realize Pam had installed one. But it also surprised me to hear Pam was putting up a fight. It made little sense. I turned and looked Hart in the eye.

"Personal liberties." Hart shrugged it off as if it was all too common of a fight.

That's when I saw arson investigator Sean "Smitty" Smith

arrive. He was one of Austin's best. If anybody could figure out how the fire started, it would be him.

I told Hart to keep me in the loop. He left me alone with my thoughts. I watched him catch up with Smitty on what happened. I had the feeling I was being watched.

I turned and found Pam perched on her front porch, glaring, making me feel uneasy. There was a look in her eyes that made me think she knew more than she was saying. I wondered what that secret was. I thought about asking her a few questions but, instead, headed to my car.

When Tex saw me leaving, he called out, "What, are you going to just leave me behind?"

"I'll catch up with you later," I said.

"Where are you going?"

"There's someone I need to talk to."

CHAPTER EIGHT

I CALLED ILENE'S SISTER, CAROLINE, IN MONTANA AND left a message asking her to call me back. I wasn't looking forward to having that conversation. Caroline didn't think too fondly of me, never had, and I was certain as soon as she heard what had happened today, she'd blame me for our house burning down.

When I arrived at the Central Command Unit of the Travis County Sheriff's Office, a handful of local city reporters greeted me, all champing at the bit to get a piece of me.

I parked my Cruiser in the back and stepped out to a light drizzle with temperatures promising to rise into the mid-fifties. I was still in a daze, thinking about what had happened between last night and this morning. Though I didn't have any evidence to back up my claim, I still thought the fire was meant to kill me.

"Deputy Payne."

When I heard my name being called, I stopped and turned to face crime beat reporter, Vincent Cruz. He rushed

over to me and accidentally stepped on my boot. I looked
down and he backed off.

Cruz asked, "Care to comment on Raymond Frank's
acquittal?"

"No, I don't."

"Are you surprised the jury sided with him?"

I stared and said nothing.

"The district attorney went into trial sounding confident
the city would get a conviction." Cruz held my eye and, when
I didn't respond, he said, "You want to know what I think?"

"Not particularly."

"I think the prosecution relied too heavily on
eyewitnesses."

I stepped forward and said, "The thing about people like
Frank is they don't stop. He might have got off this time, but
next time—and there is *always* a next time—we'll get him."

Cruz grinned. "Should I tell him you said that?"

"Tell him whatever you want." I brushed past Cruz and
caught Deputy Emily Sanchez at the door.

Sanchez said, "He thinks we're still withholding
information."

"Are we?"

"That was your case. You tell me?"

We worked our way back to Homicide. Sanchez must
have noticed I wasn't feeling myself, because she said, "You
did everything in your power to make sure the jury saw Frank
for who he was. We lost to money. Simple as that."

I wasn't so sure, but I muttered my thanks regardless.

"Oh," Sanchez turned to warn me, "heads up. I heard
Moreno got off his suspension early."

As if my morning didn't have enough bad news already, I
now had to deal with the fallout of Deputy Tom Moreno.

CHAPTER NINE

I THOUGHT ABOUT STOPPING AT MY DESK AND CATCHING UP on missed messages, but that wasn't why I was here. Needing to cool off, I got myself a coffee from the break room and headed toward Deputy Chief Matt David's office.

The only good that came from having Tom Moreno back was how it redirected my anger away from my family and back to him.

I couldn't believe it.

If what Sanchez said was true, it was another example of failed justice.

I was oh for two—oh for three if I counted my house burning—and desperately needed to get back on a winning streak.

I kept my eyes forward as I weaved my way through the department. I couldn't stop thinking about Moreno and almost wished I would bump into him so I had someone to unload on.

Moreno was the type of cop who gave us all a bad rep. I was certain he was done for. What he did should have warranted a longer suspension from Internal Affairs, perhaps even his termination. I wondered whose ass he had kissed, and what strings they pulled to get his badge and gun back.

But why was Cruz here asking me about Frank when he should be here to report on Moreno's incident of excessive force?

I rounded the corner and, when I saw Moreno leaving the deputy chief's office, I couldn't believe my eyes.

CHAPTER TEN

WHAT WERE THEY DISCUSSING?

When Moreno turned around, he eyed me and flashed a grin that made my blood boil. He knew he'd gotten off with only a slap on the wrist—and knew that there was nothing I could do about it.

I followed him with my eyes until he disappeared into the next room. I wanted nothing more than to use him as a human punching bag. Maybe then I'd begin to feel like I wasn't personally responsible for everything that had happened in the last twenty-four hours. Instead, I walked into David's office, questioning the integrity of the department.

David said, "Close the door, Jackson."

I shut the door and took a seat.

David gave me a cock-eyed look and said, "Before you jump to conclusions about IA's decision to drop Moreno's suspension, let me be absolutely clear when reminding you that the suspension could have easily been yours."

He didn't really mean that, did he? Though I whole-heartedly disagreed with the deputy chief's assessment, I kept my mouth shut, knowing nothing good would come from trying to defend myself. We held each other's stare for a moment before David continued, "I heard what happened at your house. Have you been able to reach your wife?"

"It doesn't look good," I said.

David broke eye contact and frowned. "When was the last time you spoke to either of them?"

Thinking about my visit last night and what I had said to my sleeping daughter just before I kissed her head for what might have been the last time, it occurred to me I might already be on the department's list of suspects.

Avoiding the question altogether, I said, "I intend to catch whoever is responsible."

"I'm sure you would, however, I can't have you working the case."

I knew I shouldn't be surprised, but I was. "Chief, you can't keep me out of this. It's my family we're talking about."

"You're too close to it."

Sure, there was a conflict of interest, but no one cared more than I did.

"Until we have proof this is a homicide, I'm ordering you to stay clear."

I sat back and tightened my grip on the armchair until I heard the wood splinter. It was then I realized I better keep my theory of this being an attempted hit on me to myself.

"Maybe take some personal time off?" David suggested. "Just a couple of days to get your affairs in order."

"Thanks, but I'm not interested."

"Jackson, I really can't have you anywhere near this case."

"My wife and daughter were everything to me," I said as I stood and turned to the door.

"Deputy?"

I stopped before turning to face him, and noted that he hadn't referred to me as deputy detective.

"Let the investigators do their job. I'll notify you as soon as we find anything."

CHAPTER ELEVEN

THERE WAS NO WAY I WAS GOING TO STAND DOWN. NOT even Deputy Chief Matt David could stop me from finding out what happened. This case was personal. Since I couldn't prove Ilene or Selina were actually killed, I had to start believing they were still alive.

But if they were, where could they have gone? And how did this fire start? Was it intentionally set like I thought it might have been? I questioned it all as I moved through the squad room before catching Moreno at his desk.

He was leaning back in his chair, on the phone. I didn't know what he was talking about, or who he was speaking to, but I made sure he didn't see me coming. I took the receiver out of his hand and killed the call with my finger.

Moreno jumped to his feet and barked, "What the hell do you think you're doing, Payne?"

He stood an inch taller and had several pounds on me, but I benefited from muscle and flexibility, two characteristics I knew he didn't have. If it came down to it, it would be a good fight, but I was certain I would win.

"Where were you last night?" I asked.

Moreno squinted and got a funny look on his face. He said, "Are you still upset about me beating the shit out of that scumbag?"

"I don't care that you kicked the dirt bag's ass," I said. "What I care about is how you lied about it."

Moreno almost laughed, but he knew better than to do that in front of me. He must have seen the look in my eyes, because I wasn't in a joking kind of mood. I said, "Makes me wonder what else you've lied about."

"Look, Payne," Moreno held up his right hand, "I've paid my dues. It's time you let whatever grudge you have against me go."

"You should have revised your statement when I gave you the chance."

"I've owned my mistake."

"Have you?" He gave me a knowing look, but I begged to differ. I said, "One more mistake and you're through. They won't let you back in, and trust me when I say there *will* be a next time."

Moreno latched onto his waist as he stared me down. I was already walking away when he said, "I was only doing my job, Jackson. Which is exactly what you should be doing."

I stopped, turned, and faced him. He never called me by my first name. *What was that about?*

Moreno raised both his eyebrows when he said, "You're going to have to try a lot harder than that to end my career."

CHAPTER TWELVE

VINCENT CRUZ WAS WAITING FOR ME OUTSIDE. HE LOOKED hopeful I might be ready to talk about Raymond Frank. I wasn't. Instead, I told him, "I'm not your story, and neither is Raymond Frank."

"Are you sure about that, Detective?"

"You're close, though. The story you're looking for and should report is here, inside that building. His name is Tom Moreno."

"Are you throwing another detective under the bus?"

"You didn't hear it from me," I said, walking to the Cruiser.

Once inside, I left the parking lot and circled the block, waiting to see what came of Cruz and Moreno. Something told me Moreno wouldn't be pushing papers for too much longer and he'd need to get out. He was like me, started out as a beat cop working the streets, and the streets were where we wanted to stay.

I pulled out my pack of smokes and lit one up. As I smoked, I couldn't stop thinking about Moreno and how nobody but me seemed to care that he lied about beating the shit out of a suspect. It felt like such a huge injustice to have him back on the job after being caught in a lie. But worse, it seemed as if the news cycle had moved on from him and swung over to the trial I had let slip away.

My cell rang. It was the arson investigator, Sean Smith.

"Smitty. Talk to me."

"Jackson, you sitting down?"

My brow pinched. "What did you find?"

"It's preliminary," he said, mentioning how Hart told him to call me, "but there were definite traces of accelerant found."

My vision tunneled with memories of Ilene and Selina at my side as Smitty said something about how the fire burned intensely hot and extremely quickly. He was giving me more details than I needed and, when I didn't respond, he asked, "You still with me?"

I said I was. Then I asked the question I wasn't sure I was ready for. "Did you find anything to suggest my family got caught in the fire?"

It felt like I waited forever for his response. Then Smitty said, "No."

I breathed a sigh of relief, continuing to hold on to hope they were still alive. It would be a miracle, but I still didn't know where they could have gone. Was Ilene planning to leave, knowing I wasn't ready to sign the divorce papers? Anything was possible, but if she had left, what car did she take?

When I lifted my head, I saw Moreno exit the building. He headed straight for his patrol vehicle—a Ford Police Interceptor with the Travis County sheriff's emblem on the side. I looked for Cruz, but he wasn't anywhere in sight. Where did that little weasel go?

Smitty continued breaking down the report. "But, like I said, Jackson, the fire burned extremely hot. In cases like this, intentionally set fires are a common method to disguise a homicide."

CHAPTER THIRTEEN

VIPER GOT INTO HIS VEHICLE AND CLOSED THE DOOR. HE started the engine, pulled the seatbelt across his chest, and began scanning the radio for the latest news reports. There was weather, sports, the latest happening in national politics, but not one mention of last night's fire.

He lifted his head, asking himself if it was just that no one cared, or that word hadn't yet spread about whose house had burned down? Either scenario suited him just fine. It was all good news to Viper.

The beginning of the end, he thought.

It bought him time to see if the fallout would warrant Jackson Payne's own department to look into him as a possible suspect. He certainly hoped so. But, if not, he'd nudge them closer to the truth.

Viper backed out and turned onto the main drag with hopes that he'd done his job well enough to have the fire destroy any trace evidence of him being the one who had started it. He was certain he had. After all, he was a professional who knew the system inside and out.

As for Jackson's wife and daughter, well, no body meant no murder.

Viper grinned, knowing that the unknown was ten times worse than the truth.

Psychological warfare could kill a man faster than even a perfectly planned murder, all without lifting a finger.

Viper grinned. He felt his power growing.

"Don't get too cocky," he reminded himself as he drove through the city. "There is still a lot more work to do."

He was feeling good about being back on the streets, even better about being a free man. A man born to do as he pleased. And if last night's incident didn't bring Jackson to his knees, Viper had a surprise waiting. He planned to deploy it all in due time.

He chuckled as he reached for his cellphone and was about to make a call when he noticed a light colored SUV following him two cars behind. He dropped the phone onto his lap, thinking that perhaps he was getting ahead of himself, when he said, "Let the games begin."

CHAPTER FOURTEEN

MORENO WAS WEAVING IN AND OUT OF TRAFFIC AS I fought to keep up. I wasn't certain he saw me following. But there wasn't anything else to explain his hurry.

I followed him as best as my Cruiser could, but it didn't handle the way our sheriff vehicles could. As for where Moreno was going, it was anybody's guess. There were only two possibilities to what happened to Ilene and Selina, and something told me that maybe Moreno knew more than he was saying.

Then Moreno did something I didn't expect. He cut across two lanes of traffic and took a hard right turn onto the highway offramp.

I tapped the brakes, pulled behind a pickup truck going far too slowly, and impatiently honked my horn for him to speed up. Once off the highway, I struggled to decide which direction Moreno went. I looked left, then right. Thankfully, the traffic was light, and I could spot him only a few blocks north.

I shifted gears and begged my Cruiser to go faster as I sped after him. Moreno wasn't going as fast as he was on the highway, but I struggled to make up for lost time. I couldn't lose him. Not now, and certainly not when I thought there was a chance he knew how the fire had started.

As soon as I had closed the gap between us, I hit another roadblock. Moreno drove through an intersection just as I watched the light turn yellow. I revved the engine and pushed my car to go quicker. Moreno was going to get away. The engine whined as I sped faster. I knew I wasn't going to make it, but I kept my foot on the gas pedal, regardless.

When the light turned red, I tucked my chin and said a quick prayer.

A horn blared and tires squealed. I quickly checked the mirrors to make sure everyone was safe. They were, and so was I. Then my cell buzzed with an incoming text message.

I had Moreno in my sights. He must have seen me, because he slowed down. Keeping one eye on the road, I read the text from Sergeant Hart saying Pam still wouldn't give us access to her video files without a warrant.

"Shit," I said, lifting my head, realizing where Moreno was leading me.

It didn't surprise me Pam refused to cooperate. She was there for her neighbors when they needed her, just not when it came to threatening her civil liberties.

There must have been something she was hiding—something good caught on the cameras. But it also occurred to me that she could be doing it to protect me.

Moreno slowed to a stop, and so did I.

We were now in the Westlake Highlands neighborhood, and when he parked in front of County Judge Kevin Brown's house, I knew Deputy Chief David had sent him to retrieve the warrant we were all hoping to get. Moreno wanted me to know it, too.

I called Tex from the side of the road. When he answered, I said, "There's a problem. We need to talk."

CHAPTER FIFTEEN

I MET TEX AT A COUNTRY MUSIC BAR, CREEK HOUSE, ON the south side of the city. It was fifteen minutes past one p.m., and a dozen or so people were at the bar eating lunch.

Tex was sitting at a back table working, when I slid into the booth across from him. He leaned back and never mentioned that I left him at my house to find his own way back to his car. I didn't ask for details. Instead, he asked me, "Need a drink?"

I shook my head, said, "The deputy chief thinks I did it."

Tex didn't react, but I could see the questions that reflected in his eyes.

I told him what I had just learned, what Smitty discovered about the fire, adding, "They haven't ruled out a homicide."

"But it hasn't been determined there was one, either."

Neither of us knew where Ilene and Selina could have gone. Tex didn't want to admit they might have been murdered any more than I did, but I could see it in his eyes. He knew, and so did I. Ilene and Selina were dead.

Tex sipped his whiskey, and I watched his jaw tighten just

before he asked, "Are you still thinking Frank might have done this?"

"Maybe."

"Who else have you pissed off to want to go after your family?"

It was a serious question that deserved to be explored. The list was long, and I already had a few names working their way to the top. Moreno. Frank. Apparently, according to Tex, Ilene, too. But instead of naming names, I told Tex why I asked to meet with him.

I said, "They're going after the neighbor's surveillance video."

"Is that a problem?"

"I was at the house last night."

"Jesus, Jackson—"

I knew he wouldn't take the news well. Judging by his reaction, the deputy chief wouldn't either, once he learned I kept that very important fact from him, too.

"If Pam Johnston has a security camera, like I'm told she does, I'm certain I was caught on it. I'd be surprised if I wasn't."

Tex leaned forward and spoke in a soft whisper. "And what exactly will they see you doing?"

"Nothing criminal," I said, thinking about how Moreno was going to use this to end my career.

Tex was a man who worked with facts, had an appreciation for sticking it to the justice system—which he believed was deeply flawed. Not that I couldn't agree with his viewpoint, but we worked opposite sides of the same playing field, and my case was no exception.

"On the bright side," Tex said, "hopefully the cameras can help explain how the fire started."

I had thought that, too. I said, "What if Raymond Frank

burned down the house as some sort of payback? He's the vindictive type to do something like this."

"Give it time. Let this play out before jumping to conclusions."

"I'm not sure I have the patience for it."

"If Frank is responsible, he would have had to plan this before today's verdict."

"Maybe that's exactly what he did. Maybe he was like the rest of us and thought he was going to be convicted? And maybe he planned it to happen the same day he thought his future would be decided for him?"

Tex stared into his drink and sighed. "That's a lot of maybes."

I asked, "Does Frank know we're friends?"

Tex looked me in the eye and said, "Raymond Frank knows everything."

"Then let's see if he knows about this."

CHAPTER SIXTEEN

TEX PASSED ALONG FRANK'S INFORMATION. I RECOGNIZED the address from my own files. It was the quickest way of finding him, but also perhaps the most dangerous. I stuffed the piece of paper into my pocket when Tex caught someone staring at us from the bar.

Tex said to me, "We're being watched."

I turned my head and looked.

"That we are," I said, scooting out from the table.

"Let me know how it goes," Tex said about my meeting with Frank.

I told him I would, and then made my way over to Alan Bolin, an ex-cop, who seemed surprised to see me. Bolin said by way of greeting, "I didn't take you for a day drinker."

"Depends what's being served," I said, shaking his hand. "What brings you here?"

Bolin raised his eyebrows and said, "My paycheck."

His answer caught me by surprise. It had been over a year since I'd last seen Bolin. At the time he was wearing a Travis County sheriff's uniform, proudly serving his community, and I couldn't help but think about why he had left the force. It was partially my fault, or at least that was the way I viewed it, even if Bolin insisted it was a matter of department politics.

Bolin said, "I heard about Moreno."

I shifted my eyes back to his. "Back on the job as of this morning."

"You're kidding?"

"Wish I was."

I could see that Moreno getting to keep his job while they forced Bolin out, angered Bolin.

"Just so we're clear," I said, "you did the right thing."

"Except *you* took the kill shot."

I was looking into Bolin's eyes, but I didn't see him. Instead, my brain flashed back to that deadly encounter, and I watched it play out behind my eyes as I heard Bolin say something about how he missed being a cop.

When I snapped out of it, I told him it was good to see him and started for the exit when he said to me, "Jackson. Watch your back. Moreno isn't the forgiving type. He doesn't just let things go without making sure to throw the last punch."

CHAPTER SEVENTEEN

VIPER WALKED ACROSS THE STREET AND GOT INTO HIS Ford. He was parked on a side street beneath a street lamp adjacent a popular bar, waiting for his target to show. The sky had opened up to scattered clouds, and the sun poked through for the first time today.

He spent too much time in the car, but had nowhere else to go. His legs were cramping as he reviewed his notes on Jackson Payne. A part of him wished he'd killed Jackson Payne in the fire too, but no sense in dwelling in the past. He'd find another way—perhaps even decide to make it into a game.

Over the course of the last several months, Viper had put together a thick profile on his subject. He knew everything he needed to know. There were pictures of Jackson's wife, and details of his outstanding career; but there was nothing Viper could use to destroy Jackson's reputation, and that was what kept him awake at night. He needed something—something to bring Jackson to his knees. If he couldn't physically destroy him, he'd have to kill his career.

Viper rubbed his hand over his face, growing impatient. He was waiting for his source to call back.

Just the mere thought of Jackson Payne had his blood boiling. *The self-righteous prick who could do no harm. Who did he think he was? Superman?* "I'll show him."

Viper knew the truth. Jackson was a lone wolf. A reckless cop who escaped disciplinary action from the upper brass far too many times.

"Not this time," Viper said to himself. "This time, we're going to catch you in a lie."

Five minutes passed when the call finally came in. Viper answered and the woman on the other end said, "The meeting is set. Anything else I can do for you?"

Viper sat still, thinking about how he could speed up the process of making Jackson's life miserable when Viper's target stepped out of the bar. Suddenly, he had an idea. Everything was set. Then he said to the woman, "No. That's all for now."

CHAPTER EIGHTEEN

BOLIN ONLY CONFIRMED WHAT I WAS ALREADY THINKING, and now I couldn't get Moreno out of my head.

What was his fight? How did he plan to get back at me, if in fact, that's what he planned to do? Would he go as far as killing my family? It seemed extreme for catching him in a lie. However, ruining my career certainly seemed plausible.

I drove aimlessly for the next couple of hours without having a clear direction of where to go. I tried to come up with an excuse to explain my being at the house so late at night, but nothing could escape the truth. Soon, everyone would learn about my divorce and how Ilene had requested I move out. No matter how I spun it, I looked guilty.

Now, if only I knew whether or not my family was dead.

I passed the time by speaking to CIs, and worked the streets hoping someone had heard something about anyone wanting to put a hit out on me and my family. There was nothing. No one had heard a damn thing; none of it made any sense.

I kept driving in circles, hoping an answer would come to me. I just needed to know when the fire started, and who or what to pay retribution to for taking my family away from me. My presumed innocence rested entirely on that single detail. As of now, it was in Moreno's hands.

It was dark now, and I still had heard nothing more about my wife. With no more leads to pursue, I did something I wished I didn't have to. I tried calling Caroline again. She must have gotten my message by now. As I waited for her to answer my call, I thought about Montana.

Montana was where I was born, where Ilene and I had met. I knew Ilene wanted a divorce, but now I wondered if she was planning to move home and leave Texas for good. Maybe Caroline could answer that for me.

"Hi, Jackson."

"How are you, Caroline?"

She apologized for not calling back, and added, "I'm not sure I should be talking to you."

It had been forever since we spoke. My relationship with Caroline had always been complicated. We approached the world differently and rarely saw eye-to-eye.

I said, "I'm calling because I want to know if you've heard from Ilene."

"I spoke to her yesterday."

I assumed it was about the divorce, but I couldn't say for sure. "How did she sound? Did she say where she was going?"

Caroline got worried. "Did something happen?"

I paused before saying, "The house caught fire last night."

"Oh my god," she gasped. "Is everybody all right?"

"I can't say for sure, but I think Ilene and Selina were inside."

I could hear Caroline fight back the tears. It was clear this was the first she was hearing of this. Then she said, "Please tell me this wasn't your fault."

Anger surged through my body. I knew I had let my family down, failed to protect them from the dangers that had a way of creeping into my life, but hearing it from Caroline made the sting burn. Making matters worse, I didn't know who to go after to make things right.

I merged into the right lane and watched a pair of headlights several cars back follow.

"I'm sorry," Caroline said. "That came out wrong. It's not what I meant."

"No. You're right. It's possible Ilene and Selina got caught up in my mess. I can't say for sure, but the fire may have been intentionally set."

Caroline was quiet, and I kept my eye on the pair of headlights following me off the highway and getting closer. My heart beat faster, and I instinctively touched my Sig Sauer 9mm 17 round pistol. Then Caroline said, "Jackson, swear to me. If the girls didn't make it out of the fire, and someone did this on purpose, promise me you'll make whoever is responsible, pay."

CHAPTER NINETEEN

WITH CAROLINE'S BLESSING, I PROMISED HER—AND MYSELF —I'd sort this out. Though I was mildly confused by her support, I didn't object to it either. In fact, I welcomed the change.

As soon as I ended the call, I slammed on my brakes and skidded to a stop. The car behind me did the same. Once we were both stopped in the middle of the quiet street, I jumped out with my badge and gun in hand.

"Open your door slowly and come out with your hands in the air," I yelled, squinting into the high beams.

At first, nothing happened and I stepped to the side, trying to catch a face. A silhouette sat still behind the windshield. Then the door opened and two slender hands lifted in the air.

"Jackson, relax. It's only me."

I recognized Emily Sanchez's voice and immediately relaxed. I put my gun down and made my way to her door, embarrassed I hadn't recognized her car.

Sanchez said, "You know, this is the reason you're called a cowboy."

"What are you doing following me?" I asked.

"I thought you could use some company." Her white teeth glowed in the subtle light when she smiled.

I sighed and holstered my weapon. "How did you know where to find me?"

"I didn't." She winked. "Well? What do you say? Have a drink with me?"

Sanchez had her jet black hair down and she was out of uniform. As much as I tried to deny it, she looked fantastic. I said, "Follow me."

CHAPTER TWENTY

THE ENTIRE DRIVE BACK TO MY PLACE, I KEPT ASKING myself if this was the right move or not. I'd known Sanchez for five years—since the year she came to police in Travis County—and yet something about inviting her to the apartment I was renting in North University felt premature.

I watched her follow me to the back of the building in my rearview mirror, convincing myself I shouldn't be doing this. But there was always something between us, something I knew she wanted to explore, too, but couldn't because of the wedding band I refused to take off.

Despite all that, Sanchez was right about one thing: I needed company, and not just any company, but the company of a woman.

I opened her car door for her, and said, "Welcome to my castle."

Her brown eyes swooped over my shoulder. "Lovely."

I walked her to the front door and, as soon as she stepped inside my humble abode, she shed her jacket and hung it over the back of a chair. The smell of her perfume had me wishing she was here under different circumstances.

I said, "How about that drink you wanted?"

Sanchez smiled.

She was quiet as she studied my small living quarters. It was embarrassing how little I had, but I had everything I needed, and more.

When I opened the fridge, I realized maybe I didn't have everything I needed after all. "Looks like we're drinking Coors," I said, not having an alternative to offer.

"Fine by me."

"Can, or glass?"

"Can."

We sat on the couch and drank. Sanchez commented on my minimalism, a polite way of saying I owned jack shit, but didn't seem turned off by it. I had only told her and Tex about Ilene requesting a divorce, and I appreciated that she didn't bring it up. Instead, she turned our conversation toward the fire.

"Jackson, you should have told me earlier about what happened."

I stared at my beer can, not knowing how to respond.

"David had Moreno investigating whether this was a homicide."

"I know," I said. "Smitty called me earlier."

"Have you heard from Ilene?"

I shook my head, told her neither had Ilene's sister, Caroline.

"I'm sorry, this is just awful. Who would want to do this to you?"

I lifted my head. "Really?"

"They went after your family."

I nodded. Then I told her what I was thinking, how maybe Raymond Frank did this in retaliation for building a case and testifying against him.

"And risk throwing his life away? I don't know, Jackson.

Seems like a stretch since he was just acquitted a few hours ago."

"You don't know Frank," I said, adding how maybe he wasn't planning to get off and wanted to go out with a bang.

"You think he hired someone to do this for him?"

"I don't know what to think."

Sadness filled her eyes, and I knew she was thinking that Selina was a victim of the dirty world I tried to clean up.

I said, "But then I ran into Alan Bolin. Remember him?"

"Of course. How could I forget?" Sanchez nodded, and I knew we were both remembering how that day changed how we all went about doing our police work. Then she said, "You made us all learn that we should take the shot first rather than dealing with the consequences of *not* eliminating the threat."

"Well," I said, "Bolin said something that had me thinking Moreno started the fire."

"A cop? C'mon, Jackson. You can't be serious."

I raised my eyebrows and shrugged. "We're both cowboys, and he has reason to want to get back at me for what I did."

"For the record, you did the right thing by taking a second look. IA should have taken the investigation more seriously. You showed them both to not close a case until it was thoroughly investigated. But make no mistake, you two aren't the same caliber. Moreno reacts, where you think before you act, and that makes you a professional, not a cowboy."

I appreciated her words, but it didn't stop me from thinking Moreno should at least be looked into. "Chief David sent him to the county judge's house to sign off on a warrant today." Sanchez sat forward and was looking me in the eye when I told her what the warrant was about. "I need to see who's on the tape. Maybe the person who started the fire is there. But, even more important, I need to know if Ilene and Selina escaped."

"And Moreno has the tape?"

"Who else?" This was news to Sanchez, and I made sure she understood David wasn't going to let me anywhere near this case.

"So what are you asking me to do? Get the tape?"

"At least review it," I said. "Then tell me what's on it."

Sanchez gave it some thought, then agreed. She finished her beer and was putting on her jacket when she said, "Something told me it was only a matter of time before you dragged me into one of your games."

CHAPTER TWENTY-ONE

CRIME REPORTER VINCENT CRUZ WAS TUCKED IN THE BACK of a coffee shop working on tomorrow's column about a man wanted for shooting at Austin Police, and as interesting as it was, he thought he had caught wind of something better.

Earlier this afternoon, he had received an anonymous tip saying there was a big story about a deputy that would make the Moreno story look like peanuts. Though Cruz didn't know exactly who this deputy in question was, he hoped it had something to do with Jackson Payne.

Employees called out orders and the aromatic scent of espresso was making it difficult for Cruz to concentrate. Cruz waited for his source to call him back and, as he did, he couldn't get his mind off of the conversation he had with Jackson. Something told him that the current story he was working would pale in comparison. Or at least that was the hope. But would his editor agree?

Cruz leaned back and cast his gaze to the front counter.

There was more going on with the Raymond Frank acquittal than what Cruz had been told, and he wondered if perhaps it was related to the fire that burned down deputy Payne's house last night.

But how could Cruz connect the dots, if that was all true?

Cruz reached for his cellphone and flipped it screen-side up as soon as the message came through. He read it and noted the address. Then he gathered his things and headed to an underpass on the opposite side of town.

As he waited for his contact to show, Cruz was feeling anxious as he kept looking over his shoulder. Surrounded by concrete and the hum of the highway above, he was the only car within sight.

Cruz kept looking at the clock. His contact was running late. An ill feeling fell over him and he thought about bailing. Though danger was part of the job, he had never been a target himself, but he knew other journalists who had. It was those thoughts that had him questioning if he should have ignored the call and stuck to the original script.

"Where the hell is this guy?" he muttered, continuing to look around.

He knew he was at the right location. Had his source gotten cold feet, or was simply late? Then there was the bigger question of who this person was and if what they said they had was true or simply a hoax?

A knock on the window startled the journalist and sent his heart jumping into his throat.

A man with a hood over his head peered in through the window. Only the bottom half of his bearded face could be seen. He seemed to have come out of nowhere. He motioned for Cruz to power down his window, and Cruz did. Then Cruz said, "Something I can do for you?"

The man straightened and unzipped his thick denim jacket. Then he dove his hand across his left breast and, for a split second, Cruz wondered if he was reaching for a gun.

Instead, a thick folder appeared, and the man dropped it onto Cruz's lap without saying a word.

Cruz looked down at the folder and asked, "What is this?"

The mystery man turned and walked away without ever saying a word.

Cruz peeked inside the folder and his eyes widened with what he saw. He looked one last time toward where the man had walked, but he was already gone. Cruz fired up his engine and drove away before anything else caught him by surprise.

He was in the home stretch, on his way to acclaim. But first, he had a long night ahead of him. There was work he had to do.

CHAPTER TWENTY-TWO

I GOT LITTLE SLEEP THAT NIGHT. SANCHEZ LEFT BEFORE midnight and I spent the remaining hours of the night alone, staring up into a blank ceiling, unable to stop thinking about the fate of my family. With my 9mm auto over my heart, I prayed my girls were alive. Deep down, I knew they weren't. It was the void I felt in my heart that convinced me they were gone, and again I found myself alone in the world.

Shortly before five in the morning, I made an egg bagel sandwich and was out the door to get an early start to my day. I hoped to prove Ilene and Selina hadn't been murdered because of me.

As I was walking to the Land Cruiser, I was eager to see what Sanchez would discover on Moreno's desk, hoping it could give me some sort of closure, when a pearl white Rolls-Royce Cullinan seemed to appear out of nowhere.

I watched as it stopped only a few feet from where I stood and I checked the plates before squinting through the tinted glass windows. I was intensely aware that I might be on someone's hit list, and I still couldn't say with absolute certainty the fire wasn't supposed to kill me, too. Not willing to chance it, I reached for my sidearm and prepared for the worst.

A few tense seconds ticked away before the Royce's back window powered down.

"Easy, Jackson," Raymond Frank laughed. "I'm not here to hurt you."

A woman younger than him leaned forward and said, "Hi, Jackson."

I held still and stared into the eyes of the woman who Frank murdered his wife to be with.

Frank moved, and my gaze moved with him. He gave the impression he had been partying all night—wide awake at such an early hour—happy to be free. He said to me, "I was in the neighborhood and thought I'd stop by to say hello."

I kept my mouth shut, but I couldn't help but wonder how he knew where I was living. I hadn't been in the apartment long, and though I assumed he was busy with the trial, perhaps he was busy keeping tabs on my life instead.

Frank's girlfriend had her hands all over him. She kissed his cheeks and petted his head like a lap dog while Frank stared at me, chuckling and grinning like the goon he was.

Frank said, "We lose our wives and move on. Isn't that right, Jackson?" When I said nothing, he continued, "But some of us never learn to let go."

As if they had practiced this, the woman turned her head and asked me, "What type of person are you, Detective? One to let go, or will you chase her forever?"

It took every ounce of patience inside me not to react, but I imagined what it would feel like to squeeze off a single round and put it right between Frank's eyes.

The woman lit up a cigarette and put it into Frank's mouth. He puffed away as he said, "Anyway, I hope you catch whoever burned your house down."

Then he told his driver to roll.

I could hear him laughing all the way up the street, and there was nothing I could do but wait. Had he just admitted guilt to starting the fire? I believed he had. Now, I just needed to prove it.

CHAPTER TWENTY-THREE

She took a piece of his ear between her teeth and growled as she whispered something dirty. Viper laughed and snuffed out his smoke. Then he took her face between his hands and kissed her passionately. When he pulled away, he said, "You did great."

"Thank you," she purred.

He stared into her eyes. They were dark and full of desire. She hooked her hand around his neck, pulled his forehead to hers, and mewed as she reached to his crotch, hungry for more.

As she clawed at his chest, Viper stared off into the distance, doubting she was as good as she claimed. He'd been seeing this new woman for about three months and she was everything he needed—young, long legs, thick thighs, and fake breasts—his toy to keep his mind off of all the bad luck he'd been experiencing lately. Still, something about her didn't seem right.

"Honey bunny wants to hop," she said into his ear.

Viper turned his head and chuckled. The poor little thing was begging for attention.

She sat upright and hiked up her dress, then straddled him. Viper pushed his hands under the cloth. She wasn't wearing anything beneath. Taking her breasts into his hands, Viper thought maybe it wasn't her that was causing him to feel unsatisfied, but that Jackson Payne seemed unphased by his threats.

"Really?" she said when Viper reached for what she thought was his cellphone.

Viper ignored her whine and said, "It's your phone that is ringing."

She reluctantly answered the call. After a minute, Viper asked, "Anything?"

The woman covered the phone's mic with her hand and whispered, "Just the same as before."

Which meant nothing. Viper turned his head and thought how the cops must have known by now that Jackson was at his house only minutes before the fire started. Yet he was still a free man. What were they waiting for?

Viper faced his girlfriend and said, "Today. It happens today." When she didn't respond, Viper growled, "Got it?"

"Got it."

After the woman relayed the message, Viper grabbed the phone away from her ear, killed the call, and tossed the phone to the floor as he smacked the woman's rear, getting her to squeal.

CHAPTER TWENTY-FOUR

DEPUTY SHERIFF EMILY SANCHEZ GOT INTO THE OFFICE between shift changes to minimize her chances of getting caught. She wanted to know what was on Pam Johnston's camera as much as Jackson did.

As she entered the empty homicide detective bureau, she was thinking of what she would say if someone were to see her at Moreno's desk. By the time she sat down, she'd come up with a few good excuses and went to work on her search.

She didn't like Moreno any more than Jackson did, but she also didn't need to get dragged into department politics either. Sanchez had worked hard to get promoted into the homicide bureau, and one wrong decision could set her back. Her decision to help Jackson was purely to know what happened to Ilene and Selina.

Moreno's desk was a mess. Sanchez lifted papers, opened desk drawers, and flipped through his notes, avoiding his computer—which she knew was password protected.

Finally, she found Moreno's investigation book. Her heart sped up when she looked over her shoulder before opening up the book. The information inside was telling. Someone had definitely assigned Moreno to investigate the cause of Jackson's house fire and the potential homicides that occurred.

Moreno had a reputation of not playing well with others and of being hot-headed, but Sanchez still was having a tough time convincing herself he would retaliate against one of their own, like Jackson suspected him of doing. But what she couldn't explain was why the deputy chief made this case Moreno's first assignment when coming off of suspension.

Inside were Moreno's notes, detailing important information pertaining to the potential crime scene. She flipped through the pages, took a few photographs with her cellphone, and was relieved to see no human remains had been found—yet.

But if Jackson's family wasn't dead, where were they?

Then she came to Pam Johnston's statement and the warrant to her home security system. Sanchez committed the case file number to memory, then stood to leave before anyone inside the department caught her snooping around Moreno's desk.

CHAPTER TWENTY-FIVE

An hour later, Sanchez met with the forensic video analyst, and talked him into giving her a copy of Pam Johnston's security video. With file in hand, Sanchez hurried through the department hallways, feeling like time was running out.

A few Late Show deputies were ending their shifts and greeted her as she passed. She smiled and hid her anxiety as best she could. Then, at her desk, she logged on to her desktop computer and inserted the thumb-drive into the terminal.

"C'mon. C'mon," she whispered impatiently as she waited for it to load.

When the file appeared on her screen, she clicked her way to Pam Johnston's security tape and navigated to the estimated time and day of when the fire was thought to have started. The angle on Jackson's house wasn't perfect from the lens's vantage point, but Sanchez could see enough of the front of Jackson's house to build a clear picture of what might have happened.

The clip rolled. She couldn't believe her eyes.

"You have to be kidding me." She leaned back and looked over her shoulder. Then she rewound the film and watched it for a second time.

"What are you doing there, Jackson?" She whispered her disbelief.

Sanchez stared as she watched Jackson arrive on foot and enter the house shortly after midnight. She noted how he entered through the front door and disappeared into the dark.

She let the film continue to play, thinking how there was nothing suspicious about his entry. Jackson certainly wasn't trying to hide that he was there, but why hadn't he mentioned this to her last night? A heads up would have been nice.

Several minutes passed where nothing happened. Then Jackson's eggshell white Land Cruiser clipped the bottom of the screen, driving directly in front of the camera's lens before disappearing in the next frame.

"How did you get out of the house?" Sanchez asked herself.

She never saw Jackson leave. At least not through the front door—the door he had entered only twenty minutes before. Now she wondered if Jackson left the house at all or if he had someone with him.

She let the video play. Nothing happened for another ten minutes, then the house went up in flames.

CHAPTER TWENTY-SIX

SANCHEZ STILL COULDN'T BELIEVE WHAT SHE WAS SEEING when she heard Moreno's voice appear in the hallway behind her. Not wanting to get caught looking at the files, she quickly clicked out of the browser and brought up a recent case file, pretending to work on it, when she heard Moreno approach.

His footsteps got closer and she fought off the nervous sweats beading beneath her uniform. Had he known she was at his desk snooping? She suspected he did. It was possible the forensic tech had mentioned what she requested.

When she felt Moreno standing behind her, her heart stopped.

"You're in early," he said.

Sanchez swiveled her chair around and faced him, hoping not to look as surprised as she was. She said, "I think better when it's quiet."

Moreno held her eyes with his own but said nothing.

Sanchez said, "If you're going to distract me, you could have at least brought me coffee."

There was no reaction from Moreno. Then he asked, "You heard about the fire at Jackson's place?"

"Devastating."

Moreno seemed indifferent when he asked, "Jackson mention it to you?"

"He may have mentioned it to me." Sanchez paused to read him, but his look gave little away. "I heard Smitty was suggesting it might be a homicide."

Moreno said, "What do you know about his relationship with his wife?"

"Oh my god, it was a homicide, wasn't it?" Moreno didn't answer. "Does Jackson know this?"

Again, Moreno didn't answer, instead he responded by saying, "I know he wasn't living at home, and I'm trying to understand how this fire may have started."

"You can't be serious. Jackson had nothing to do with it," Sanchez said, then silently thought, *these two cops are out to destroy each other.*

"Never said he did." Moreno flashed a knowing look, then walked away. "If you see Jackson, tell him I'd like to speak to him. And tell him, it's important."

CHAPTER TWENTY-SEVEN

I WAS THINKING ABOUT FRANK'S INTENTION FOR HIS surprise visit to my apartment when Sanchez called my cellphone.

"What did you find?" I asked.

"You were on the video, Jackson. How could you have not warned me that might happen?"

She wasn't yelling, but she definitely sounded angry. I drove with one hand and thought that perhaps it was unfair of me not to at least warn her what I thought might have happened. But I didn't want her to go in with any expectations, and I certainly couldn't afford to have any early assumptions made about me, either.

"Moreno is on to you, and once the deputy chief sees this, they will come for you." Sanchez spoke forcefully. "Jackson. You still there?"

"I'm here."

"You have nothing to say?"

I checked my mirrors and asked, "Did you see Ilene or Selina? Were they anywhere in the video?"

"Please tell me you didn't do this."

"I didn't do it," I said, but I wasn't sure Sanchez believed me. Even though I knew this was coming, I just couldn't understand how I had been set up.

"I never saw Ilene or Selina," she whispered.

I tightened my grip and my knuckles went white on the wheel. "What else did you see? Was there anybody else besides me around the time the fire started?"

"Nothing. You went in and never came out. Your car drove away. Then ten minutes later, the fire started."

I tried to make sense of it. How was it possible I was the only one who got caught in Pam Johnston's new security system? I drove with tunnel vision and my head felt dizzy. It made little sense. I needed to see the video for myself.

"Are you sure there was no one else?" I asked. *There had to be someone else.*

"It was only you, Jackson."

My thoughts drifted back to Frank's visit this morning.

"Come see for yourself."

I knew I needed more than what Sanchez said she found. I silently listed off other neighbors who might have seen something, but the angles on my house were all wrong.

I said, "Make a copy. I want nothing to get deleted."

"I'll do my best, Jackson."

I knew I was asking a lot, and I certainly didn't need my problem to become hers, too, but then Sanchez surprised me. "Moreno is going around asking people about why you weren't living at home with your wife and daughter."

"How did he know that?" I barked into the phone, pissed my secrets were getting out.

"I don't know, but he knows."

Then Sanchez told me Moreno was looking for me.

CHAPTER TWENTY-EIGHT

AFTER MY CALL WITH SANCHEZ, I STARTED MAKING A LIST of who might be keeping tabs on my life. I wasn't that popular, and didn't have many friends, but I had plenty of people who would like to see me dead.

I didn't like being locked out of my family's investigation. It felt like a secret was being purposely kept from me. What was that secret?

Moreno must have known before yesterday about my pending separation with my wife, but how did he know I had already moved out? Had he kept eyes on me during his suspension? It was possible, but Frank knew about me living in North University, too—proved it by his brief visit this morning. Tex was the only other person who could have known, but he wouldn't have told a soul. As for Sanchez, well, I had her on the inside and risking her own career to save mine, so I didn't see her gossiping about my secrets, either. That left only one other possibility. That weasel Vincent Cruz.

I turned into a quiet side street, parked on the side of the road, and unlocked my cellphone.

Cruz's Twitter feed gave me a glimpse into his work, and it was there I began my search.

It didn't take me long to know he was at it again. Cruz couldn't shut up about speculating about what went wrong at Raymond Frank's trial. He was hounding me yesterday about it, and someone seemed to pressure him to keep after it.

I didn't want to blame him entirely for Frank's acquittal, but his reporting certainly impacted the outcome. If he didn't put down the pen soon, he'd also mistakenly implicate me for a crime I didn't commit.

But perhaps that was the point—to get me to look the other way.

A call came in from deputy chief David's desk, and I elected to ignore it. Instead, I clicked on a link to a web article Cruz published yesterday morning to the *Chronicle*.

A lot was said about the district attorney's failure to convict Frank, as well as directly mentioning how badly I handled the case from the very beginning, saying what I already knew; that I relied too heavily on eye-witnesses.

I lifted my head and gave it some further thought.

Cruz seemed to create a narrative that I was mentally unfit for the job. At least, that was how I interpreted it, and I found it ironic that he'd hardly said anything about Moreno and his use of excessive force. Coincidence? Only if I believed life was full of extraordinary accidents, which I didn't.

A new Tweet was posted, and I was surprised by what he said.

Travis County sheriff's deputy may have been last to see his family alive. More to come. Stay tuned...

Was Cruz suggesting I had gone off the rails and set fire to my own house after Frank's trial went south? It certainly seemed like a possibility, but the fire was started before Frank's acquittal.

Frustrated, I squeezed my phone and heard the plastic casing crack.

Was it possible he knew about my wife's request for a divorce? He never said it in any of his reporting, but that didn't mean he didn't know. That might also explain Moreno's line of questioning with Sanchez.

Just when I was thinking I needed to speak with Cruz, a siren blared behind me.

I flicked my eyes at the rearview mirror and watched as an Austin PD patrol car turned and flicked on their lights. I held still, worried they were coming after me, but I watched them race past.

I didn't want to believe it was possible, but I certainly felt it. Soon, my department would come after me if I didn't set the record straight with what really happened to my family and how this fire got started.

CHAPTER TWENTY-NINE

CRUZ WASN'T AT THE NEWSROOM, DIDN'T ANSWER HIS phone, and no one I spoke to knew where he was. That made me suspicious of what exactly he was hoping to prove.

It seemed he couldn't let the Frank case go. Why was that? And what was his infatuation with me? I drove aimlessly, thinking about all these things, before I moved down my list of things I should do instead.

My next best option was a hard decision to make, but I knew I needed to do it sooner rather than later. I headed home to see what I might find.

Traffic was congested but moved at a steady pace. I wasn't in a hurry. It gave me time to think.

My thoughts were mostly consumed by happy memories of my wife and daughter, and the life we could have had if I wasn't a cop. I wasn't one to beat myself up, but reality was setting in and I blamed myself for inviting danger into my family's life.

But a cop was who I was, and crime was my beat. There was no other way to spin it. I just never imagined I would have to solve my family's murder—especially from the outside.

I imagined what might have happened. Nothing could erase the screams of my daughter from my head. To die in a fire was the worst outcome imaginable, and when my imagination became too real to cope with, I shifted my thoughts to something more productive.

I knew I had to speak to, and make peace with, Pam Johnston. Without another suspect or eye witness to chase and prove I didn't do this, I was toast. I just hoped that she could forgive me for whatever seeds Ilene had planted inside her head.

Soon, I was weaving my way through the neighborhood Ilene had chosen long ago for us to live. When I passed the park where Selina learned to ride a bike, I felt my throat constrict. I was feeling a flood of mixed emotions the closer I got to the house.

If only I would have known, I could have got them out of the house before terror struck.

If only I had never let my marriage get lost in the job.

If only we had never left Montana.

If only...

As soon as I rounded the bend on the street where I once lived, I hit the brakes and swung the wheels to the curb. Keeping my engine running, I couldn't believe who I saw speaking to Pam Johnston.

"You little sonofabitch," I said.

Now I knew I was in trouble. Pam had nothing good to say about me, and neither did the person she was speaking to. This was going to blow up in my face if I didn't stop it before it happened.

I monitored them both, then I watched Cruz get into his little blue Prius and leave. I held back one long second, then decided I had no choice but to follow.

CHAPTER THIRTY

I DIDN'T HAVE THE PATIENCE TO WAIT AND SEE WHERE Cruz was going next. Didn't really care. I punched the gas and rode his tail to make sure he knew I had seen him speaking with Pam. When we stopped at a red light, I pulled up alongside him, rolled down my window, and motioned for him to do the same.

Cruz smiled, as if excited to see me.

Once his window was down, I said, "We need to talk."

"You read my mind."

We met at the nearest park and I surprised him when opening his door. I told him, "Let's take a walk."

We walked around the playground, next to the closed swimming pool, and headed toward the baseball diamond, when I looked behind us and saw a waxed black Range Rover with tinted windows stop next to my Cruiser. I didn't think too much of it, but kept one eye on it without alerting Cruz to what I was doing.

I turned to Vincent, and asked, "What were you doing speaking with Ms. Johnston?"

Cruz said with a raised eyebrow, "She had some interesting things to say about you."

"I bet she did," I muttered, staying on the lookout.

I'd been especially paranoid since Frank's visit this morning, and I was believing the world had flipped upside down on me. I still couldn't understand why any of this was happening, but I wasn't willing to take any chances, either.

"Any leads on who started the fire?" Cruz asked.

I kept walking, but I turned to him when I said, "What makes you think it was started by someone?"

"A little birdy told me you were seen minutes before the fire began."

"Did Pam tell you that?" Cruz never said, but I could see the headline now: *Wife and daughter of Travis County sheriff's deputy, suspected dead after horrific fire. Police are investigating.*

"Did you start it?"

I looked back to the Range Rover without making it obvious and was surprised to see it gone. I kept flitting my gaze between the swings and chain-link fences to keep a lookout for who might be watching.

"Listen to me," I said. "Your reporting is getting out of hand."

"Is that an admission of guilt?"

I stepped directly in his path and we both ground to a halt. I said, "Quit speculating, and start investigating." Cruz said nothing, but I could see he knew what I was thinking. That if he didn't shape up, his stories would spin out of control, confuse evidence, and perhaps spawn hoaxers. "Are you sure you want to make that mistake again?" I asked.

"No one has seen your family since, and there is talk that maybe you did it because your wife requested a divorce."

That got my attention and Cruz knew it. I saw the Range Rover circling out of the corner of my eye. Its movement had

me feeling nervous, and it definitely felt like they were monitoring us, but Cruz seemed oblivious to the wagon circling.

Cruz asked, "Where are you living now?"

I met his eye and thought about the questions Sanchez
said Moreno was asking her earlier.

Cruz gave me a knowing look when he said, "In a garden
level apartment, isn't that right? North University, where the
rent is cheap? Did your wife ask you to move out, or did you
decide yourself?"

"Since when did you become so interested in my family
affairs?" I asked, thinking about the timing of Moreno's
suspension and the acquittal of Frank. Were they working
together? I doubted it, but anything was possible. But I
couldn't reveal my suspicions to Cruz about who might actually want me dead, without first having the evidence to back
it up.

Cruz took my statement as an admission to guilt. Then he
said, "Tell me, Detective, what was the purpose of your visit
the night your wife's house burned down?"

"It was my house, too," I reminded him.

Cruz didn't seem to care. He said, "Explain that to me,
and we move on."

A few seconds passed, and I had nothing I wanted to say
that might get printed in tomorrow's paper.

"I guess, since you can't," Cruz said, "perhaps my sources
are right in thinking you did it."

"Who is your source?"

"You know I can't reveal that information."

"Then you should be careful with what you write. It could
get you killed."

"Are you threatening me, Detective?"

When the Range Rover parked, I got nervous.

Cruz now saw what I had been watching.

A window rolled down on the Rover and I couldn't place

the bearded driver's face, but my gut said he might have been connected to Frank. Hiding behind mirrored pilot sunglasses, the driver made a gun with his hand, and shot at me.

Or was it Cruz he was shooting at?

I turned to look at Cruz. His lips were parted when he asked me with a pale face, "Do you know him?"

I said, "I was hoping you did."

CHAPTER THIRTY-ONE

VIPER PARKED IN FRONT OF THE HOUSE AND REACHED across the seat for his hat. He pushed his fingers through his hair as he pulled the bill down over his eyes. One look over his shoulder and he was opening his car door, grabbing his jacket on his way out. It was a navy blue windbreaker with the words Travis County Sheriff printed on the back, and it matched his cap.

It was all part of his plan. To fool and manipulate; to cause the greatest confusion possible.

Viper chuckled at his ingenuity. Then put on a pair of aviator sunglasses.

He stood at his car, *wanting to be seen,* and stared at the modest two-story house across the street. The once working class neighborhood of East Austin was now home to crime beat reporter Vincent Cruz, and Viper was here to make sure Cruz had taken his bait.

He crossed the street with a confident stride. He wasn't worried about being recognized because he knew it was the words Travis County Sheriff that people would remember. Almost like he was invited and was supposed to be here.

Viper looked both ways as he climbed the concrete steps to the front door. The neighbors were oblivious, keeping their eyes down and their focus short. He pretended to knock before discretely working to pick the lock. He had done his research, knew that Cruz didn't have a home security system.

"After tonight, he might." Viper chuckled.

The lock clicked over and he let himself inside, pretending that someone had opened the door for him.

He stood at the door for a moment to take in the house's layout.

An amazingly clean kitchen to the left, a narrow flight of stairs leading to the upstairs off to the right. Viper knew Cruz slept upstairs, but he was most interested to see his desk.

Viper wiped his feet on the doormat to be polite and walked through the living room with a large flat screen TV mounted to the wall. A Bose stereo system connected to the TV, and an acoustic guitar leaned against the wall in the corner, near Cruz's work desk.

The extensive research he'd given Cruz last night was spread out and organized into three piles. Nothing had been reported yet. At least officially. But Viper was pleased to see Cruz was definitely calling Jackson's intention into question.

Cruz laid out the motive—divorce—and had it circled next to the word *revenge*.

Viper was pleased. His hard work was coming to fruition. Maybe his day of reckoning was closer than he originally thought.

"Now, where do we go from here?" Viper asked, knowing once the public opinion shifted against Jackson, the deputy chief would have little choice but to make an arrest.

Then Viper saw something that surprised him. He lifted the paper and read Cruz's chicken scratch. It was difficult to decipher, but Viper got the gist. He had laid out an alternative theory, a twist Viper hadn't expected, but should have.

Stunned, Viper said, "You're smarter than you appear."

He lifted his head and stared blankly at the wall. His thoughts churned over, thinking circumstances might have changed. If the death of Jackson's family didn't end the detective, Viper's next move certainly would.

CHAPTER THIRTY-TWO

CRUZ SEEMED CLUELESS AS TO WHO THE MAN WAS, BUT HE showed enough fear for me to suspect he might have found an enemy himself.

"Get out of here, now," I said.

Cruz didn't react. He stood and stared, clearly stunned by what he just saw.

I didn't enjoy pretending to get shot at any more than he did, but if we didn't move soon, we might find out if the man was serious about his threat.

I grabbed Cruz's arm and shook him hard. "Vincent." He blinked and looked at me. "You need to leave, now!"

I broke free from Cruz and turned my attention toward the Range Rover. Mr. Aviators didn't seem to be in a rush. I liked his show of overconfidence in my ability to react. Whoever he was, I was going to find out.

He let off the brakes and eased into traffic as I ran to my Cruiser, making sure I saw which direction he went. Once behind the wheel, I turned the key, slammed my foot down on the clutch, and sped after him.

I flipped a U-turn and listened to the tires squeal. When I

glanced in the rearview mirror, I glimpsed Cruz leaving the scene.

I don't know why, but suddenly I was worried about the kid. I knew I had somebody wanting to kill me, but did he have someone wanting to kill him, too?

With that on my mind, I circled the park and turned north, looking for the Rover.

Thinking I lost him, I weaved through the city streets using only my instinct. I went where my gut told me to, and soon, I spotted Aviators speeding onto the Expressway.

I dropped the gear, sped forward, and worked my way through traffic. As soon as I hit the on-ramp, I went even faster. It wasn't easy, but I managed to catch up to him. He drove a tight weave between traffic and then, after a few miles of jockeying for position, he exited the Expressway and raced through the red light.

I had little choice but to stop. When I did, the next thing I heard was the sound of police sirens behind me and a voice telling me to pull over.

CHAPTER THIRTY-THREE

I WAS PISSED I LET AVIATORS GET AWAY. I ONLY GOT CLOSE
enough for a partial plate number. But I was even more angry
when I saw who pulled me over.

As soon as I saw Moreno get out of his Ford Interceptor,
I punched the dash. Then I jumped out of my car and hurried
to meet him at the back.

"Finally, some backup," I said.

"You chasing someone?" Moreno asked.

I looked him in the eye and something told me he was
hoping to catch me in a lie.

"What is it you want, Moreno?"

"Besides saying you were speeding twenty above the speed
limit?"

"Yeah. What about it?"

"Deputy Chief asked me to bring you in."

"Bring me in?" I didn't have time for this bullshit and I
could have sworn Moreno thought it amusing. "You couldn't
have called to tell me this?"

"Like you would have answered. Besides, Deputy Chief
called."

The prick was enjoying this, but what I couldn't believe was Moreno's impeccable timing. "What's this about?" I asked.

"The fire."

My gut clenched. "Then, let's get this over with," I said, telling him I would follow him to the office.

"No," Moreno said. "I'll follow you."

As if I would run.

CHAPTER THIRTY-FOUR

THE MOOD AT THE STATION WAS TENSE. NO ONE WANTED to look me in the eye.

Moreno walked behind me and I was sensing my worst fear had come true.

I looked for friendly faces in a sea of glares. Though no one said it, I could read their faces. They thought I had killed my family, but there was no way they were going to pin my family's murder on me. Instead, I concentrated on my efforts to be sure I did everything in my power to walk out of here without having to first post bail.

As soon as I stepped foot into the detective bureau, Sergeant Ty Hart motioned for me to follow. He led me to the interview room and told me to take a seat.

"Is there something I should know?" I asked.

"It's about the fire."

I said I still hadn't heard from Ilene and Selina, then added, "I'm afraid they didn't make it."

The door opened, and Moreno entered the box. I watched him give a knowing look at Hart. It was subtle enough to nearly be missed, but now I suspected I had even lost the trust of my commanding officer.

"I want my lawyer," I said.

"Jackson—" Hart sighed. "Hear us out first. Will you?"

"I'll listen to you, but not him." I jutted my jaw toward Moreno. "Forget about it."

"Moreno stays."

That's when I knew the deputy chief had assigned him lead detective. It was a gut punch that had me imagining how I could fight back. I wanted to take a swing at both of them for insulting my integrity.

"You made him lead?" I said to Hart, nearly jumping out of my seat. Hart's silence spoke volumes. I slammed my fist on the table and said, "If my family is dead, I need to know about it."

"Tell him," Hart said to Moreno.

I shifted my eyes over to Moreno. My anger was boiling hot.

Moreno said, "The judge signed off on the warrant. We got footage from your neighbor's security camera the night of the fire."

"And?"

Hart said, "We'll show you the video, but first we need to ask you a few questions."

I knew this was coming and had prepared for it. I said, "Make it quick."

What they promised to be short, turned into three hours of questioning. Even worse was I did it all without Tex by my side.

Moreno tried to play me at my own game—I suspected he was hoping to catch me in a lie—but after the first round of questions, I could see him getting frustrated with me. I stuck to the script and told the truth. They knew I was at the house shortly after midnight, and I didn't deny it.

"Ilene wanted a divorce," I finally admitted. "I went there to collect a few important belongings and talk to my daughter."

Hart looked on with familiar eyes. He'd been through a couple difficult divorces himself. It was a sacrifice many cops shared, one I did my best to avoid, but the job took root and made it impossible to share my work with my wife. Not because I didn't want to, but because I loved her enough to want to protect her from the evil I knew lurked around every corner.

Moreno seemed troubled by the timing of my visit. He asked, "Why so late at night?"

"I'm a night owl."

"Were your wife and daughter awake?"

I stared, thinking about the last thing I said to Selina. I shook my head no and asked to see what they had found on film.

Hart brought in a laptop computer, placed it on the table in front of me, and hit play. I hovered over the machine and observed.

I knew from the angle it was taken from Pam Johnston's house. Moreno skipped to the important parts and, when it finished playing, I said, "Just like I told you. In and out. Now tell me what you're hiding. Because I don't understand why you dragged me in here, treating me like I'm some kind of suspect in my own family's murder."

Hart said, "Jackson, you have to understand. We had to ask you why you were there."

"Are they dead?"

Hart said, "At this point, the only crime that has been committed is arson. They found traces of accelerant at the scene. We know someone did this intentionally, and we'll catch whoever did, but we're afraid of how the public might view this video if it gets into the wrong hands."

I shifted my eyes to Moreno. He looked away. Had he leaked the video to the media? When I thought back to my meeting with Cruz, something told me he already had—or certainly would have liked to if he hadn't yet.

I pushed back from the table and stood. The chair crashed to the floor. I pointed my finger at both of them. "That's what you're worried about? Public relations?"

I couldn't believe it. My own people couldn't even sympathize.

When I headed for the door, Hart called after me. "Jackson, wait—"

"Forget about it," I said, opening the door and sending it flying into the wall. "You've given me no choice but to investigate my family's murder myself."

CHAPTER THIRTY-FIVE

IT WAS WELL AFTER MIDNIGHT BY THE TIME I LEFT THE station. I was beyond pissed off. It seemed like no one but me was convinced a murder had occurred. There was no sense of urgency, and nothing was being done about finding out what happened to my girls.

I was convinced they were dead. Even when Ilene was angriest with me, she'd call.

She'd always call...

I crossed the parking lot and a pair of headlights flicked on as soon as I went to open my car door. I froze like a deer in headlights, but I couldn't see who was hiding behind the bright beams of light. I was certain they could see me.

The brakes released and the SUV rolled forward before it turned up the street. Though I never caught a face, I was certain it was Frank. It was the same high-priced Royce I saw him happily rolling around the city in when he showed me his face outside my apartment nearly twenty-four hours ago.

But why now? And why continually stalk me? Was it possible he had spoken to Moreno before Moreno tracked me down? If Aviators from the park was one of Frank's men, like

I thought he might be, that would explain how Moreno could find me.

I followed Frank's taillights with my eyes until they disappeared. How long had he been waiting for me? It must have been hours. It made little sense. As unnerving as it was to know I was being stalked, at least he was making it obvious.

I stayed alert, constantly checking my mirrors as I made my way across town.

Twenty minutes later, I was knocking on Vincent Cruz's door.

A light flicked on a second before he opened the door. His eyes were groggy, and sleep-filled.

I slammed my hands into his bare chest and pushed him inside. Then I tossed him up against the wall and asked, "Where is the video?"

Cruz's eyes were suddenly wide awake. "I don't know what you're talking about."

I was so angry; I felt myself on the edge of blacking out in a fit of rage. "Did Moreno give you Pam Johnston's home security tape?" Cruz was mumbling something I couldn't understand. "Is that why you went to speak with Ms. Johnston today? To check if the video was authentic?"

Cruz told me to fuck off and I punched him in the gut. I heard the air get knocked out of him before he crumbled to the floor. I stood over him with clenched fists, ready to beat the truth out of him.

Cruz coughed and held his hand in front of his face, as if that would be enough to protect him from the beast inside me. "Just listen, will you?"

I said, "You better speak clear and fast, because I'm running out of patience."

Cruz said, "I don't have any video. I don't know what you're talking about."

"Who told you I was at my house the night of the fire?"

"I don't know."

I kicked him again.

"I swear."

"Are you sure it wasn't Moreno?"

"He had a beard. Walked like a cop. That's all I know. There. It's all there." He pointed across the room to his desk. "Everything I was given is there. Go ahead. Look for yourself."

Two giant steps later I was at his desk, assessing what lay there. I was breathing hard, and my heart beat faster. Cruz had copies of my divorce papers, pictures of Ilene and Selina. Intimate moments of my life. Without looking at him, I asked, "How did you get this?"

Cruz was still on the floor, up against the wall, when he said, "It happens more than you think. Anonymous sources give me tips, send me information. I was investigating the fire. Isn't that what you told me to do?"

Cruz wasn't telling me anything I didn't already know, but why me? This felt like payback. I was once again thinking about Raymond Frank and Mr. Aviators at the park.

My blood boiled over. Cruz hid this from me earlier. I turned and faced him. "You're making a case against me?"

"On the contrary," Cruz said, pushing himself up on his feet. "I think someone wants to set you up."

I stared into his eyes to see if he was only telling me what he thought I wanted to hear. I saw nothing to suggest that. Surprised to have suddenly found myself an ally, I asked, "Who? And why me?"

He must have seen the look in my eye because Cruz told me what I had already thought myself. That Frank had started the fire as some sort of payback.

"Do you have proof?"

"Not really. But I was working on it."

I turned back to the desk and picked up the papers about my family and me. I asked, "When did you get this?"

"Last night."

"And you didn't think it would be important for the investigation? You could have told me earlier."

"Take it. I'm done. This is way above my paygrade, and something I'm not willing to die for."

I thought about Aviators pretending to shoot at us with his hand. When I mentioned it to Cruz, he said, "Exactly. I don't know what the hell is going on, but if Frank did this, I want no part of what he's planning next."

"C'mon. Let's go. You're coming with me," I said, reaching for his arm.

Cruz jumped back. "I can't."

"What do you mean, you can't?"

"I'm done, Detective. This time you're on your own."

CHAPTER THIRTY-SIX

I SAT IN MY CRUISER GOING OVER CRUZ'S NOTES, READING the file about my family. We'd come up with the same theory on our own. That was enough for me to think we could be right. But how could Frank have pulled it off when the world was watching his every move? And did he plan for me to be set up, or was he hoping to kill me, too?

Frank was taunting me, perhaps taunting us both. But why do so when he won his trial? The only explanation I could come up with was that Frank was preemptive in his attack and was now following me, hoping to learn where the investigation was going. Though that only made him suspicious, and Frank wasn't stupid.

Something inside me said he was going to kill me.

Determined to stop it before it went any further, I retrieved the information from Tex. It was the name of a popular nightclub Frank frequented on the east side of Austin. After committing the address to memory, I stuffed the piece of paper back into my pocket and started my drive.

I didn't know exactly what I planned to do, but I needed Frank to know I would not allow him to intimidate me.

At the club, I spoke with the bouncer working the door. He was a large, muscular Black man who was careful with his words. His eyes were alert as he listened to my request to know whether or not Frank was inside the building.

"Don't know," he said in a cool baritone.

Suspecting he was bullshitting me, I stuffed a twenty-dollar bill into his hand and asked again. "Is Raymond Frank here or not?"

He said, "He was here earlier with his entourage, but has since left the building."

"How long ago was that?"

"Maybe thirty minutes."

I wondered about the purpose of Frank's visit. "Any idea where he went?" I asked.

The bouncer gave me a look that told me he'd need more money to answer that. I gave him the rest of what was in my wallet. Two tens.

"Home," he said.

"I won't forget this," I said as I walked away.

Finding Frank at the club would have been easier. Less hassle, too. It wouldn't be easy getting close to his house, but I had no other choice than to try.

Frank lived in a ritzy part of town and there was only one way in and out of his neighborhood—through the security gate, guarded by a duo of wannabe cops I showed my badge to, to little fanfare.

"Is there a problem, Sheriff?" the gate attendant asked.

"No problem. Just need to ask Mr. Frank a few questions."

"May I ask about what?"

"No, you may not. It's a private matter."

After I threatened to make a scene, I was told to go through. There was no way to eliminate the element of surprise. In a matter of minutes, they would tip Frank off that I was coming for him.

The nicely paved road snaked, climbed, and led me to another gate at the end of a cul-de-sac that prohibited me from going any further. It was Frank's gate, and one I suspected I would have to jump in order to get to Frank's front door.

I parked in the shadows and stepped out onto the street, staring up the drive. Frank's mansion shone down upon me like a castle on the hill. It was lit up with hundreds of lights, and the air was eerily silent. I assessed the layout of the grounds, the height of the hedge, chambered a bullet, and went to jump the gate.

Once I was over the barrier, they tackled me as soon as my feet touched the ground.

CHAPTER THIRTY-SEVEN

I QUICKLY MANEUVERED TO GET ON TOP OF THE MAN WHO had tackled me and was about to throw my second punch when another man took me down again. They had me pinned, and I was receiving a good beating when suddenly a knee fell hard on my neck.

The pain was sharp and I winced.

The tips of my fingers were tingling; every breath of air became a struggle.

I felt them take my gun, then they zip tied my hands behind my back and tossed me into the back of a Toyota Tundra. I sat up before the wheels rolled and met the narrow eyes of the two faces staring back. Neither of them seemed concerned to have just assaulted a cop, and certainly weren't afraid to show their faces.

"You boys help Frank murder his wife, too?" I asked. They continued to stare without reaction. "I bet you did," I said. "You two look crazier than a run-over coon."

When we reached the house, the truck stopped and Frank was outside waiting for me. His men reached for my ankles and dragged me to the edge of the truck bed. I slid off the back, looking around.

Frank lived in a sprawling five-thousand square foot mansion with a manicured lawn. There was a powerful scent of chlorine in the air, and I assumed by how Frank was dressed that he'd just gotten out of the hot tub.

"Nice place, Frank. I'd love to shake your hand, but your boys took that ability away from me."

Frank said, "Untie him. He's a cop, for Christ's sake."

One of his goons stepped in front of me, flicked open his knife blade in front of my face, and warned me that he wouldn't be afraid to use it if I tried anything funny.

When my hands were freed, I said, "And my gun?"

The big guy turned and looked at Frank. Frank debated my request. He said, "I suppose your uninvited visit should only be expected."

I nodded and agreed as I flitted my gaze between the men, hoping to see Mr. Aviators somewhere in the light. None of them had beards. Then I turned back to Frank and said, "You're looking more like a gangster every time I see you."

"With all the wild pigs in Texas, security detail is a commodity I unfortunately can't afford to live without."

His men laughed.

Getting to the point, I asked Frank, "Who told you where I was living? And why do you keep following me?"

"Is that what this is about?" The crease between his eyebrows deepened. "No, Jackson. You don't come here asking the questions. Not until you apologize for the trial you made me go through and admit you were wrong."

"That's why you're following me?"

"It's not because you're cute."

"We both know you murdered your wife. And something tells me you murdered mine, too."

Tension escalated quickly and, before I knew it, they shoved me in the back with a couple muzzles pointed at my face. I didn't let it get to me. What more did I possibly have to lose?

"How could I do that, Jackson? Until yesterday, I was the most talked about face in Texas. You really think that I would be stupid enough to seek revenge?" When I didn't answer, Frank said, "You're losing your head, Detective."

"That may be," I said, thinking about his girlfriend's words this morning. "So, does that mean you're denying you had any involvement in my family's murder?"

"Don't come here again." Frank told his men to lower their weapons and give back mine. Then he said to me, "You'll regret it if you do."

I nodded like I accepted the terms to his challenge. Then I pulled out my pack of smokes, lit a single cigarette, and flicked it at Frank's feet. "Next time it will land in a pool of gasoline."

CHAPTER THIRTY-EIGHT

VIPER SPLASHED COLD WATER ON HIS FACE. THOUGH refreshing, it did little to damper the anxiety he was feeling. Leaning forward, he hovered over the sink, staring at himself in the mirror. He needed to take a good, hard look at the person he was becoming. Inside those once tormented blue eyes was a spirit that had been reawakened.

He liked what he saw. The feeling of purpose; a reason to get out of bed in the morning. Until recently, he forgot what it felt like. And damn did it feel good to be back.

But his next move was bigger than his last. He couldn't afford to make a mistake. Not in the second quarter of his game when the stakes were growing increasingly higher. One wrong decision, a slip in his plan, and he'd be caught.

"No matter what they say about you," he said to himself, "you're a winner."

He straightened his shoulders and untied his belt. His bathrobe opened to reveal his chest. Viper was in incredible shape. That was the one daily routine that hadn't changed for him. He kept strong, flexible; maintained a soldier's body.

He pounded his chest with his fist as he moved to the

closet. Sifting through clothes, Viper was certain Jackson would eventually make his way to Cruz—either by invitation or request—if he hadn't already. Either way, Viper planted the motive and now needed to execute on his plan by committing another murder.

The thought was invigorating, and he had the perfect plan.

He turned and faced the bed. On the nightstand was the wooden box he'd taken from Jackson's house the night of the fire. Viper opened it up and peered down at the magnificent weapon. It was beautiful and strong, just like him.

Viper visually stroked the barrel, wondering if anybody had died because of its extraordinary fire power. "Or will tonight be the first?"

The excitement was growing when he heard the front door open. He quickly shut the wooden box and heard his girlfriend call out.

"In the bedroom," Viper responded.

She entered the room and kissed him on the lips. Then she gave him the keys to the Range Rover.

"Everything work out as planned?" he asked.

"He loved the car." She smiled. "Wanted to borrow it longer."

Viper chuckled. "I bet he did. Who wouldn't?"

She said, "They were together. At the park. Just like you said."

"And your friend doesn't know I'm involved?"

"Not a trace." Then she pointed to the box and asked, "When are you going to let me shoot that thing?"

"This *thang* sweetheart, is a Walker Colt." Viper grinned, thrilled to be telling her about the pistol's history. She stared with wide eyes as he told it, but all Viper could think about was how he wanted to frame Jackson with his own gun.

When Viper was finished with his story, he told his girl-friend to take the gun into her hand.

Her eyes lit up, and she said, "It's heavy."

"Four and half pounds and a nine-inch barrel."

"When can I shoot it?" she begged.

Viper made her put the gun back. "Patience young grasshopper. Your day will come. Believe me. Now, go, draw yourself a bath. Daddy has work to do."

She leaned against him and planted her lips on his. "Join me?"

"I have to go out tonight."

She pouted and he told her to go. He watched her do as she was told and thought nothing was more fun than this.

CHAPTER THIRTY-NINE

TEX TOLD ME TO MEET HIM AT A LOCAL ALEHOUSE NOT FAR from Frank's place, and I caught sight of him shortly after I arrived. He was on the dancefloor twirling a good-looking brunette around. They were both laughing, having a good time.

I ordered myself an old-fashioned at the counter, thinking what to do about Frank.

Things were getting out of hand. I just needed to know how I could speed up my plans to settle the score, and what that might look like when I did. Either way I spun it, tonight, I'd failed. Miserably.

Tex slid up next to me at the counter and requested water from the barkeep.

I asked him, "What brought you here, cowboy?"

A silly grin stretched to his ears when he pointed to the cute woman he had just been dancing with. "Jackson, this woman," he wiped the sweat from his brow, "I'm telling you, she can move like a snake."

I assumed that was a good thing. Not how I would have

described a woman as beautiful as her, but Tex knew what he liked. Apparently, so did she.

Tex was four inches taller than me, standing at six foot two, he was lean and muscular. A real charmer, too. He had all the qualities the ladies couldn't resist. He was intelligent, single, and had lots of money to go along with his killer smile.

Not wanting to take his spotlight away, I said, "I was right."

Tex looked confused by me changing the subject.

"I got caught on camera, just as I thought."

When I told him I was brought in and questioned by my team, Tex said, "Why didn't you call?"

"I've got nothing to hide."

Tex asked if I met with Frank. I told him about the guy at the park, and how I chased after him. Then added, "Even the reporter Vincent Cruz thinks Frank is setting me up."

After I mentioned what I took from Cruz, Tex slid off his stool and said to follow him. We took a table in the back. I showed him the files. Tex reviewed the information with his lawyer eyes and I could see he was as surprised as I was by the details of what Cruz had been given.

"Not only did word about my divorce get leaked," I said, "but Cruz even knew how Ilene was putting me at fault and planning to take everything we owned."

Tex lifted his gaze. I knew by his look that he was worried about me.

I said, "Lucky me, Cruz has integrity and did his due diligence before putting them to print."

Tex asked, "And the theory is what? Frank supplied him with these documents?"

I shrugged, said we weren't sure. "Frank was never supposed to be released, but what bothers me more is that I'm losing the trust of my colleagues."

Tex knew I was referring to Moreno without having to

spell it out for him. My gut instinct was rarely wrong, but now I just couldn't decide whether to go after Frank, Moreno, or the both of them.

"Either way," I said, "someone was hoping Cruz would slip up and rush to print the story so the entire city of Austin could see I had motive to kill my family."

"We don't know they are dead," Tex reminded me.

I gave him a sideways look. We both knew the odds of them being alive were slim.

Tex leaned back and said, "I can have one of my PIs watch Frank. See what he's up to."

I thought about what happened at Frank's tonight, and I wasn't sure I was ready to complicate matters by involving more people. I said, "I understand if you don't want to get involved."

Tex held up his hand and said, "I'll make some calls. Put a feeler out and have somebody on standby in case we need them."

I nodded. Tex shifted his eyes to my right and looked over my shoulder. His lady friend was beckoning him with her slender finger. "Better not leave her waiting," I said, sending him off so I could finish my drink alone.

As soon as Tex was gone, my cellphone rang. It was Sanchez.

"Jackson, you available?" she asked.

"Depends."

"It's about Vincent Cruz. He's dead."

CHAPTER FORTY

I KNEW I SHOULDN'T GO, BUT I HAD TO SEE IT FOR MYSELF.

The entire drive to Vincent Cruz's house, I tried to think what I had missed. When I left Cruz's house earlier, I thought I was doing him a favor by staying away. Now I knew I was wrong. I may have been the reason they killed him.

I didn't have to ask who *they* were. I already knew—Frank. But why drop Cruz now instead of waiting until after his story was complete?

As soon as I turned the bend, my instinct to fight kicked in. Several media vans and their accompanying reporters crowded the street on what would have otherwise been a quiet night.

I parked a half-block up the street from Cruz's front door, thinking how the investigation was now fully in the public eye.

I badged my way through the police line and walked between a couple Austin Police officers who assisted on the call. I registered my name at the door with a deputy and entered the house, hoping that it would be obvious I wasn't the only person to have visited Cruz tonight.

The techs were working the scene. They were dusting for prints and taking pictures. All I could hear were Cruz's last words to me: *"I'm done, Detective. This time you're on your own."*

It would only be a matter of time before my prints were lifted, pulling me once again into a mad sea of questions and accusations. More worrisome was how, yet again, I had been at the victim's house only moments before they were murdered.

Sanchez caught sight of me and met me at the door. She said, "A neighbor heard fighting. Then, about a half-hour after, they came to check it out and saw that the front door was ajar."

"And they discovered the body?"

"Never went inside. Only called it in."

I continued to look around. Cruz's bags were packed. Where was he going to go? I regretted not making him come with me. I turned my attention to his desk. It was a mess. Papers had been scattered, his drawers tossed as if someone had been looking for the same documents I now had myself. A tech was taking pictures of it all, though I was certain Cruz already gave me everything I needed to figure out who wanted to destroy my reputation.

Sanchez said, "The initial feeling is that this was a robbery gone bad."

I said, "Where is he? I need to see him."

I followed Sanchez into the living room. Cruz was lying on his side, his back pushed up against the wall. I kneeled over him and made mental notes of what I saw. He was still shirtless, and I could see the marks on his arms I had left on him earlier.

Sanchez said, "He was strangled to death."

"Petechial hemorrhage," I said, pointing to the burst blood vessels on his eyelids. "Caused by asphyxiation."

As I looked for other clues, I wondered what happened between the time I left and now. Did his killer know I was here? My heart was pounding. Something inside me told me they did.

"This wasn't a robbery," I said, standing. Sanchez was looking at me funny, like she knew I was thinking this was the job of Frank's hands, but I kept my secret to myself. At least for the time being. Then Moreno's voice cut through the air.

"Care to tell us where you went after you left the station?"

I turned and faced him. "I could ask you the same."

As I stared into Moreno's blue eyes, I looked for any sign he had set me up—knowing I would come here right after he hinted that Pam Johnston's security tape might just find its way to the media.

"Correct me if I'm wrong," Moreno shifted his eyes to Sanchez, "but wasn't Cruz investigating whether you started your own house fire?"

Moreno laid out the motive, and it got the attention of a few techies who stopped what they were doing to glance in my direction. I took a step forward and asked, "You have something you want to get off your chest?"

Sanchez jumped between us and reminded us we were on the same team.

Moreno stepped away. I watched him exit the house as I stood near Cruz, thinking about the mystery man in the park who pretended to shoot at us. It was the only lead we had. Then Sanchez told me that Cruz's notes were filled with Frank's and my names.

I whispered to Sanchez, "I talked to Cruz, here, only two hours ago."

Her eyes widened with disbelief. "Jackson—" After she collected herself, she said, "Why did you tell me that? Now I'll have to put it into my report."

Then a uniformed APD officer burst into the room and told us something that neither of us wanted to hear.

"Neighbor two houses up the block swears the only person in and out was a Travis County sheriff's deputy."

Sanchez couldn't even look me in the eye. It was clear she thought I had done Cruz myself.

CHAPTER FORTY-ONE

VIPER DIDN'T GO FAR. HE SAT IN HIS FORD, STARING AT the clock. An hour passed before the first sounds of a siren broke the still night air. As soon as he heard it, he cranked the engine and made his way back near Cruz's neighborhood.

He parked a block to the west and stepped out to stand beneath the crimson and blue strobe flashing in the sky as he took off his sheriff's windbreaker and exchanged his regular ball cap with the sheriff's cap. Finally, he reached into the backseat for his digital Nikon camera. Then he slung the bag full of lenses over his shoulder, closed his car door, and circled his way back to Cruz's while listening to the sounds of more sirens heading his way.

He smiled and whistled a tune as he calmly walked without worry. There was nothing like a murder and he was about to prove that once again tonight.

Porch lights flicked on. Neighbors peeked behind closed blinds to see what was happening in their rather dull neighborhood.

Viper continued whistling, surprised it had taken this long for Cruz's body to be discovered.

"I made it obvious," he muttered to himself. A city of fools, he thought. "Everyone is looking, but no one actually sees a damn thing."

The closer to the crime scene he walked, the more excited he got. He liked the thrill; the ability to know exactly what happened—before, during, and after—where the crime was committed.

But it was Cruz who decided to die, not him. All Cruz had to do was write the stupid story. Yet he couldn't. His hesitation got him killed. Because of it, he deserved what he had coming.

Still, there was a snag Viper couldn't explain.

Where did the notes and files of Jackson Payne's divorce go? Cruz wouldn't tell him. Even as he dangled over the edge of death, he stayed silent until the moment he passed.

Had Cruz given them to Jackson when Viper wasn't looking? Entirely possible. But when? Viper knew he should have monitored Jackson himself. He couldn't trust others to do the job for him. No one cared more than he did.

He took off his black leather gloves and stuck them in his back pocket as he approached the scene. TV news crews were getting set up, preparing to broadcast as the first inspectors entered the house to learn the reason they were called. No one but Viper knew what had happened, and he stood taller because of it.

The power.

The control.

The selfish urge to share his secret with the world. It was so difficult to contain and keep a tight lid on his spiral of excitement.

A fake press badge hung from his neck and he began snapping photos as all those intense emotions crashed to the forefront of his mind.

No one paid him any attention. No one asked him who he was or who he was with. He blended in like a chameleon and slithered his way to the front of the line like the snake he was.

"Yes. That's what I'm telling you. A cop was here, inside his house, before all this happened."

Viper glanced in the voice's direction. The woman spoke loudly, swinging her hands through the air with grand passion. It was a witness telling her story to the female journalist who soaked up every detail.

"No. We don't say that," the journalist said to her colleague. "If a cop killed a reporter, we'll run it. But we will not speculate until we have the facts."

Viper grinned at the irony. He continued moving around, taking pictures. It seemed everyone wanted to know what story Cruz was working, how that piece of information might explain why he was murdered.

"Should we be worried, too?" Viper heard someone say.

Yes, he answered silently. An attack on one is an attack on all.

He lowered the camera lens and stared at the incredible sight. In that moment, his work became real. He recognized the stakes. His need to plan the perfect crime was greater than ever before.

"You've really outdone yourself," he whispered, proud of what he had accomplished. This was so much better than the fire because this he could see.

This went on for over an hour. Then, finally, Jackson Payne exited the house and he didn't look happy.

Viper grinned and stepped forward. He began aggressively taking pictures, acting like he knew something the other reporters didn't. Soon, they followed his lead and someone finally made the connection.

"That's the deputy whose house just burned down. You don't think—"

"Yes. I do think," Viper said, acknowledging the man. They both stared at each other, sharing a look that said they were onto something big. And they were. Something larger than life.

CHAPTER FORTY-TWO

A LOUD BANG ERUPTED AND STARTLED ME AWAKE. THE walls shook as I snapped to attention and had my gun aimed at the front door, ready to drop whoever might come through. A few breathless seconds passed before I heard it again. Then I took a deep breath, realizing it was only the trash truck doing its morning rounds.

I laid my gun on my chest and dropped my head back to the pillow.

Cruz's murder left me feeling on edge. I still couldn't make sense of it. I'd been careful when covering my tracks, but I wasn't going to be able to hide my involvement in this for long. I was there, but not the one the eyewitness saw. The fact that I felt like I'd been set up again had me reeling for the truth. Was it Frank? If so, how did he pull it off? And if it wasn't, who murdered Cruz?

We tried to answer those questions last night but got nothing in return. I spoke to the APD officers who responded to the call. They did everything according to the book. Once they knew Cruz was dead, they blocked the entrance to his house and didn't let anyone inside until the first detective arrived, which just so happened to be Moreno.

Go figure.

Not only did I find it interesting that Moreno was the first detective on scene, but he quickly claimed the title of lead detective and already had his finger pointed at me.

Something told me he knew I had visited Cruz but couldn't prove it. I regretted revealing my secret to Sanchez. That report was going to cause problems. My saving grace was that I wasn't in my sheriff's windbreaker at the time, but wearing civilian clothes.

If it wasn't me the neighbor saw enter Cruz's house, then who was it? Moreno? Or someone impersonating a deputy? Either scenario, it was frightening to think who we might go up against.

I slung my leg over the side of the couch and planted my foot flat on the floor.

There was also someone else I couldn't get out of my head —Mr. Aviators.

I set my gun on the coffee table and dug out the crumbled up note in my jeans pocket, staring at the partial plate number from the black Range Rover. Not only did Mr. Aviators make it clear he wanted one—or perhaps both of us— dead, but he was also the only solid lead I had to go on.

I took a picture of the plate number with my cellphone to act as a backup file, then called Smitty's mobile to see what more he might have found when digging through the house ash. He didn't answer. I left a message and told him to call me back. Then I reviewed Frank's wife's murder book, trying to make a connection to either of the murders.

As I flipped the pages, old wounds opened up. I spent over a year of my life working this trial, banking on the fact we had our guy. Frank was as guilty as they got, and it was a long and laborious investigation, a trial the DA was pissed we'd lost. Nothing suggested Frank's case was related to the two I was currently working, but that didn't mean he wasn't trying to frame me.

By the time I was finished, I still couldn't explain why Frank would want to pick a fight so soon after he was acquitted of murder—if in fact that was what he was doing.

I showered, grabbed a quick bite to eat, and then was out the door calling Tex.

"What did you find, cowboy? Was he murdered?" Tex answered his cellphone.

I jumped behind the wheel of my Cruiser and Tex took my silence as a resounding yes.

I said, "I think Frank might have someone on the inside."

"Are you sure?"

"I'm not sure about anything anymore."

Then I told him my plans. I was calling as a way of keeping records of what I was up to in case I needed a defense.

CHAPTER FORTY-THREE

THE AUSTIN *CHRONICLE'S* NEWSROOM'S MOOD WAS SOMBER. It was clear the moment I entered, that the news of Vincent Cruz's murder hit too close to home. I knew little about Cruz's career, but I hoped to learn more today.

A heavyset woman showed me to the newspaper editor's office, and I thanked her for being so kind. I knocked on the editor's door. His name was Maxwell Sheldon, and he told me to come in. I introduced myself and said, "I'm here to ask you a few questions about Vincent Cruz."

He motioned for me to sit. I took the chair across from him. He looked me in the eye and said, "It's heartbreaking what happened to him. We're all surprised by the news. Shaken up as well." He sighed heavily, cleared his throat, and continued, "Have you any leads on who might have done this?"

"I can't comment on the specifics."

"Of course. The investigation is ongoing."

"But that is why I'm here; to see if maybe Cruz had unknowingly stumbled onto something he shouldn't have."

Sheldon locked eyes for a beat, then he said, "I'm surprised you're here, Deputy Payne."

"Call me Jackson."

He gave me an incredulous look, a look that suggested he might have heard what we all had last night. That a sheriff deputy might have been the last to see Cruz alive.

Then, Sheldon said, "I spoke to Deputy Tom Moreno already."

I hid my surprise.

"He called me last night. I was one of the first to learn what happened. Broke my heart."

"Is that all deputy Moreno said?"

Sheldon shook his head. "He asked something similar. He even asked about you."

"What about me?"

"Cruz was investigating your house fire." He said it as a statement, not a question. Sheldon looked into my eyes for the truth, then continued, "I suppose you knew that already?"

"We'd met," I said, looking for any kind of reaction. "Had a pleasant discussion about it yesterday."

Sheldon gave me a knowing look and then showed me today's paper. It was surprisingly thin, and I couldn't recall the last time I held a paper in my hands. It had been a while, but I didn't like what I was seeing. A picture of me exiting Cruz's house was printed on the front page with a headline that had me lifting my gaze. "That, sir, is a big allegation, and one that could get the newspaper in trouble."

"We're just reporting the facts. The connection you make is all your own." Sheldon's eyes sharpened when he said, "But I have to ask. Were you at Cruz's last night?"

I said, "Isn't that what the picture suggests?"

"You know what I mean."

I changed the subject. "Besides Raymond Frank, what other stories was Cruz working, and were they dangerous?"

"They're all dangerous. Cruz wasn't one to let up off his pen once he got writing. He pissed off many people because of it." He broke eye contact and leaned forward. "Don't worry, Detective. He liked you. Admired your work ethic. Thought you were a good cop."

He stood and motioned for me to follow him. We left his office and weaved between cubicles, moving across the newsroom floor. As I followed Sheldon to Cruz's desk, I thought about Moreno and what it was he was trying to prove.

"Cruz was young, but he worked like an old school reporter."

"What do you mean?"

"He hounded his sources for information before jumping onto the Internet. It's the opposite of what a lot of these new kids coming out of university do. Not Cruz. He had a knack for getting to the truth, sniffing out stories before they even happened." A remorseful look crossed his face. Then he looked at me and said, "It was refreshing. Gave me hope that our industry might find a way to survive."

I glanced at the clock on the far wall, and Sheldon saw me do it.

"Anyway," he inhaled a deep breath, "let's not waste any more of your time." He turned to Cruz's desk, said, "Peek around. See what you can find. I can't promise you'll find anything useful, but I had IT unlock his computer. There's a lot there, but maybe you'll see something I couldn't."

"Thank you."

Sheldon nodded and said, "Take all the time you need."

"Do me a solid?" When I had his attention, I said, "Keep this between you and me?"

His face softened. "Your secret is safe with me."

CHAPTER FORTY-FOUR

Two hours later, I climbed into my Cruiser with a thick file of papers and a thumb-drive tucked beneath my arm. Before I left the newsroom's parking lot, I called into the station.

Captain of the Command Staff, Alice Dupre, answered. "Hey Jackson. You staying out of trouble?"

"Doing my best," I said. "Did you see when Deputy Moreno left the building last night?"

"Let me think. Not long after your little powwow."

I wasn't surprised. It was just what I suspected.

"What was that about, anyway?"

I stared ahead and let my thoughts flash back to last night. It was clear, even before yesterday, the upper brass was afraid of bad publicity, and we all had Moreno and his excessive force to thank for that. But had Moreno manipulated Sergeant Hart into making me believe the media already got hold of Pam Johnston's security tape, thinking I might take my questions—and my frustration—straight to Cruz? It was certainly something he would chance, but how could he have known I would? I wasn't that predictable.

"Nothing," I told Alice. "Forget I called."

If Moreno left the building not long after I did, it gave him plenty of time to murder Cruz, while I was getting my ass kicked by Frank. But was that what happened? I wished I didn't think it was possible, but I did. Moreno didn't hide the fact he was making this investigation about me. The question was, how far would he go to seek revenge?

I let that thought sink in as I drove across town. Making matters worse, I knew I shouldn't have told Sanchez about stopping by Cruz's house. Now I wondered if she had let my secret slip to Moreno.

CHAPTER FORTY-FIVE

THE SMELL OF DARK ROAST COFFEE FILLED THE KITCHEN and drifted into Viper's face. The smell invigorated him, jolting him awake. He took a sip from his cup and stared into his backyard. It was fenced in with a six foot tall privacy fence, and he was trying to decide which was most intense; the house fire, or strangling that mole reporter?

The morning news played on the TV behind him as he thought how both crimes had their merits. Though he had certainly showed himself a good time last night, perhaps the most fun was manipulating the media into believing they had the story of their lives.

Soon, the rumor would grow that it was Jackson there to visit Cruz, not Viper. And when it did, Viper would fan the flames until the truth would be harder to believe.

With his coffee getting cold, he zapped it in the microwave, continuing to obsess over Jackson's next move. It was imperative he stayed one step ahead of him.

Think like Jackson. Act like Jackson. Be like Jackson.

Imagining Jackson suffer was thrilling, but Viper desperately needed to prove he was the better man. When Viper reached inside his jeans pocket, he suddenly remembered what he had taken from Jackson the night of the fire. A smile sprouted, and a new idea presented itself. But making it happen wouldn't be easy. Jackson wasn't entirely predictable, and that made him difficult to catch.

"Like me," Viper said, aloud.

"Like you, what?"

Viper turned fast, forgetting he wasn't alone. His girl-friend pranced into the kitchen wearing only her underwear. She was holding her cellphone with one hand, messaging a friend. Viper never understood how someone could be so connected to a device and actually want to share their life with the outside world.

What was she typing now, and to whom?

Enjoy youth while it's on your side, he thought, letting his eyes lazily drift down her backside. She never asked where he was last night, but knew the routine. If anyone asked, he was with her—always with her.

Instead of answering her question, he asked, "Plans today?"

"Meeting a friend," she said, stopping to glance at the pile of outgoing mail.

Viper stared and wondered if she knew what he was planning to send.

"Going to get my hair and nails done." She turned to him and smiled.

He called her over and, when she was within reach, he gripped her wrist and yanked her to his chest. She clawed her way up to his shoulders and took his face into her hands. With heavy eyes, she purred, "Unless you had other plans for me?"

"Meet me in the bedroom."

"What about the guns? You have them all over the bed."

Viper laughed. "Ah, yes. The guns." He'd nearly forgotten

he'd laid them out. "Don't worry about them. They won't hurt you." Then he reached behind him, grabbed the sheriff's cap he wore last night, and put it on her head.

"What's this?" she asked.

With his hand on her hip, he said, "I thought maybe we could do a little role play before I go to work."

CHAPTER FORTY-SIX

I TOOK TEMPORARY RESIDENCE AT A BAR AND GRILL WHERE I ordered lunch. Then I got to work on Vincent Cruz's notes. It didn't take me long to separate them into three piles. Three possibilities I believed may have been a deciding factor in Cruz's death.

First, there was my neighbor Pam Johnston's testimony. She was convinced I killed my wife. After I read Cruz's notes, I better understood his need to vet me before highlighting his concern about Raymond Frank and that Frank was the one to give him the idea, laying out the motive why I would have started the house fire that killed my family.

But Cruz said his source *walked like a cop*.

Did Frank have that kind of swagger? I believed he did.

Then there was the story on Moreno's excessive force. Though it was just a blip in the scheme of Cruz's career, it reminded me of the piece Cruz had written about my own police shooting last year, the incident that got Alan Bolin terminated. Though Moreno's excessive force incident happened before the fire, his exoneration hadn't.

That had me thinking.

I lifted my head and was reminded how Bolin had warned me about Moreno. Though I couldn't be sure it was him who gave Cruz my divorce papers and the pictures of my family, I certainly thought it was possible.

Moreno should have never been asked to come back to work until after he went through a proper internal investigation. Instead, he was given the keys to investigate my family's murder. Now, ironically, Moreno seemed to be doing a good job of convincing the same upper brass—who should have terminated him—to turn their focus on me instead.

I read through Cruz's notes for a second time, thoroughly confusing myself to the point of second guessing everything. I needed to get this right—especially if Moreno was somehow involved. But was it possible that Cruz and I had it all wrong? Perhaps it wasn't Frank seeking revenge, but instead Moreno?

But the third pile had me wondering if the district attorney who prosecuted Frank for the murder of his wife pressed Frank's current girlfriend, Candy Scott, hard enough when testifying on Frank's behalf. It wasn't the first time I read her conflicting testimony. What I wasn't sure about was if she purposely lied for Frank, or if they had threatened her to lie before taking the stand?

Either way, something told me Cruz's work on Candy was left unfinished, and now, it was up to me to see whether Candy could be the wedge needed to get to Frank.

CHAPTER FORTY-SEVEN

CANDY SCOTT WASN'T HARD TO FIND. SHE HAD MADE A name for herself in the lead up to—and during—Raymond Frank's murder trial. In the end, she was his number one supporter who basked in the media spotlight which she then turned into her own personal brand.

Candy was an unemployed socialite who kept her whereabouts well known. Her various social media feeds left little room for secrecy, but what made her public image even more interesting was knowing how much she had to lose if Frank's trial had gone the other way.

Was it possible Candy had started the fire, thinking Frank wouldn't get off? It made more sense than having Frank take the risk himself, but why hadn't I thought of that before?

I parked out front and entered through the glass doors. A strong chemical smell hit me in the face as soon as I entered the day spa. A woman in her thirties worked the front desk and laughed. "You'll get used to it. This your first time?"

She wore entirely too much makeup, and hairspray froze her hair in place. It wasn't my type of establishment, but it wasn't like men didn't come to these types of places, either.

I said, "That obvious, huh?"

Her lipstick was so bright it hurt my eyes.

"Did you make an appointment?"

When I shook my head no, she asked what I would like done. She seemed too eager to get the virgin in the chair and begin grooming him. I crushed her dreams by saying, "I'm here to speak with a friend, Candy Scott."

Her lips closed as she pointed over her shoulder.

Candy looked relaxed as she leaned back in her chair, her nails being worked on. Her eyes were closed and she was busy chatting up the man sitting in the chair next to her. He wore a beard, and I stared, thinking it was Mr. Aviators from the park. Maybe he was, maybe he wasn't.

I started heading their way. He stood, and they hugged. Then he passed by me as if I didn't exist.

"Hey," I said, turning to him. "Do I know you from somewhere?"

He turned around. Gave me a questioning look. "Can't say I've seen you before."

I believed him.

"Must have you mistaken with someone else," I said, making a gun with my hand and pretending to shoot him. "Sorry, partner."

He squinted his eyes and looked even more confused. I watched him all the way to this car. A silver Lexus. It would have been too easy to cross paths with Aviators. I turned back to Candy. She was on her phone when I took the seat next to her.

I said, "Hi, Candy."

She startled. Surprised to see me. She didn't even take the phone away from her ear when she said, "What do you want?"

"Thought it was time I properly introduced myself."

"I know who you are."

"But I don't know who you are."

She rolled her eyes as if not in the mood for my bullshit. Then she told whoever she was talking to on the phone she'd have to call them back. She said to me, "Then let's keep it that way."

"Mind if I ask you a few questions?"

"Do I have a choice?"

"Any of your friends drive a black Range Rover?"

"What's it to you?"

"Why did you and Raymond stop by my place the other morning?"

"You'll have to ask him."

"I intend to, but while I have you here, what did you mean when you said, '*What type of person are you, Detective? One to let go, or will you chase after her forever?*' Was there something you were referring to?"

Candy sat forward and looked me in the eye. She reached for my hand and curled her bottom lip. "We just don't want to see you suffer any longer. You must be devastated. I know I would be."

"Care to elaborate? I'm not sure I know what you're talking about." She pulled her hand away, and when she didn't respond, I asked, "Where were you the night my house burned down?"

She leaned back and closed her eyes. "You want to know what I think this is really about?" One eye opened. "Last night."

Of course she knew about my brief visit to Frank's and how I had my ass handed to me. She was probably there, watched it all go down so she could throw it in my face, like she was doing now.

I said, "If Frank had anything to do with burning my house down, or killing Vincent Cruz, we'll get you on co-conspirator charges. That's three counts of first degree murder, Ms. Scott."

Both her eyes snapped open. That got her attention.

I softened my tone, and said, "Unless, that is...you cooperate."

I handed her my card. Her cheeks flushed and she didn't look happy. She asked me as I stood, "What is it you have against Ray, anyway?"

"Besides him being a murderer? Nothing." I turned to leave, told her to have a nice day.

Candy called after me, "My Frankie didn't do what you think he did."

Without looking, I continued toward the exit, saying, "Don't go down with Frank. Do the right thing. You have my number."

CHAPTER FORTY-EIGHT

RAYMOND FRANK WAS LINING UP HIS TARGET WHEN HE GOT the call from Candy. But, before answering it, he took a shallow breath, held it, and then fired his weapon.

A blast of fire left his muzzle.

A clink followed.

He hit his target—bullseye.

Then Frank set his rifle down on the bench in front of him and answered the call.

"Hey baby." Candy was frantic. She seemed spooked. "Slow down and tell me what happened."

Frank ground his teeth as Candy told him about her visit from Jackson Payne. *Who did that pig think he was? He had no right harassing Candy. This beef was between me and him.*

Candy said, "He was asking about the house fire and the murder of print reporter Vincent Cruz. Apparently he's dead, and Jackson said you did them both."

"Ridiculous. I wouldn't be so stupid."

"That's what I told him, baby. You're smarter than that."

Frank felt his blood pressure spike to new levels when he asked, "What else did you tell him?"

"Nothing. I didn't tell him shit."

Frank promised to take care of it, and said, "It's nothing for you to worry about, but if he comes back, don't tell him anything. Got it?"

"Got it."

"He's only trying to get you to confess to something you didn't do."

When Frank ended the call, he was livid. First, Jackson had the balls to come to his house and jump the gate. Now he was going after his girlfriend? He tried to think what Jackson might have on him. There must be something, but the only explanation he could come up with was vengeance; retribution for a murder trial that failed to convict. That had to be it.

"But two can play the game called revenge," Frank said out loud.

He stepped to the side and picked up an AR-15. He squeezed off a fast clip, then did it again. After hundreds of rounds fired, Frank took a moment to breathe. Movement caught his eye and he removed his earbuds when he saw his associate arrive.

"Now what?" Frank barked.

His associate handed him an envelope.

Frank asked, "What the hell is this?"

"It arrived at the office early this morning. It says it's important."

Frank tore open the envelope and ripped out the papers from inside. He read them over and showed his associate what he received.

The associate said, "If you do anything with this, Jackson will come for you."

"He already is," Frank said, picking up the AR-15 once again, thinking how he'd like to put Jackson directly in his field of fire.

CHAPTER FORTY-NINE

I FELT LIKE I WAS ON TO SOMETHING. CANDY WAS definitely harboring a secret. But did it have something to do with her, Frank, or both of them? That, I didn't know.

I climbed into the Cruiser, thinking I needed to keep an eye on her and apply more pressure if needed. Candy was smart, but fragile. And until that time came, I expected to receive a visit from Frank.

Then my cellphone rang. It was Smitty.

"Did you get my message?" I asked.

"Have they not told you?"

"Told me what?"

Smitty cursed under his breath.

"What's up? What did you find?" I could sense he was having difficulty finding the words. I knew the news couldn't be good. "You can tell me. Even over the phone. What is it?"

"We found something," Smitty finally said.

A bubble closed over my head as Smitty explained the details of carbonized bones found in the ashes. As I listened, I clutched Selina's compass rose pendant.

"It was Ilene, Jackson. I'm sorry. I was really hoping it wouldn't come to this."

I closed my eyes, bowed my head. Then, after a moment of silence, I asked, "What about Selina?"

"Nothing."

But I was certain she couldn't have escaped the blaze. I kept the phone pressed to my ear and sat quietly for a half-hour, blankly staring ahead, thinking about how this officially marked the beginning of a new homicide investigation. Smitty never hung up and occasionally asked if I was all right.

I wasn't sure I was—if I would ever be again.

But, before I let him go, Smitty said, "The ME will complete the report and pass along the details to Detective Moreno. Call me if you need anything, anything at all."

"I will. Thanks."

"And, Jackson, good luck catching the brute who did this. It was one of the worst fires I've ever seen and they deserve to die."

CHAPTER FIFTY

I FELT EMPTY. MY BUCKET HAD BEEN TURNED OVER. THERE was nothing else for me to give. I blamed myself for letting it come to this.

Ilene's biggest fear had always been having Selina grow up without a father. Mine had always been that the bad guys I chased would go after my family. And now they had.

My hand shook as I refused to let go of Selina's pendant. I cleared my throat, attempting to keep my emotions checked. I listened to my shaky voice promise to kill whoever had murdered my family, wishing there was something worse than death itself.

I sat quietly with my thoughts for several minutes before finally dialing Ilene's sister.

Caroline knew as soon as she picked up. "They didn't make it out, did they?"

"I'm sorry," I said.

The news deeply saddened Caroline. Saddened both of us. Caroline didn't need to know the details, but I told her anyway.

She asked, "How is the investigation coming along?"

"I'm working some leads," I said. "Not sure how long it's going to take. The fire destroyed most of the house and we have little evidence to work with."

"You take as much time as you need, Jackson, and I'll take care of the rest."

A couple minutes passed where no one spoke. Then my heart broke when I said, "I'd like Selina's headstone to be next to her mother's."

CHAPTER FIFTY-ONE

THIRTY MINUTES LATER, I WAS WALKING THROUGH THE corridors of Central Command trying to keep my head up when faced with the dark glares and sideways looks from my colleagues. Again, they didn't seem to want to look me in the eye. What was it this time? I thought.

They ducked their heads and looked away, acting as if I didn't belong. I ignored it and marched right into Deputy Chief Matt David's office. He was on the phone and motioned for me to sit down.

I said, "This won't take long."

David cut his call short.

"I talked to Smitty," I said. "When were you going to tell me Ilene was killed in the fire?"

"I just learned of it myself."

"Then consider this my official notice that I'll be taking over the investigation."

"You were never off of it." David gave me a knowing look that suggested he knew what I had been up to. "But, Jackson, what were you thinking going to Raymond Frank's house?"

I could only stare. David didn't look happy.

He said, "Frank is meeting with an IAD officer now, and let me say, it's not looking good for you."

"Frank's here?" I needed to speak with him myself. Listen in on the conversation. "Which room?" I asked.

David shook his head and continued giving me that look that said he didn't know who I was anymore. "He's filing a complaint against you, Jackson."

I had to admit, of all the moves I anticipated Frank making, this wasn't one of them.

David knew I was monitoring Frank's movements, had harassed him, and even showed up at his house armed. "With the intention to do what, Jackson? Your behavior is unacceptable."

"You don't understand; Frank has been stalking *me* since the morning of the fire. Not the other way around."

"Where's your report?" David glanced down at his desk. "I don't see it anywhere."

"If I reported every low life that threatened me—"

"The trial is over. Whatever you have—or think you have —against Frank, you need to let it go and move on."

A deputy entered the office behind me and interrupted. I turned, and he hesitated when he realized it was me who was standing there.

"What is it?" David asked.

"Sir, it's the news."

"What about the news?"

The deputy shifted his eyes to me, and said, "There is talk that the sheriff's office might be involved in the coverup of Deputy Payne's house fire."

CHAPTER FIFTY-TWO

THE PERFECT TIMING WAS NOTHING SHORT OF SUSPICIOUS. Pam Johnston's security tapes had been leaked to the press. As if the deck hadn't already been stacked against me, I now had this to deal with, too.

After the deputy left the office, David quirked an eyebrow as if asking why I hadn't followed. "Don't you want to see yourself on TV?" he asked me.

"I've seen it already," I said. "Moreno and Hart made sure of it last night."

David didn't let on that he knew about my interview last night, but I was certain he'd seen the report. But who had leaked the footage? Something told me it was Moreno, and when I put him at the scene of Cruz's murder, it only made further sense. I had taken Cruz's notes and, along with them, the narrative to suggest I was the only one with the motive to murder my family.

I said, "Last night when Moreno dragged me in here, they even hinted that this might happen."

"Are you implying they leaked the video to the press?"

"Do you think one of them would?"

I had suspected Moreno since they shortened his suspension, but where did David stand on the issue? I thought I knew, but didn't want to make any assumptions.

"Jackson," David lowered his voice to a whisper, "I'm worried about you."

"I'm fine."

"I can only imagine what you must be going through."

He was referring to the obvious stress and not allowing myself time to properly mourn. If I stopped now, I'd lose the little momentum I had. David stared and I suspected what he was getting at. I wished he'd stop dancing around the bush and just come out and ask what it was he was thinking. Then he did.

"I know you've recently been in contact with Vincent Cruz."

"It wasn't me the eyewitness was referring to."

David looked me in the eye and slowly nodded his head. "That's what I wanted to know."

I noted how I was dressed in civilian clothes, then I said, "Cruz was an ally. He made the same connection I did."

"Which is what?"

"That someone was trying to set me up."

David listened with an attentive ear as I laid out my theory. I spoke about Cruz's source and how Cruz was given private information about my divorce. David never asked how I got the information, and I never told him.

"These two cases are linked," I said. "I'm sure of it, Chief. Give me time and I'll prove it, but I can't do it alone. I need your support to ease the friction."

He took his time to think it over before saying, "You can stay on and work Cruz's case."

It was David's way of saying I could also work on my wife's case, too.

"But I need you to stay clear of IA."

I agreed and turned to the door.

"And, Jackson?"

I turned my head to look.

"Don't make me regret my decision."

CHAPTER FIFTY-THREE

It seemed the entire unit stopped what they were doing to watch the news. I stood at the back wall, catching a piece of it myself. The TV news anchors were busy putting the spin on what little they knew.

First, they showed a video clip of me on Pam Johnston's home surveillance entering my own home, quickly followed by images of the fiery aftermath. Then they jumped into coverage of Vincent Cruz's murder and how it was thought a Travis County Sheriff Deputy had been seen entering Cruz's home shortly before he was killed. But it was that they were blaming me for both crimes that really grated on my nerves.

Moreno was standing below the TV next to Hart. They both had their arms crossed. Moreno turned around and was surprised to see me standing there. He pointed at the TV and lifted both his eyebrows as if to say, *get a load of this*.

I ignored him and went back to staring at the screen. The news was eating this up like it was the greatest thing to ever cross their desk. Thing was, I knew none of it was true.

"Are the two cases connected?" the anchor asked. "That is

what the Travis County Sheriff's Office is trying to find out. If you have any leads... please call..."

Sanchez entered the room and caught my eye. I didn't need to hear any more lies. I headed for the exit. Sanchez followed. When it was just the two of us, she caught my arm and said, "Heads up, Jackson. The forensic analyst who gave me Pam's tape told Moreno about my request."

"How did Moreno respond?"

Sanchez shrugged. "Moreno hasn't spoken to me about it."

I knew the coward wouldn't. I looked her in the eye when I asked, "But who leaked the tape?"

Sanchez looked hurt I'd even suggest she might have been the one to do it. Her eyes told me everything I needed to know. It wasn't her. There was something else I learned today that made me know I could trust her.

I said, "I read your report on Cruz's murder."

"I couldn't," she said, referring to her deliberate omission of me going inside Cruz's house perhaps only minutes before he was murdered.

"Thank you."

"Don't thank me yet. Eventually the truth will surface, but at least it will buy you some time."

She was right. I was on borrowed time. Soon, the prints would come back and place me inside Cruz's home. Then the assumptions about my being there would really begin to fly.

"Do me a favor?" I asked.

"Will this favor get me in trouble?"

I dug out the piece of paper I'd been carrying around in my pocket and handed it over to Sanchez. "Try to complete the puzzle?" She looked at the partial plate number and I said, "Goes to a black Range Rover. 2019. Maybe a 2020."

"And which investigation will this be attached to?"

Without going into the details, I said, "I think whoever the owner is, might also know why Cruz was murdered."

CHAPTER FIFTY-FOUR

I COULDN'T THINK AT THE OFFICE, SO I HEADED FOR THE exit, thinking about how Moreno knew about Sanchez reviewing Pam Johnston's security tape—the same tape that was now playing nonstop on the news.

Coincidence? I thought not. But was he planning to frame Sanchez, too? I hoped not. She didn't need to be dragged into my mess, but I was warned more than once about Moreno's ability to hold a grudge.

As soon as I stiff-armed my way through the back door, I squinted into the light and couldn't believe what I was seeing. The first press van had arrived and, instead of coming after me, they had found my first critic to talk to.

There was Raymond Frank in the spotlight. The microphone jammed in front of his face. He looked so sure of himself; happy as a clam to speak freely without having to defend his own actions.

This time I was the one on trial. A trial by media.

I circled the wagons and stayed off to the side to get close, but not close enough to be seen. I was curious about what Frank had to say, what he was telling them so animatedly. His hands waved wildly and his voice boomed loud enough for me to hear his words.

"I don't have to tell you that Jackson Payne is a dirty cop," Frank said. "We've all seen enough to know it's true; the evidence against him speaks for itself. And, to tell you the truth, I'm happy to see his true character has finally come to light, because this is what I have been saying all along."

The reporter's questions were harder to hear. As I stood behind them in the shadows, I wondered if Frank would have filed a complaint against me if I hadn't spoken with Candy earlier this morning. But if that was his reason for doing this, it meant they were scared. And scared, I liked.

Frank said to the cameras, "I came here today to reiterate the point I've been making since day one. Deputy Jackson Payne is a liar who will do anything to win. Including tampering with witnesses to say I did something that I didn't. But this isn't about me; it's about a corrupt cop out for revenge."

The reporter asked another question. Again, it was muffled.

I couldn't hear what was being asked, but I could hear Frank say, "I can't comment on the specifics. But I will say this. Jackson Payne had you all fooled. He had you looking at me when you should have been looking at him."

That was enough for me. But Frank wasn't done. This time I caught the question: *Do you think deputy Payne started the fire that took his house?*

Frank caught sight of me and said, "The video speaks for itself."

I held still as he stared. None of the reporters seemed to notice. They were too focused on Frank. Then, with a glimmer in his eye, Frank said, "Do I believe I'm in danger? Yes, I do. As long as Deputy Payne is hiding behind the badge, no one is safe."

CHAPTER FIFTY-FIVE

I JUMPED INTO THE CRUISER AND SPED OFF BEFORE THE media circus could catch up to me.

It felt strangely odd to not have Cruz waiting for me outside the station. He was always there, had a knack for sniffing me out, and I could never escape the office without first having to dodge his questions.

Cruz was also the reason I headed back to my neighborhood. It was time I confronted Pam Johnston and sat down for a one-on-one, hoping she'd reveal what might have been said between her and Cruz when I saw them talking yesterday.

Several minutes later, I was parked in front of Pam's house. I got out and stared at the gaping hole between the trees where my house once stood. It was easy to imagine it still there. Even easier to imagine a six-year-old Selina running from the house and into my arms after a long day at work.

Now, crime scene tape fluttered in the gentle breeze and my house was abandoned. Like me.

I glanced at Pam's front door. Her curtains were drawn,

and there was little sign of life to be found. I knew she was reclusive, so I assumed she was home. But it was her security camera—pointed right at me—that gave me a moment's pause.

It was the same camera that proved nothing of who had started the fire, yet managed to make my life a living hell.

With thoughts of Selina, I walked across the street thinking about the irony of working the case the public now suspected I might have committed myself. If the media kept at it, it would only make my job more difficult.

I poked around, kicked the ash, and stood in the approximate location of where Selina's bedroom would have been, wondering if I would ever find any evidence of her death.

I stared into the blue sky, smelling burned chemicals and wood, imagining Selina's bedroom as if it still existed. Soon, I could feel her soft hair on the tips of my fingers, feel her arms tighten around my torso as she gave me one of her world-class hugs.

"I'm sorry, darling," I cried, wanting to believe she might still be alive.

My head was telling me one thing, my heart another, and as I looked around me, I just couldn't imagine how she'd have survived this fire. When I was certain there was nothing left for me to find, I said my goodbye and went to knock on Ms. Johnston's door.

CHAPTER FIFTY-SIX

NOTHING HAPPENED AFTER I RANG PAM'S DOORBELL. I
speculated if she was home. The neighborhood was unusually
quiet. Something told me it had to do with the fire—the
belief that two members of the community had been
murdered for no apparent reason.

Then I heard footsteps inside the house.

I turned and faced the door.

The lock clicked over. I watched the doorknob twist
before the door cracked open. Pam greeted me with a seven-
shot tactical shotgun and said, "I've got nothing to say to
you."

"Ms. Johnston, please, lower your weapon so we can talk."

She raised it higher and pointed it directly at my face. I
stood on solid legs and stared her in the eye. Her arms were
as steady as her trigger finger, and I kept my palms faced out
to show I came to speak in peace.

"Did you kill that reporter, too?"

"I didn't kill anybody," I said.

"That's not what the news is saying."

The news hadn't said I was a murderer but, instead of

arguing, I said, "Yesterday, Vincent Cruz came to you. What did he ask you?"

Her eye squinted as she said, "He asked about you."

"What about me?"

"Wanted to know why you would want your wife and daughter dead."

"I didn't want them dead."

"I always knew you would eventually bring danger to the neighborhood. You're a dangerous man, Mr. Payne."

Pam was getting wild, the tip of the barrel getting closer, but I didn't move. She started telling me about the long hours I worked and how I made Ilene raise Selina alone. Soon she was relating Ilene's story to her own divorce and that was when I realized this was more about her and the resentment she felt for her own broken marriage than it was about me. But what really threw me for a loop was how Cruz had more dirt on me than I cared to admit, yet he still hesitated to write the story. Why was that?

I said to Pam, "The security tape, who did you give it to?"

"The only one who had a warrant. Deputy Tom Moreno."

I thanked her for her time and stepped off her front porch, praying she wouldn't shoot me in the back. Then Pam called after me and said, "Ilene knew you would eventually kill her."

I stopped, turned, and stared with a broken heart. Had Ilene really said that? I didn't ask because I didn't want to know. Maybe things were worse than I thought.

Pam said, "Now get off my property before I drop you dead myself."

CHAPTER FIFTY-SEVEN

Viper dropped off mail at a nearby post office but, before leaving, he made his way to an empty mail truck parked in the back. Inside was a jacket and cap. Before snatching them for himself, he looked around to make sure no one was watching.

The key to not getting caught was pretending like you belonged. No one questioned confidence, and Viper was good at pretending.

He had years of practice building up his ego that could never be deflated. Yes, there were hiccups along the way, like the last sixteen months of his life, but he always got up each morning with renewed determination to show the world who was boss.

He slipped into his Ford with his new cap and jacket and drove away.

A mile down the road, he checked his rearview mirrors. No one was following.

He then turned on the news radio and caught commentary on the murder of crime beat reporter Vincent Cruz. He enjoyed being in the spotlight, and listened to more news as he drove, soon arriving at North University, otherwise known as North Campus, home to mostly calmer and older graduate students serious about studying.

Viper cased the place Jackson Payne was renting and noticed his Land Cruiser was gone. He was certain Jackson was out policing, possibly even looking for him.

"Here I am," Viper said. "Find me if you can. I'm the gingerbread man."

He parked a block over from Jackson's apartment, thinking it was an interesting location to live. Vastly different from the neighborhood he had lived with his wife and daughter. Perhaps Jackson had been expecting a costly divorce—another reason for him to sever his ties by the strike of a match.

He leaned over, opened the glove-box, and took the small velvet box into his hand. Then he walked to Jackson's place while dressed as a postal service employee, acting as if he belonged.

Always acting...

He edged the house and put on his gloves as he approached the front door. He tested it. It was locked. So he picked the lock with surprising ease. Viper entered and closed the door behind him.

"What a pitiful existence," he mumbled.

There was nothing of real value to speak of. As sad as it was, it meant Jackson had only his job left. And, even that, was close to being taken away from him.

After a quick sweep of the place, Viper dove his hand into his jacket pocket and left Jackson a gift that was sure to get his attention. "For you, detective."

CHAPTER FIFTY-EIGHT

IT WAS EVENING NOW, AND I HAD MANAGED TO AVOID THE media the entire afternoon. After my visit with Pam, I tracked down Candy doing some shopping downtown, then watched as she ate a late lunch with a girlfriend. After that, she went home to Frank's for a couple hours and was now leading me to the same nightclub Frank had briefly visited last night on Red River.

It seemed to be a popular place between them, and with Frank's legal troubles now behind him, I suspected I might be able to use it to my advantage.

Candy entered the club alone and I wondered if Frank was waiting for her inside. I waited another thirty minutes before going inside myself. The same bouncer from last night was working the door and, though he didn't act it, I knew he remembered me.

"Your shoes are looking a little shabby," he said, giving me shit. "I'm not sure I can let you inside."

I looked down at my boots. "They're the best I've got."

He stared at my boots and shook his big disapproving head.

I dug out a twenty and stuck the crisp bill into the palm of his hand. "Good enough now?"

"I know you can do better." He lifted his gaze and looked me in the eye. "We have a strict dress code and those boots don't meet it."

I pushed another twenty into his hand and said, "Now?"

"Be good," he said without a smile, tucking his forty-dollar extortion tip into his back pocket.

I entered the club and listened as the music bumped. I never understood the dress code requirements when the entire club was as dark as it was. Then again, I preferred bars like Creek House to places like this.

I ordered a drink at the bar—an old-fashioned—and took my time drinking it.

Candy was in the back at a reserved table doing lines with her friends. I didn't recognize most of the faces she was with. I didn't see Frank, or Aviators from the park, but I saw the man from the day spa.

Interesting...

I finished my drink and approached their table just as Candy came up after doing another line. Her eyes widened when she saw me, and she glanced away. I flashed my badge to the bearded man next to her and told him to take a hike.

He looked to Candy for permission and she nodded her head. He scooted out and I scooted in, brushing Candy's shoulder.

"Funny seeing you here," I said.

Candy wouldn't look at me. She knew I had her on possession charges if I needed it. The evidence was all over the table in front of me, but I wasn't here to bust her. Instead, I leaned back, slung my arm over the back of the booth, and asked, "Frank know you have a boyfriend on the side?"

"He's not my boyfriend."

"Doesn't matter. Frank will tell me who he is, after I show him the photos I took of the two of you."

Candy sneered, "He's gay."

That would explain things, I thought. "Where is your Frankie, by the way?"

"What is it you want from me?"

"I got to thinking about our talk earlier, and I was hoping you had more for me?"

"If I did, I would have called you."

"I thought the same, but life happens fast."

"I don't know anything."

"Are you sure? Have you given it some thought?"

She angled her body toward me and said, "Actually, I have."

"And?"

"What I think is exactly what the news thinks."

I saw Candy's eyes drift over my right shoulder. When I turned to look, Bearded Man was back with some added muscle. I could tell by the looks on their faces that this was going to get ugly.

"I'm not going to waste my time busting you for blow," I said to Candy as I scooted out from the table, "because I'd rather get you on second degree murder."

CHAPTER FIFTY-NINE

THE MUSCLE PLAYED IT COOL AND LET ME LEAVE WITH NO added trouble. But Candy was making the wrong decision by staying quiet. I left the club feeling like I was spinning in circles, and I was nearly to my Cruiser, when two men came out from the shadows.

They were Frank's men from last night.

The big guy flicked a butane lighter and lit his smoke while the little guy flexed.

I said, "You fellas come for another rodeo?"

"And get caught up on battery charges? I don't think so," the small man said.

Then Mr. Big blew smoke in my face, and Smalls took a swing at me the moment I blinked. I ducked and lunged forward, landing a gut punch to Smalls that made him squeal. Mr. Big came in over my head just as I twisted around, landing an elbow to his face that made his nose crack. His cigarette went flying from his mouth and blood gushed out both of his nostrils.

By the time I came up for air, our dance had caught the attention of a few people.

Mr. Big charged me like a bull. He slammed into me with his entire weight and picked me off the ground, driving me straight back onto the hood of a nearby pickup truck. I grappled for position as he jabbed my ribs. Then I put him in a chokehold that took away his breath.

The crowd circled and taunted for more.

When Mr. Big went limp, I kicked him off and watched his big body flop to the ground like a dead fish. Then I went after Smalls, who was still working to catch his breath. He was bent over with his hands on his knees. I kicked him in the back of the knee and watched him crumble to the ground. Then I finished the job by slamming the heel of my boot between his shoulders. Smalls toppled over and kissed the pavement.

I was really getting into it when a hand landed on my shoulder. Without thinking, I reached around, grabbed a wrist, twisted around, and was about to snap the bone when I realized it was a friendly.

Bolin.

The moment I saw the look in his eye was the minute I knew I had made a mistake. Still clutching onto his wrist, I looked around. People smiled and cheered as if they had scored front row seats to a private fight.

"Go on, get!" The bouncer told everyone to move on. "Show's over."

Mr. Big came to, pushed himself to his feet, and said, "It's not over, Jackson."

"I agree. Let's mutton bust again sometime soon. That was fun," I said.

I turned to Bolin, who didn't look too impressed. The crowd chanted my name, and I heard someone yell, "You should have killed them, too!"

Bolin asked, "Where's your car?"

I pointed to the Land Cruiser. Bolin hurried me away,

opened the driver's door, and got me inside. But, before closing it, he said, "I know what you're going through, Jackson. Trust me. I do. And I know what it feels like to have lost control of your career, but these people aren't worth it."

"That's not what this is about," I said.

Bolin disagreed. "If you ever want to have a fighting chance at learning who murdered your family, you need to play this smart. Now get out of here before you end up like me."

CHAPTER SIXTY

I TOOK THE LONG WAY HOME TO MAKE SURE I WOULDN'T BE tailed. The raw ache in my hand had spread, and I needed to clean up. Mr. Big's blood was all over my shirt, and Bolin had left me with a lot to think about.

Things were different now that my name was in the news. I had a more recognizable face than I cared to admit, and anonymity would be in short supply. Where I could once rustle a few hotheads, Bolin made me realize that time had come to an end. At least temporarily, until I could figure out why someone wanted to set me up for the murders of my family and Cruz.

The apartment was dark when I arrived home. The neighbor above had a few people over. They were playing music, and scents of barbeque were in the air. I wanted nothing more than to kick back with a few beers before falling asleep.

I dug out my house key at the door, surprised to find my apartment already unlocked. Without hesitating, I reached for my gun and looked over my shoulder. Then I nudged the door open with the toe of my boot and flicked on the light.

"Please don't shoot me. I'm not armed," a woman's voice said from the couch.

She was in her mid-forties and she wore her red hair down. Her leather jacket was unzipped halfway down her chest, revealing her voluptuous figure. I knew who she was, and I also suspected I knew why she was here. But what I didn't know was how she knew where I lived.

"How did you get in?" I asked, lowering my gun and closing the door behind me.

Whitney Voak said, "The door was unlocked when I arrived. Thought I'd let myself inside and wait until you came home."

"You should have called," I said.

Whitney was an eyewitness who testified against Frank. I had no reason to suspect her, but with everything else going on, I remained hesitant.

"I did," she said. "You didn't answer."

"I'm glad you're here," I said. "There're some questions I'd like to ask you."

"It's about the fire, isn't it?" When I gave her a funny look, she added, "I knew I needed to speak to you as soon as I saw the news."

She looked at me for some kind of confirmation. I asked, "Why is that?"

"There's no way you did it."

"We don't know who did."

"But you think it might have been Frank?"

I stared without giving away my thoughts. Her eyes drifted to the bloodstains on my shirt. Indeed, that was exactly what I was thinking, but I couldn't tell her that without first knowing why she was here.

Whitney calmly said, "The question is, how? If Frank would be acquitted hours later, why would he take the risk by doing something so brazen as attacking your family?"

Whitney had been my strongest eyewitness, and though she was convincing in her delivery, unwavering when cross-examined, she was also Frank's wife's sister who had seen Frank exit the house after the murder, still holding the murder weapon in his hand. Still, with all that, it wasn't enough to seal the deal. So we were here, having to decide what Frank might be up to next.

I said, "It crossed my mind."

Her gaze was steady; there wasn't an anxious bone in her body. Had the trial numbed her? Or had she not yet made the connection that she might be Frank's next victim?

"That's what made me believe he did it." Whitney paused. "Or had someone do it for him. The perfect alibi."

She stood. Walked around the room. Checked out the white walls, stopping occasionally to stare as if a prized painting hung instead of only painted sheetrock. I didn't tell her I was working on Candy, because I didn't want another secret of mine to get revealed.

Whitney turned to me and said, "The news reported a Travis County sheriff's deputy was seen shortly before they found the journalist murdered. The reporter was investigating the house fire, wasn't he?"

She couldn't know I was wearing civilian clothes, but she certainly acted like she knew.

"What are you getting at?" I asked.

"What I'm telling you is, Frank likes to use disguises. He did it when killing my sister and nearly got caught. He won't get fooled again. Killing my sister was only practice for what he's capable of doing now."

My heart was hammering when she closed the gap between us. Her green eyes shined; she smelled beautiful. Lifting her gaze to mine, she said, "He won't make the same mistake twice."

"Are you saying Frank killed the reporter?"

"I'm saying it's possible."

"If you know something, you can tell me."

She touched my arm and stared into my eyes. "I've already told you everything, but if I'm right, I imagine your job is about to get so much harder."

CHAPTER SIXTY-ONE

SHERIFF DEPUTY TOM MORENO WAS PARKED ADJACENT TO
Jackson Payne's apartment with a pair of binoculars in his
hand. From behind the steering wheel of his civilian Ford F-
150, he peered through the optics and watched the shadows
move behind closed curtains.

Two people were inside the apartment, but he was certain
he'd seen Jackson arrive home alone.

Who was with him? How had Moreno not known
someone else had entered the apartment?

Moreno lowered his binoculars away from his eyes and
thought about his mission. It was the greatest irony having to
survey the man who could once do no wrong. Something
about it felt right. Like the pendulum had shifted off
Moreno's shoulders and onto Jackson's.

But was Jackson working to cover his tracks, or looking to
solve a murder?

Moreno couldn't decide.

He lifted his binoculars and pointed the lenses to Jackson's neighbor's barbeque. The party was spilling outside and
Moreno wondered what they thought about Jackson—if

anything at all? Had they seen the news? Were they aware that a killer might be living below?

Moreno made a mental note to come back and speak with them at a later time. Then he flipped on the dome light and once again reviewed Raymond Frank's initial complaint before it had been passed on to Internal Affairs.

He shook his head at the absurdity. But it was the feeling that Jackson handled the recent string of homicides that kept Moreno focused on connecting the dots. They had one commonality between them, and that was Jackson Payne.

"What happened to you?" Moreno muttered.

A pair of headlights caught his attention. He turned off the dome light and let the car pass. A hint of paranoia had him tense. Then it all went away the moment Jackson's front door opened.

Moreno paused and stared as a red-headed beauty exited the apartment. She pivoted on a pair of glowing white pumps, as if expecting Jackson to give her a kiss goodbye.

Moreno knew her face, knew her name too, and her connection to Jackson. What he didn't know was why she was here tonight.

He took a couple photographs for his files and liked how the two of them were back at it—reunited against what he assumed was a common enemy; Raymond Frank.

"What are you two planning to do? Anything?" Moreno could only assume.

Jackson watched Whitney Voak walk to her car and slide into a cherry red Camaro only one-hundred yards in front of where Moreno was parked. After she sped away, Jackson barely looked to see who might be watching. Then Moreno left before Jackson caught him casing his house.

CHAPTER SIXTY-TWO

WHITNEY HAD LEFT ME WITH A LOT TO THINK ABOUT. SHE was the second person to come to me, suggesting Frank was the killer I should be chasing. Frank knew about the house fire well before it caught the attention of the media, but did he also kill Cruz?

I showered and changed shirts, then opened my laptop computer and reminded myself that what Whitney had said was absolutely true. Raymond Frank liked to use disguises, and certainly wouldn't make the same mistake twice. But did he pose as a sheriff's deputy when entering Vincent Cruz's house? I wasn't so sure. What I did know was that Frank was playing offense.

We all wanted to see justice served, but Frank wasn't an easy target. He had money and connections, and a river of momentum on his side. Basically, everything I lacked.

I leaned back and was thinking about Candy Scott when I received a call from Sanchez.

"What are you doing?" she asked. "Are you busy?"

"Just reviewing cases."

"Mind if I stop by? I have dinner."

"Dinner sounds good," I said.

There was a sense of urgency in her voice and I hoped she had linked the partial plate number to a name. I closed the lid on my laptop, cleaned up a bit, and opened the door as soon as I heard her arrive.

"In the neighborhood?" I asked.

"I knew you wouldn't say no to food."

"And if I had?"

"Then I'd have to eat it all myself."

Sanchez entered my apartment and set the food bag on the kitchen counter. Incredible scents of brisket sandwiches and home fries filled the air, but Sanchez smelled something much different.

She asked, "Who's the woman you're seeing?"

"Excuse me?"

"That scent in the air. It's a woman's. Who is she?"

Impressed by her awareness, I told her about Whitney Voak's visit and tried to change the subject.

"You two been seeing each other a lot?" Sanchez asked.

"There's nothing going on between us," I said, trying to change the subject again. "Talked to Smitty earlier."

"I heard. I'm sorry, Jackson."

"It's not like we didn't know what was coming."

"So, if nothing is going on between you and Whitney, then why was she here?"

Sanchez couldn't let it go. I said, "She saw the news about Cruz and it made her think about Frank."

"What, she thinks he might have been the one to have whacked Cruz?"

"In fact, she does," I said, mentioning what Whitney said about Frank's appreciation for disguises.

"Just a hunch feeling she had?"

"That's all it is," I confirmed. "Frank did it once before, why not do it again?"

Sanchez said she heard about Frank filing a complaint with IA. "He's smart, Jackson. Whether he did it or not, he's out to make your life miserable."

"I know it," I said, asking if she had heard if the prints were back from Cruz's house.

"Haven't heard."

"There's no sense of urgency," I muttered, "because no one thinks the cases are linked."

She opened the to-go box and told me to eat. I retrieved a couple Lone Stars from the fridge and set the beer on the counter next to Sanchez. After my first bite, I thanked her for the meal.

"You need to eat, Jackson."

She was right. I hadn't been eating. I was too consumed by thoughts of Frank—too sick that my wife and daughter had been murdered in cold blood.

"He finally stopped stalking me," I said.

"Who? Frank?"

I nodded and Sanchez saw my swollen hand.

"Did you get in a fight?"

"It's nothing," I assured her, hiding my fist under the counter.

She sighed and stared. I couldn't look her in the eye. I knew she was worried about me and what I might do. I was worried about myself, too.

I said, "I spoke with Candy Scott today."

"And?"

"She had everything to lose if Frank was convicted."

"Do you think she started the fire?"

"I don't know, but it makes sense, right?" I said, recalling how she and Frank stopped by my new apartment the morning after to send their condolences.

"Anything is possible, but I will tell you this: that woman is an embarrassment to Whitney's family. Can you imagine the loss of dignity they all must have felt, knowing Frank murdered your sister to be with a woman like Candy?" Sanchez took a bite of her sandwich, then said, "But do your homework, Jackson. Whitney wants to see Frank put away as much as anybody else."

I said I trusted Whitney, then added, "She didn't seem scared or worried Frank might come after her too. Whitney was confident, like she—"

"—had a plan?"

"Yeah." We locked eyes, and I asked, "Do you think Moreno leaked the security tape?"

"I don't know. He certainly seemed to enjoy himself."

"When I spoke to Ms. Johnston today, she said something about how Ilene knew I would eventually kill her."

"She said that?"

I nodded. "Could be the reason Moreno is focusing his investigation on me?"

Sanchez dove her hand into her jacket pocket and handed me a folded piece of paper. She said, "You were right, the partial plate goes to a 2020 black Range Rover, owned by a man named Steve Eli." She told me the address and said Steve had no criminal record. "But get this, he reported his car stolen five days ago."

CHAPTER SIXTY-THREE

VIPER PULLED THE CAR OUT FRONT, PARKED ALONG THE curb, and messaged his girlfriend to meet him on the street. Two minutes later, she trotted to the car and climbed inside.

"Where did you get this piece of junk?" she asked.

"You calling this car junk?" He revved the engine, listened to it purr.

Viper's girlfriend laughed. "I am."

"That's because I spoil you."

Her eyes drifted to his lap. "What are you going to do with that?"

Without taking his eyes off of hers, Viper firmed up his grip on the butt of his nine-millimeter, and said, "Nothing, if I don't have to."

She lifted her eyes and Viper watched the color drain from her face. She asked, "Why are you looking at me like that?"

"Like what?" He grinned.

"You're acting strange." She looked away. "There was a fight at the nightclub. Did you hear about it?"

Viper set his hand on her thigh closest to him. "That's why I called."

She turned her head and he watched her smile disappear.

"I did something tonight," he said.

"What did you do, baby?" she mewed, sensing something was wrong.

"I'll tell you about it later, but nothing will ever be the same again."

"You're scaring me."

He smiled, flashed a look that said everything would be okay. "There's nothing to fear, but I need to know that you're all in?"

"You know I am. There's no one I'd rather be with; nothing I'd rather be doing."

"That's good." Viper smiled. "Because now's the time to duck out if you're not."

She leaned across the center console and took his face between her hands, kissing him on the lips. "I'm not going anywhere. I wore what you told me to, didn't I?"

Viper glanced down at the black form-fitting dress and told her to open up more of her jacket. "Good," he said, reaching into a paper bag in the backseat. He handed her a blonde wig and said, "Now, put this on."

"Who am I dressing up for?" she asked.

Viper put the car in gear and said, "You're doing it for me."

CHAPTER SIXTY-FOUR

"It's like they didn't know Cruz wrote for the *Chronicle*," Sanchez said, looking at me. "This is nothing more than tabloid fodder."

We were still at the kitchen counter, discussing what to do about Steve Eli and his missing black Range Rover when our conversation circled back to Vincent Cruz. Now Sanchez was reviewing the files Cruz had given me just before he was killed.

I said, "Divorce is a motive for murder."

"Except it didn't work."

"Maybe not this time," I said, pointing to the papers in Sanchez's hand, "but the media found their angle with the leaked security tape."

Sanchez said she was tired and moved to the couch as I cleaned up. I grabbed two more beers from the fridge and, when I turned around, I noticed Sanchez holding something in her hand.

"Jackson, is there something you want to ask me?"

It was a black velvet box. Not mine. I asked, "Where did you find that?"

Her smile vanished. She said, "I found it here, in the couch."

My heart was beating faster. It could have fallen out of Whitney's pocket. I set the cans on the counter and sat next to Sanchez.

"Should we open it up?" she asked.

I nodded yes. "But don't touch whatever's inside."

As soon as she had the lid off, Sanchez said, "It's beautiful."

Indeed, it was, but I also knew that this couldn't be a coincidence. When I cursed, Sanchez asked, "What?"

I stared at the royal sapphire rose and said, "It's Selina's birthstone."

I took the small box into my hand, thinking about its cousin, the compass rose pendant I had found in the ash, amazingly still intact. Though this was a different kind of rose, it was still a connection to Selina. I was certain, however it got into my apartment, and whoever left it behind, wanted me to think of my daughter.

"Did you bring that?" I asked Sanchez. "Is this some kind of joke?"

"Jackson, I found it on the couch. Between the cushions. Just like I said."

I stood and moved to the window to cool my anger. Was Whitney playing a sick joke on me, or what? It made little sense. Frank had murdered her sister and we both wanted to see him put away for life. Why bring me something to make me remember what I had lost, too?

"Jackson, is it possible Whitney left it behind on purpose? Did she sit on this couch?"

I hadn't told Sanchez how I found Whitney already in my apartment when I got home, but I was certain I hadn't left my door unlocked. Could I trust her? I thought I could, but maybe not.

"What would she be trying to prove by leaving it behind? And why not mention it to me while she was here?"

I turned and started looking for other clues that could have been left behind. I checked the locks to make sure they hadn't been broken, then I opened and shut closet doors. Sanchez followed, calling after me, wanting to know how she could help. When I stopped, I said, "It was him. He was here."

Sanchez asked, "Who?"

"Frank. It had to be him. He was here."

"Tonight?" Sanchez looked worried. Not scared, just worried I was losing my mind.

I stared at the front door, thinking how Frank might have somebody working for him from the inside. Then I looked at my bruised knuckles and thought about the fight I had had with his boys outside the nightclub.

"None of this was a coincidence," I muttered to myself.

The fight wasn't chance, nor was it payback for last night, or have anything to do with my conversation with Candy. It was simply to buy time so Frank could plant this present inside my house without me knowing about it.

"You need to go now," I said to Sanchez.

"Jackson—"

I gathered her things and pushed her toward the exit. "It's not safe for you to be here."

CHAPTER SIXTY-FIVE

I TURNED OFF THE HOUSE LIGHTS AND FROM BEHIND THE
curtain, watched Sanchez drive away. I needed to be certain
she left me alone to deal with whatever fallout was to come of
this. Then I looked up and down the street, feeling like my
cover was blown and I might be being watched.

The party upstairs was getting louder. I needed to think
this through.

I moved to the couch and sat, staring at the piece of
jewelry. I couldn't be certain it wasn't ever something Selina
had owned, but I believed that it was left by whoever
killed her.

Whitney's visit was too coincidental and suspicious. Was
it possible she knew more than what she was saying?

My heart pounded.

Before tonight, I had found comfort in not knowing the
specifics of my daughter's death. I had accepted the fate of
what happened and understood they were never coming back.
But now I wondered if maybe I shouldn't have. Why give me
Selina's birthstone? If it was to torment me, they succeeded.

But did they also want me to believe my daughter was still alive? There was no evidence she wasn't.

I reached for my cellphone and called Whitney. When it clicked to voicemail, I hung up and dialed again. This time, when she didn't answer, I let it go.

CHAPTER SIXTY-SIX

When she slammed the door shut, it nearly hit Raymond Frank in the face.

He lunged forward and caught her by the arm. "You have every right to be mad," he said, "but don't think for one second I'll allow you to take it out on me."

Candy looked him in the eye and said, "It was your fault this happened."

"My fault?" Frank's eyes widened and he tightened his squeeze around her arm.

"You just couldn't keep your mouth shut."

"I was doing you a favor."

"Some favor." Candy snapped her elbow, punched him in the chest with her other hand, and broke free from his grip. "If you haven't noticed, I can take care of myself."

Frank laughed. "You need me, and you know it, too."

Candy stormed up the flight of stairs and, a second later, Frank heard another door slam.

The woman didn't know what she was talking about, he thought on his way to the wet bar where he made himself a stiff drink and flicked on the TV, turning on the news. He watched the recap—the continuous news cycle stating their assessment of Jackson Payne. Public opinion of both Jackson and the sheriff's office was shifting. Frank liked what he heard.

"Prick had it coming," he said into his glass. "They all did."

Frank was livid about how Jackson was putting the pressure on Candy. She was about to snap, do something stupid. He could feel it. Worried that Jackson had already gotten inside her head, Frank was even more pissed that Jackson had put two of his associates on the ground in what was an embarrassing display of power.

"The Travis County Sheriff's Office has refused to comment on the allegations of their deputy detective," the TV journalist said.

Frank muttered, "If IAD doesn't finish the job, I'll do it for them."

CHAPTER SIXTY-SEVEN

TWENTY MINUTES AFTER I CALLED WHITNEY, I EXITED MY apartment and climbed the stairs to knock on my neighbor's door. The music was still playing, but the party had since moved inside. A young woman in her early twenties opened the door and I caught scents of marijuana.

I flashed my badge and said, "Is the owner of the apartment home?"

Her eyes widened and she nodded. "Let me go get him."

She closed the door and I turned around to face the road below. There was my Cruiser, parked in front of a dark Camry. I could see everything from up here. I hoped someone from the party saw whoever came to pay me a visit tonight.

I listened as the music was turned down and the door opened to the sound of hushed conversation. "Can I help you?" the young man said.

"You the owner of this apartment?" I asked.

He shook his head no. "I rent it."

I asked his name, and he said, "Ronnie Gould." Then I introduced myself, told him I lived downstairs. Judging by his expression, he didn't know who I was, but had seen me around.

"I'm sorry for the noise," he said, running a hand through his thick hair. "We're celebrating a friend's birthday. Didn't mean to cause a disturbance to you."

"No trouble at all."

"You're new to the building, aren't you?"

I said I was, then added, "I'm curious if you saw anything unusual tonight?"

"Unusual? Can't think of anything off the top of my head." He turned and glanced through his front window with a curious look on his face. "What sort of something did you have in mind?"

"I found my door unlocked when I came home."

"Anything taken?"

Just the opposite, I thought. "You didn't see anybody stop by, did you?"

"Can't say I did, but I can ask my friends? They might have seen something?"

I nodded and Ronnie opened the door, stuck his head inside, and relayed the message to his friends. The woman who had answered the door came out and said, "Earlier, when I arrived, there was a mail carrier at your door."

"From the post office?"

She nodded, briefly described his attire. "Thought nothing of it, except that it was a little late for him to be working."

"Anybody with him?"

She crossed her arms to ward off the chill. "No. I didn't see anybody with him. I think he was alone." She paused and glanced at her feet. "Can't be sure, but I thought I heard him knock on your door."

"Is that right?"

"I guess I assumed he lived there, but he didn't stay long

either. Left a short while after that and I never saw him again."

"Did you see where he went? What kind of car he drove?"

She said, "Watched him walk up the street and disappear around the corner. If he drove a car, I didn't see it."

CHAPTER SIXTY-EIGHT

I WOKE TO THE SOUND OF MY MOBILE PHONE RINGING. I checked the time—8:27 AM—and answered. "You have anything you want to say to me?"

Whitney's tone was friendly when she said, "I'm surprised to be hearing from you so soon."

I got straight to it. "I think you left something here last night."

"Not to my knowledge. Did you find something?"

I stared at the velvet box, thinking about how Selina had come to me in my dreams. We hugged. We cried. And I felt re-energized by the prospect she might still be alive. But before I could tell Whitney about the sapphire rose, I asked, "How long had you been waiting for me last night?"

"Not long. Maybe thirty minutes."

"Where were you before that?"

"Jackson, if this is about me letting myself into your apartment, I'm sorry. I didn't think it would be a big deal after everything we've been through."

I asked again. "What were you doing before you waited for me to come home?"

"What's this about? Did something happen?"

I told her about the piece of jewelry, and said, "I found it in the exact spot where you had been sitting on the couch."

"It sounds beautiful, but it's not mine."

"Then whose is it?"

"Seriously? How could I possibly know? Maybe check with one of your girlfriends." Whitney laughed.

Not finding it funny, I said, "There is nobody else."

"Sad. Your wife clearly didn't know what she had, did she?"

I lifted my gaze and stared across the room. My instinct was to believe Whitney. I just didn't see any point in her doing this. I said, "I still can't understand how you knew where I was living."

"It's no secret, Jackson. Turn on your news and you'll see what I'm seeing. The entire world is watching."

CHAPTER SIXTY-NINE

I COULDN'T TURN ON A TV BECAUSE I DIDN'T HAVE ONE.
But Whitney was right. The world was watching because the
media and their microwave jungle were parked outside my
front door.

Keeping the curtains drawn, I hurried to get ready. Then I
grabbed my phone, gun, and the velvet box before having to
face the cameras.

As soon as I opened the door, I heard my name being
called.

"Did you start the fire that burned down your house?
Why did you start the fire? Was it to bilk the insurance
company, or simple vengeance?"

There were dozens of them, all wanting to get a piece of
me. I pushed my way to my Land Cruiser with lenses and
microphones jammed in my face. A thought crossed my mind
that said maybe the person who left me Selina's birthstone
was watching.

"You were the last to speak to Vincent Cruz? What did
you two talk about?"

I didn't even pause for consideration. As bad as the question stung, I wondered if they knew it as fact, or were simply using it to hook me into answering a question I otherwise wouldn't have answered.

The circus followed me across town and watched me enter the medical examiner's office, where I dropped off the birthstone, with a fingerprint analyst in the crime lab. They said nothing about Cruz's case, and I didn't ask. Then I led the same train to Central Command, where they continued to hound me with questions I refused to comment on.

Inside wasn't any easier. I was still the odd man out. But, at least here, I could work at my desk alone.

I picked up the phone and called the Auto Theft Task Force in the East Command office and spoke with deputy Tony Olivas. I told him about the black Range Rover. Tony was aware of the case but said they hadn't any luck in locating the vehicle.

"Most of the time, these cars get put through chop shops and moved across state lines," he said. "Why do you ask, anyway?"

"Might be connected to a homicide we're working."

"If that's the case, chances are, we'll never see the vehicle again."

It wasn't what I wanted to hear, but it wasn't a surprise either. I hung up the phone and looked up Steve Eli's home address and jotted it down. I thought I'd speak to Steve myself, see what he had to say about his missing Rover. Maybe he knew something I didn't. As soon as I turned around, Moreno was there to block me.

"Just the man I wanted to see." He smiled and mentioned something about how nice it was to have the media off his back.

"Did you leak Pam's security tape to the press?" I asked.

"Now why would you say that?" Moreno tucked his chin, appearing to look offended I'd ask. "How about this? I'll tell you if I did or didn't, but only after you tell me why you went to Frank's house the other night."

"Who says I went to Frank's?"

"It's in the IA report," Moreno said, listing off the complaints Frank had filed against me.

Moreno wasn't going to rope me into playing his game. I kept my mouth shut, thinking what an embarrassment I had become. I asked, "Anything else you'd like to waste my time on?"

Moreno stepped closer and said, "Frank said you were there to kill him. Is that true? Were you going to kill him?"

My memory flashed back to the other night and how Mr. Big and Smalls tied me up and took my gun away from me. Then I remembered flicking my cigarette at Frank's feet, threatening to add fuel to the fire the next time I visited. I could see where Frank might have thought that I was going to kill him, but I didn't admit it to Moreno.

I said, "And what? I couldn't kill him, so I whacked Cruz instead?"

Moreno asked, "Did you?"

"Don't be an idiot," I said, slamming my shoulder into his as I moved past him. "You're wasting my time."

Moreno still hadn't answered for his whereabouts on the night Cruz was murdered, and something told me he never would. I kept that in the back of my mind as I heard him say, "It doesn't look good, Jackson."

It never did, I thought, just as Sergeant Hart called across the bullpen.

"Moreno? Payne?" We both turned to look. "A call just came through. Some asshole is down near the waterfront impersonating a cop. You better get down there and get him before he slips away. This could be the guy who dropped Cruz."

CHAPTER SEVENTY

I JUMPED INTO A SHERIFF'S VEHICLE AND MORENO followed. He sat in the passenger seat as I fired up the engine and sped past the first unit out of the lot that had stopped to put up a blockade between me and the media vans. With lights flashing and sirens blaring, I led the procession of sheriff's vehicles across town, all traveling in one direction.

The two-way radio chattered and I turned the volume up to listen. Dispatch was giving a physical description of the suspect.

"White male. Late teens to early twenties, seen wearing a Travis County Sheriff's Deputy windbreaker. Last seen heading northwest on the trails at Emma Long Metropolitan Park. Suspect was carrying camera and gear, may be armed, and considered dangerous."

I tightened my grip on the steering wheel and sped faster. The sea of cars parted in front of me as they heard me coming.

Moreno held the radio in his right hand and kept his eyes forward when he said, "I know what you're thinking, but I didn't do it."

I checked my mirrors and felt him turn his head to look at me.

He said, "It wasn't me who leaked Pam Johnston's security tape to the press."

My thoughts jumped back to my conversation with Cruz, our shared suspicion I was being set up. I thought about who might have given him the details of my divorce. Everything inside me wanted it to be Moreno.

I asked, "If it wasn't you, then who?"

"Your guess is as good as mine. Perhaps it was Pam? Maybe Sanchez?"

That got me to look.

Moreno raised an eyebrow and had a knowing look on his face when he said, "You knew it too, didn't you?"

"Knew what?"

"That Sanchez went around me and got to the tape before I reviewed it myself." When I didn't respond, Moreno suspected I had asked her to do it for me. I didn't tell him he was right, and he asked. "Did she give you a copy?"

He couldn't possibly think I had leaked the video myself, but maybe he did.

The radio chattered. An update came from dispatch, and I adjusted my plan according to the additional information coming in. Though we were making good time, I wondered if it would be enough.

I asked Moreno, "Where were you the night Cruz was murdered?"

"You can't possibly think I did it." He chuckled.

I said, "Did you?"

"Wasn't me," he said seriously.

I reminded him of his excessive force incident and said, "Doesn't matter. Your word means nothing to me."

"You don't have to believe me, but see how it looks from where I'm sitting." Moreno told me what he found in Cruz's notes, repeating the words I had said to Cruz in the park. *"Then you should be careful with what you write. It could get you killed."*

I should have known Cruz would have quoted me, but was Moreno aware of the full context of our conversation? I doubted it. If he was, he was no different from the media who cherry picked soundbites accordingly.

"Surprised?" Moreno asked. "So was I. Now you understand why you're the focus of the investigation."

"Am I the focus?"

"Everything points to you, Jackson."

I concentrated on my driving, and though Moreno had gotten to me, I didn't let it show. What else had Cruz written in his notes? I didn't know, but something told me Moreno did.

"What did Cruz have on you to make you want to kill him? It had to be something big." Moreno stared and nodded. "Any idea what that might have been? Did Cruz tell you what it was?"

My look said it all. I didn't murder anyone.

When I didn't answer, Moreno continued, "You want to know what I think? I think it had something to do with Raymond Frank."

We were a mile away from the park and Moreno seemed more focused on me than the task at hand. He kept pressing me for information, hoping to get me to talk.

Moreno said, "I was thinking about our long talk the other night, and I recall you said something about going home to get a few important things and to talk to your daughter. What was so important that couldn't wait?"

I shut off the sirens as we entered the park. Moreno wouldn't shut up.

He asked, "Was it something you didn't want your wife to have? Something you couldn't afford to lose in a fire?"

I drove at a steady pace and kept my eyes peeled for our suspect, trying to decide what exactly Moreno was getting at —if anything at all, other than to annoy me.

"Whatever it was," he said, "it had to be something so valuable that it would make the divorce from your wife easier, especially if she was planning to take everything from you."

I didn't bother to look, but I was wondering where he was getting his information from, because he definitely had something in mind. That's when I spotted our suspect. He was wearing a sheriff's jacket, just like the one reportedly seen being worn the night Cruz was murdered.

CHAPTER SEVENTY-ONE

THE SUSPECT HAD HIS HAND WRAPPED AROUND A WOMAN'S wrist when I kicked the door open and sprinted after him. He saw me coming, turned and ran. I ran faster and, after a one-hundred yard dash, I tackled him to the ground and threw some cuffs onto his wrists.

Belly down, he turned his head, looked me in the eye, and started laughing.

"It's you," he said. "I can't believe it. Are the media here, too?"

Feeling like I was part of some prank, I said, "It's illegal to impersonate a cop, but impersonating a suspect involved in a robbery homicide makes it look like you might be the person we're looking to arrest."

That wiped the smile off his ugly face. His eyes widened and he glanced at Moreno who was standing behind us, comforting the young woman the kid just had his hands on, while he called it in.

"I didn't rob or kill anyone," the kid said, jutting his jaw to a camera perched on a tripod near an enormous tree. "You can check it for yourself. I'm just trying to get laid."

"Looked to me a lot like harassment," I said, searching his pockets. I opened his cellphone before it locked and then opened his wallet. Reading his driver's license, I said, "Who did you get the jacket from, Samuel White?"

"What?"

"The jacket. Where did you get it?"

"Bought it off some couple online," he said. "I didn't murder anybody."

"You sure about that?"

"I'm sure."

I was flipping through his phone messages when I dropped Vincent Cruz's name. He had no idea what I was talking about, even less of a clue that his jacket might have been linked to an imposter. Samuel White seemed to be nothing more than a nineteen-year-old kid caught up in being at the wrong place at the right time.

"Describe the couple who sold you the jacket," I said.

"What? I don't know. It was a man and a woman."

"Who did the talking?"

"The woman."

"What did she look like?"

"Blonde hair. Average height."

"What color eyes?"

"I don't know, they were both wearing sunglasses."

I glanced at Moreno. He was at the camera. The woman sat on a nearby bench, squeezing her knees together. I turned back to Samuel, opened my cellphone with thoughts of a postal worker and how Frank used disguises. I showed Samuel a picture of Raymond Frank. "Was this the guy?"

"I don't know. Maybe."

"What about her?" I showed him a picture of Candy.

"No. The hair color is wrong. Did they kill somebody? Oh, God," Samuel moaned as if suddenly realizing the seriousness of his arrest.

I took the kid's picture, picked him up off the ground, and walked him to another sheriff's vehicle.

"You're arresting me?" he asked.

"What you did is illegal."

I instructed the deputy to collect Samuel's jacket and cap as evidence, then turned and walked away while thinking about my conversation with Whitney. Though I suspected Samuel was innocent of Cruz's murder, I was certain the news had somebody worried.

When Moreno joined me, I asked about the woman. He said, "She'll be fine."

Then I told him, "The killer could be offloading evidence." He gave me a sideways glance as if he didn't believe me. I said, "Doubt we'll get any forensic evidence off it now that it's covered in the kids slime, but it's worth a shot."

"It's a convenient theory," Moreno said. "Especially for you."

I watched Moreno walk away. I didn't know why I thought I could trust him. Before he got too far, I called after him and told him to hitch a ride back with someone else.

He asked, "And what are you going to do?"

"Keep the TV news crews off your back."

CHAPTER SEVENTY-TWO

I LEFT THE SCENE BEFORE THE NEWS CREWS KNEW I WAS there. It was good to be alone and have a vehicle all to myself. Moreno left me a lot to think about and, once again, I wondered what exactly he was hinting at on our drive to apprehend Samuel.

It bothered me to think he knew something I didn't.

When I thought back to the night of the fire, I recalled my brief stop in my study to grab important paperwork I might need for the future, but I took nothing Ilene didn't already know herself. Moreno had something else in mind and, though I had lost a lot in the fire, nothing compared to the loss of my family.

My cellphone rang. It was Tex. When I answered, he asked, "Now a good time?"

I could hear the concern in his voice. "You saw the news?"

Tex said, "Do you know who is behind the leak?"

"I have some ideas." Then I told him about Ilene.

"Jackson, I'm sorry." A brief pause before he asked, "What about Selina?"

"No sign she was ever there," I said, catching him up on

how someone left her birthstone inside my apartment. "I'm getting it printed now and am waiting on the results."

"How the hell did Frank get inside your apartment without you knowing about it?"

"I don't know," I said. "But Whitney Voak found a way."

"She broke into your house, too?" Tex sounded shocked.

"She said the door was unlocked. If that's true, Frank was there before her."

"Why was she there at all?"

"To warn me about Frank."

Tex asked if it could have been Whitney who had left the stone behind, and I brought Tex up to speed. I told him that a mail carrier was seen near my place earlier in the night, and that we had just apprehended a kid impersonating a cop at the park. "It appears that whoever is behind the murders is now working to unload the evidence."

Tex said, "I talked to my private investigator. He's ready when you are."

"I don't think it will help."

"It sounds like you need all the help you can get."

"Whether or not Frank is behind this, I can't escape the truth," I said.

"Which is what?"

I briefly mentioned how I was working on borrowed time, and said, "Soon, forensics will link my fingerprints to those inside Cruz's house and, when they do, Moreno will pile that on top of whatever else he has on me."

"Jackson, what else aren't you telling me?"

"Moreno has something," I said, mentioning the conversation I had had with Moreno on our way to the park. "I don't know what it is, but he seems confident it's enough to give a reason I would want Ilene dead."

Tex was quiet for a long while, then he asked, "What did you ever do with your Walker Colt forty-four?"

CHAPTER SEVENTY-THREE

TEX MIGHT HAVE BEEN ON TO SOMETHING. THE WALKER Colt made perfect sense. There were about a million reasons Ilene would want it because, if auctioned correctly, that would be how much she could get for it.

But who else knew about the rare gun besides Ilene? Was that what Moreno had been referring to? If so, how did he know about it?

I couldn't recall seeing it in the study the night I went home, but I wasn't looking for it, either. And I certainly didn't see it yesterday when searching through the rubble of what was left of my house, but that didn't mean it hadn't survived the fire.

These thoughts traveled with me all the way to Vincent Cruz's neighborhood. Now that I had Samuel White's picture on my phone, I was hoping I could get a neighbor to identify him as being the deputy seen the night of Cruz's murder.

I parked in front, got out of the Ford Intercept, and looked around, aware I might be being watched as I climbed the concrete steps. Then, at the door, I punched in the key box code, retrieved the key, and unlocked the front door.

Once inside, I stood at the door for a minute and gloved up.

The air was still while I imagined the last conversation I had with Cruz and how fearful he was of Mr. Aviators. If Frank found out about what he'd discovered, he'd come after Cruz, too.

I walked across the floor and passed the wall where he had died. The light was different, giving a new perspective to everything.

When I lifted my gaze, I saw his desk had been cleared and cleaned. Most of what he had was taken into evidence, and I assumed it was also the reason Moreno was asking me all those questions.

I thought I had Cruz figured out. Now I wasn't so sure I did. What other pieces of our conversation had Cruz recorded? I had to assume he made notes of everything and even kept some of his most valued secrets safe at home with him at all times. Whether Cruz was right about someone wanting to set me up, whoever supplied him with the documents to my divorce must've had him killed, too.

It all made sense, except the timing of his death.

Nothing came of it.

The story that was supposed to end me was never written. Perhaps it was never meant to get written and, again, I asked who would want to set me up for murder.

Moreno wouldn't be so stupid to come here dressed in uniform, but Frank would, if it shifted the conversation toward the sheriff's office.

A knock on the front door took me out of my thoughts and I went to see who it was.

CHAPTER SEVENTY-FOUR

THERE WAS NO SENSE PRETENDING I WASN'T HERE. I answered the door. The woman on the other side smiled and said, "I saw there was a sheriff here, so I thought I'd poke my head in and see who it was."

She was a middle-aged woman in tight spandex leggings and a colorful light jacket. She had her hair tied in a loose ponytail that swished from side to side when she talked. It looked like she was on her way home from a run, or about to embark on one.

"I'm Misty Summers. I live just over there." She pointed diagonally through the trees behind her.

"Detective Jackson Payne," I said.

She worked hard to keep her lips curled, but I watched her smile disappear from her eyes the moment my name registered. Her look told me she knew who I was, and I hoped it was only because she'd heard my name mentioned in the news, not because she had seen me here with Cruz.

"I really can't have you here," I said, exiting the house, closing the door behind me.

"Of course," she said, taking a step back, obviously embarrassed by her intrusion. "The neighborhood won't ever be the same again," she said as she looked me in the eye. "You hear about these types of events in the news and never expect it to happen in your neighborhood."

I wanted to tell her the community would move on, eventually forget all that had happened; but I didn't. Instead, I just stood and stared toward the street, formulating the questions I wanted to ask inside my head.

"They are saying he was strangled. Is that true?"

I turned my head and asked, "Ms. Summers, has anyone come to speak to you about that night?"

"Yes. I gave my statement. I'm the person who saw one of your deputies visiting earlier in the evening with Mr. Cruz."

She eyed me hard and I wondered if she had placed me at the scene. I asked, "You saw one of our deputies with Mr. Cruz?"

"Not exactly. I'm not sure Vincent was home. I assumed he was, but I am certain the deputy entered Vince's house."

"And what happened after that?"

"I don't know. Nothing, I guess."

"You didn't hear them talking, maybe arguing about something?"

"No. Nothing like that. I assumed it was work related. Vince was a reporter, you know."

I nodded, and she continued to stare deep into my eyes. I kept thinking she would recognize me, call me out as being the one to have pushed Cruz into his own house to beat the shit out of him. But she never did.

"I read his stories online." She looked away when saying, "I'm going to really miss him."

"Was the deputy you saw male or female?"

"Definitely male."

"What car was he driving? A squad car or an SUV like the one I have there?"

Her eyebrows knitted. Then she said, "Come to think of it, I saw nothing of the sort."

"There was no car?"

She looked me in the eye and shook her head, no.

I pulled out my cellphone and showed her a picture of Samuel White. "Was this the deputy you saw that night?"

Misty took my phone into her hand, stared at the screen for a second, then said, "No. This wasn't him. This man is too young to be the deputy I saw."

"About how old would you say the man you saw was?"

"Maybe forty, forty-five. Dark hair stuffed beneath a ball cap."

"Beard?"

"No. I don't recall seeing one."

I needed to make sure there wouldn't be any surprises coming down the pipeline, and asked, "Did he look like me?"

She angled her head and squinted her eyes as if digging deep into her memory. The look she was giving said she knew what the news was suggesting—that I was the one who killed her neighbor—but she never mentioned it.

"About your height, but heavier. Not as lean."

Misty mentioned the hair color again and said that he walked like a cop. It was a similar description to how Cruz described his source, the person who leaked the details of my divorce, minus the beard. I didn't want to believe it, but it sounded like she was describing Moreno.

Then she said, "Odd thing was, he wore a pair of aviator sunglasses. Can you believe it? Sunglasses at night. Who does that? Just when you have hope for the world, people can't even look you in the eye when they speak."

CHAPTER SEVENTY-FIVE

JUST WHEN I THOUGHT THERE WEREN'T ANY MORE questions to ask, Misty told me something I hadn't heard before, and I knew just who I needed to speak to next.

Steve Eli's house was west of Vincent Cruz's and in the area known as Silicon Hills. I knew the neighborhood for its high-tech companies and startups. After I double checked the information Sanchez provided about the black Range Rover, I rang Steve Eli's doorbell.

He answered shortly after the bell chimed.

"Mr. Eli?"

"That's me."

His eyes drifted to my sheriff's vehicle and he had a hopeful look on his face. I told him who I was, why I was here, and Steve asked me, "Did you find my car?"

"No. We haven't." I didn't mention the obvious; that locating stolen vehicles wasn't what homicide detectives did. Instead, I said, "But I would like to ask you a few questions. Mind if I come inside?"

He opened the door wider and motioned for me to follow. "I'm between conference calls."

"This shouldn't take long," I said. "Do you work from home often?"

"When I can."

Steve led me to the front living room and told me about his busy schedule of juggling business with family. I remembered the days when Selina was young and I tried not to think about it too hard.

I stopped near the couch when I spotted a pair of pilot sunglasses on the side table. Behind them were pictures of Steve with his children, and it occurred to me he had a beard in most of the photos, too. I tried to place him at the park, but couldn't.

"Why did you lose the beard?" I asked, pointing to his picture.

"Grew tired of it." He offered me a drink, and I declined. Steve said, "I recognize you from the Raymond Frank trial. Heard he got off."

"Jury found him not guilty."

"Shame," he said.

"Did you follow the case closely?"

Steve sat on the couch and crossed his left leg over his right knee. "I did."

"Were you surprised by the verdict?"

"The glove doesn't fit argument always works on rich assholes like him." Steve shook his head and said, "But you and I both know he did it."

Steve lived in a nice big house, and though there were pictures of him with his children, I didn't see any signs that they lived here with him. There were lots of rooms, and the house was well kept and clean. Not the kind of house you would expect to see with young children.

I asked, "Why do you say that?"

"Am I wrong?"

"The jury thought so."

Steve grinned. "We live in a world of injustice, and they tried Frank in a system not offered to most of us."

I sensed he knew Frank on a personal level, and I asked about it.

"You'd be correct," Steve said. "I know more than I care to know about Raymond Frank."

Steve never tried to hide his resentment, and he told me about how Frank was born into a life of wealth and privilege. There was a hint of jealousy in his voice and I knew everything he said, but then he told me something I didn't know.

"Five years ago I had an idea for an online university teaching young entrepreneurs ecommerce solutions." Steve smiled at his brilliance. "It was going to change many people's lives. Except I didn't have the capital it needed so I went looking for venture capitalists. Frank made me the best offer."

"Did you take it?"

"I did."

"And?"

"Never received a penny. Instead, Frank stole my concept and developed it himself." Steve stood and pushed his hands deep into his pants pockets. "I sued, he counter sued, and guess who won?"

"Frank."

"I couldn't compete. Hell, how can anyone compete against that asshole? He has bottomless funds. Frank does whatever he wants and gets away with it because he can. And, to top it off, he still takes full credit, as if the idea was his."

"What kind of work do you do now?" I asked.

"Enterprise application software." I must have had a funny look on my face because Steve added, "It's a way for computers to report tasks within a business."

"Frank know about that?"

"That asshole knows everything about his enemies," Steve said. "Frank would like to see me fail, just so I would go away."

"Has he harassed you recently?"

"No. He was on trial for murder." Steve grinned, then said, "It was the best thing that ever happened to me and my business. Too bad it wasn't for life."

I thought the entire story was ironic. I wondered if Frank was getting back at everyone who'd wronged him. There was no proof it was happening, but it certainly felt like that was the case. I asked Steve about the park I had met Cruz at, asked if he'd ever been there.

"It's possible," Steve said. "I like to run. But what's that have to do with my Range Rover?"

"I think your vehicle might have been involved in the homicide of crime reporter Vincent Cruz."

Steve sat forward and stared. "Jesus."

"You wax your ride?"

"Yeah."

I asked what he was doing the afternoon of Cruz's murder and Steve said he was at the office. "My employees can vouch for me," Steve said, giving me their names and contact information. "But my vehicle was stolen before that."

"You recognize him?" I asked, showing Steve a picture of an out-of-uniform Moreno.

"No. Who is he?"

I never said. Then I showed him pictures of the two goons I fought last night.

"You're kidding, right? They're Frank's thugs. He uses them to intimidate anybody he doesn't like. You think they stole my car and used it to kill that reporter?"

"Not sure," I said, but Steve could read the situation for himself.

"Damn," he said, shaking his head. "I should have assumed Frank would start up the war between us once he was free. But I never thought he'd try to frame me for murder."

CHAPTER SEVENTY-SIX

DEPUTY CHIEF MATT DAVID STARED THROUGH THE ONE-
way glass at a young kid, slouched in a cold metal chair,
looking scared. Samuel White would be charged with impersonating a public servant and harassment, and they would cut
a deal with the district attorney. But David was certain he
wasn't the person who murdered Vincent Cruz.

David gave the signal that the interview was over. Samuel
had caused enough damage already. There was no need to
drag this out any more than what was needed.

A second later, Deputy Moreno exited the interview room
and said to David, "Kid hasn't a clue who Vincent Cruz is."

"No, but he got our jacket from someone," David said,
clearing the room so it was just him and Moreno.

Moreno said, "Jackson might be right. It's possible the
killer is unloading the evidence."

"As long as there isn't any other sheriff's gear still out
there," David swiped his hand over his face. "Who might this
couple be that sold him the jacket, and how can we find
them?"

"I'll dig online, try to retrace Samuel's steps to see if they lead me to the seller."

"Good."

No one mentioned what they were all thinking—that it could have been Raymond Frank and Candy Scott who could have sold it to Samuel. But Moreno admitted, "There's also another theory I'm exploring."

David arched an eyebrow.

Moreno said, "I saw Whitney Voak visiting Jackson last night."

"And you're just telling me this now?"

"I was still trying to figure it all out."

David cursed under his breath. Moreno didn't need to explain it to the deputy chief; the chief already knew what it meant.

"Chief," Moreno said, "there's no evidence Frank is still stalking Jackson, or that he ever did."

David held up a hand; he didn't need to hear the commentary. IAD was working behind the scenes, and the deputy chief would let them do their job. Though he felt like he was pinned between investigations, David was feeling the pressure to decide soon—whether to support one of his best detectives, or admit that one of his men was close to going rogue.

David asked Moreno, "You rode with Jackson to the scene, correct?"

"That's right."

"And? Did you ask him about what we discussed?"

Moreno said, "Jackson isn't telling the complete truth."

"Where is Jackson, now?"

"No idea, sir."

David gave an arched look. "You let him get out of your sight? Find out what he's up to, and what's so important he can't share with the rest of us. We need to bury this before it gets too big."

"Copy that, Chief," Moreno said, moving toward the exit.

"And let me know as soon as you learn something. I need to be certain I don't have a lone wolf seeking justice on his own terms."

CHAPTER SEVENTY-SEVEN

MORENO SMILED AS HE WALKED TO HIS DESK. HE WAS MORE than willing to accept the task to keep a close eye on Jackson. He'd been dealt the hand he'd been waiting for and it was time to clean house.

"A lone wolf, you say? I think you might already have one." Moreno chuckled.

He sat in his chair, picked up the phone, and checked his voicemails. Nothing that couldn't wait. Then he called Maxwell Sheldon at the *Chronicle* to follow up on their conversation from the night Vincent Cruz was murdered.

As the line rang, Moreno asked himself where Jackson went, who he was after, and why he wanted to keep it a secret. The harder the media pressed, the deeper underground Jackson would go.

When Sheldon answered the phone, Moreno asked, "Any luck getting into Cruz's files?"

"Yes. Haven't you heard? I gave them to Detective Payne."

"Payne?"

"Yes. Jackson Payne. Yesterday. Doesn't your department coordinate?"

This caught Moreno by surprise. He leaned forward, perched an elbow on the desk, and said, "A case of miscommunication."

Moreno requested remote access to the files and Sheldon agreed. "I'll email the details shortly."

"The sooner the better."

Sheldon said, "Give me five minutes."

Moreno hung up the phone and leaned back in his chair. He didn't like how Jackson seemed to be walking a step ahead of him. He had a feeling Jackson knew something he didn't. Did it have something to do with Cruz's files? Moreno thought it might.

He pulled out the file on Cruz's murder and began sorting through the notes taken from Cruz's home desk. On a separate legal pad, Moreno put together a timeline of events.

Cruz spoke with Pam Johnston in the afternoon and mentioned the name of the park he spoke to Jackson at. What they discussed, Moreno didn't know because Cruz didn't put it in his notes. All Moreno knew was that Cruz had made a strong connection between Jackson and Raymond Frank. What exactly that meant, Moreno also didn't know. The specifics were vague, and he thought out loud, "There has to be more to it than this."

Cruz had mentioned a black Range Rover. Then, later that same day, Moreno pulled Jackson over. A thought struck.

He picked up the phone and called the Auto Theft Task Force in the East Command office and spoke with deputy Tony Olivas, asking Tony what he knew about a black Range Rover.

Tony said, "Besides it being extremely popular with your office, not a lot. It was reported stolen five, six days ago and still hasn't been found."

"Popular? Why do you say that?"

"Everyone in your office is calling me about it. Deputy

Payne, Sanchez. They both recently inquired about it. Then I come to find out it might be related to a homicide."

"A homicide?"

"Yeah. That reporter. Apparently it's somehow linked to him."

Tony gave Moreno the details and Moreno jotted down Steve Eli's name and address. Then he told Tony to keep him in the loop if anything new popped up.

"You got it," Tony said, ending the call.

Moreno stared at his notes, asking himself, "Was that who you were chasing when I pulled you over?"

He then checked his email. Sheldon's message came through.

Moreno entered the access code into his computer and began searching Cruz's files. They were well organized and things were easy to find. Soon, he was searching through photos Cruz had taken with his cellphone and stopped when he found one of the black Range Rover in the same park he met with Jackson in.

He zoomed in on the image of the driver's face.

Moreno's heart started beating faster.

"Christ, you know who he is," Moreno whispered. "And that's who you're going after."

CHAPTER SEVENTY-EIGHT

A HALF-HOUR AFTER MY VISIT WITH STEVE, I GOT A CALL from Candy saying she wanted to meet. I didn't ask what about, because I got the impression she couldn't say—at least not over the phone.

I gave her instructions to meet me at Butler Metro Park downtown and told her I'd find her there. Once we connected, we sat on a bench and I asked her, "What is it I can do for you, Candy?"

Candy couldn't sit still. She was making me nervous. I kept looking for Frank, expecting his men to ambush me from behind any second. But I saw no signs of that happening. After I made sure she was sober, I knew it was nothing more than a case of anxiety that kept her squirming.

I dug out my pack of smokes and offered her a cigarette. She took one from the box and, to her surprise, I lit it for her. Together, we smoked, and I could see it was relaxing her.

Candy stared at the burning tip, then she said, "I want to talk but I need you to promise me immunity."

I said, "You only need protection if you have something good to trade it for."

Candy turned her head and looked me in the eye. Her eyes were tired, but unwavering, and I could see she believed she had something she thought worth trading. I hoped so. Without it, she was still at the top of my list of suspects.

I asked, "Does Frank know you're here?"

She sucked hard on the cigarette, then aggressively blew out the smoke. "No."

"What about a lawyer? You have one of those?"

Candy nodded. "I've talked to them already."

"Good. Then immunity might be something that can be worked out, but I need to know what it is you have to offer."

She stuck the cigarette between her lips, twisted around, and dove her hand into the tote bag at her side. With her back toward me, Candy said, "I found this on Frank's desk."

She spun around and placed the documents into my hand. I calculated the weight of the nine-by-twelve bright white business envelope and watched as she kept looking around with a worried expression on her face. I dropped my smoke on the grass in front of me and opened the envelope. After quickly flipping through the top pages, I knew what it was.

"Why does Frank have this?" I asked.

"Beats me." Candy looked me in the eye. "Will it be useful to your investigation?"

I peeked inside the envelope again and asked, "Does he know you took these?"

She shook her head, then locked eyes. "And he'll kill me if he finds out about it."

I'd scared her good, but this wasn't proof of anything concrete. Frank had lots of people who wanted to see him put away—me included—but no one was in deeper danger than Candy. Candy was in bigger trouble than I imagined.

I kept scanning the field in front of me and glanced over my shoulder more times than I cared to admit before my attention was back on what was inside the envelope. Finally, I

pulled out the stack of papers and began scanning the documents. It was an exact replica of the papers I had taken from
Cruz that detailed Ilene's strategy for our divorce. I didn't
know which of the two was the original, or if either of them
were, but I wondered if Frank had given a copy to Cruz. With
what Frank was saying about me in the news, it made sense.
But the only thing that mattered right now was that Cruz was
given something Frank apparently had, too.

I said to Candy, "This proves nothing."

She said in a meek voice, "I'm sorry about what happened
to your family."

"Yeah. Me too."

"I can't go to prison. I didn't do anything wrong."

Feeling myself getting angry, I asked, "What did
Frank do?"

Candy was squirming again. Then she admitted Frank
wasn't home the night of the fire.

I asked, "Where was he?"

"I don't know."

"You lied to me."

Candy's posture shrunk; I could see the teenage girl she
once was. "I made a deal with Ray that if I'm ever asked, I'm
supposed to always say that he was with me, even if he
wasn't."

"How convenient," I said, turning my attention forward.

I thought about the security tape, then back to the night
of the fire and how Frank was about to be acquitted by a jury
of his peers only hours after the fire ripped through my
house. If Frank was innocent, why did he need to ensure he
always had a quick alibi?

Candy snubbed out her cigarette and tossed the butt to
the ground. I was wondering what I should do with her when
she said, "I brought you those papers to show you I can be
trusted."

With thoughts churning, I exhaled a breath and looked her in the eye.

What was Frank planning to do with the information he was given? Or had he done everything he was going to do already? Maybe Frank was the one who had given Cruz a copy and knew I'd eventually learn about it so he could once again frame me for another murder I didn't commit.

I asked, "Did Frank tell you about the house fire, or did you tell him?"

Candy said, "Frank told me. He's obsessed about it. You're all he ever talks about anymore." Then she looked me in the eye and said, "He's not remorseful about what happened, either, and won't stop doing whatever he's doing until you're out of the picture."

CHAPTER SEVENTY-NINE

I CLOSED UP THE ENVELOPE, STOOD, AND TURNED TO LOOK behind me. Candy had put everything on the line for me. But what still made little sense was how Frank got his hands on the documents that should have been kept sealed.

I said to Candy, "C'mon. Let's go."

She looked up at me and blinked her brown eyes from behind a curtain of thick eyelashes. "Does that mean we have a deal?"

I didn't know what to do about Candy, but I couldn't leave her here.

Worried this might be part of Frank's offensive strategy, I thought through every angle, trying to find a conclusion to how this could come back to bite me in the ass. In the end, I came up with nothing. The way those innocent doll eyes were looking at me, I believed Candy's motivation today was honest as a nun. But I needed her to prove she was willing to take it the whole nine yards.

I said, "It's not for me to decide."

"Then where are you taking me?"

"You're going to tell the same story you just told me to the assistant district attorney."

Candy's face flushed and she looked scared.

"The sheriff's office can protect you, but only if you come with me now."

Candy wrung her hands and shook her head. Then she said, "I gave you what you needed, and you can do what you want with it, but I can't come with you. Ray will be looking for me."

"If you want to avoid second degree murder charges, you don't have a choice but to come with me."

Finally, she stood and nodded her head. I asked where she was parked, and we decided it best to leave her car here. "No sense in showing it off at the station."

Candy called her lawyer on our way to Central Command and, after a quick discussion, she told him to meet us there.

Twenty minutes later, I walked her through the front doors and led her down the hallway, through a couple corridors, and into an empty interrogation room where I told her to wait. I closed the door on my way out and stared through the one-way glass, asking again if she could be trusted. I never expected Candy to break so easily, but her vulnerability was my only way out from the mess I'd found myself in.

I went to look for Sergeant Hart and ended up speaking with Deputy Chief David instead. He wasn't my first choice but, as soon as he saw me, I knew he would ask to be briefed.

"Where have you been, Jackson? You apprehended a suspect then disappeared."

"Tying up loose ends," I said, handing him the files Candy had given me.

"What's this?" he asked when looking at the nondescript white envelope.

I briefed him on what was inside, then added, "They're exactly the same as the documents given to Cruz."

David lifted his gaze and looked me in the eye. "The papers you still have?"

I confirmed with a single nod of my head.

David sat down and leafed through the stack. A minute of silence passed, then he asked who else might have copies.

"I don't know. I assume my wife's lawyer. Until recently, I hadn't even seen these myself."

"And they came from your house?"

"Possibly," I said, mentioning where this specific copy had come from. "Not sure who had them first—Cruz or Frank—but Cruz was worried about what might happen to him if he wrote the story."

David said something about how Cruz was never given the chance. Then he asked, "Candy Scott came to you with this?"

"Yes."

"Why?"

I purposely omitted the details of my threats against Candy, instead focusing on how Frank taunted me. "They came to my apartment, celebrating that my house had burned down."

"Is he still harassing you?"

I thought about it before answering. "Only in the news."

David had a skeptical look on his face; I could read him like a book. His distrustful eyes that looked at me like he couldn't decide whether or not I was fit for duty. Everyone knew how badly I wanted Frank to get convicted.

David jabbed a finger into the stack of papers and asked, "You sought this after Frank filed a complaint?"

I knew what the deputy chief was thinking; that I was playing defense. But Frank was on the offense and I couldn't just ignore the enormous coincidence that had landed in front of me. I said, "I spoke to Candy before Frank came here to whine about me. He's only doing it to take his name off our list of suspects."

"What do you want, Jackson?"

"A warrant to search Frank's property. Connect him to the murders of my family and that of Vincent Cruz. Look for evidence he's the arsonist—"

Dave lifted his hand and got me to stop. He said, "As interesting as it is, I can't do anything with this, and you know it."

"Go ask Candy yourself," I said, pointing my finger at the door. "Frank wasn't home the night of the house fire. Would you like to know where he was? Because I would."

"If he has something to do with it, yes. Of course I do. But all you have right now is speculation."

"Which is the reason I want to question him. I deserve as much."

David pressed his hands together and stared at his desk. After a moment of thought, he said, "Question Candy first, make sure she wasn't the one who did it. She had a lot to lose if Frank was convicted."

Just when I was about to tell the deputy chief it was a waste of time, the assistant district attorney barged into his office.

"I just spoke with Candy Scott's lawyer," the ADA said, latching his hands onto his waist. "You offered her immunity? Have you lost your mind?"

David had a puzzled look on his face. He stood and said, "I haven't offered her anything."

I said, "It was her idea."

The ADA turned to me with disgust pulling at his lips. "Her idea?"

"That's right."

He barked out a laugh. "And you said yes?"

"Not exactly."

He stepped forward and got in my face. "Need I remind you, Detective, that we just went through this? Our office isn't looking to retry Raymond Frank anytime soon."

"Would you rather have him murder again?"

His eyes squinted. "Even if you came in with a golden ticket, Candy can't be trusted. She lied once before...may have done so on purpose to sabotage the trial. Remember that? We charged Candy Scott with perjury and she paid a four-thousand dollar fine, probably using Frank's money to do so. Or have you forgotten already?" When I didn't respond, he said, "Don't waste my time again with this bullshit. You've got your own problems to worry about."

The ADA left in a hurry, but not without first giving David a look on his way out. There was something they weren't telling me and I thought I knew what it was, but I wanted to hear what David had to say first.

CHAPTER EIGHTY

I waited until the ADA was well out of earshot before I asked the deputy chief what I wasn't being told. David leaned forward, hung his head, and perched himself up on the tips of his fingers. My heart was knocking. I had a bad feeling about this.

David picked up the divorce papers off his desk and, without looking me in the eye, asked, "Cruz gave you the same copy?"

"He did."

His gaze lifted. "But you never mentioned when?"

David was nailing down the specifics, finally doing a little detective work of his own. I knew what he was after—wondering if I could be trusted. He told me to not let him down, and though I intended not to, apparently I had.

I had my response ready before stepping foot inside his office, but I took a moment to explore the Internal Affairs angle one last time before I answered his question. I hadn't heard whether they were going to pursue Frank's complaint against me and wondered if they ever would, considering who it came from.

David quirked an eyebrow and asked, "Well?"

Apparently my reassurance before wasn't good enough. He wanted more. I said, "The night he was murdered."

David slammed the stack of papers hard on his desk and ripped out a curse. He bowed his head with grave disappointment. His reaction was expected. With his hands latched onto his hips, he asked, "You know how this looks?"

"Like I murdered him."

He pushed his fingers through his hair and I thought he might pull a clump out before he was done with me. He pointed to the divorce papers and said, "Was this what was missing from Cruz's notes?"

"Possibly."

"You know damn well whether it is or isn't."

I wasn't certain, so I reminded him, "All that matters is that we learn who Cruz's source was. If we do that, we find our killer."

"Why were you at his house, Jackson?"

He wasn't listening. Once again, he seemed to only care about perception and how my actions would reflect on his department. I answered his question. "I thought he might have Pam Johnston's security tape."

"Did he?"

"No."

"Instead, he gave you this," he said, pointing to the stack of papers once more.

"Yes," I said, adding, "Cruz led me to believe it was Frank who gave him the files." I paused for a moment to give David a chance to react. He didn't. So I continued, "Then, sometime after I left that night, he gets whacked."

"And an eye witness swears the only visitor Cruz had that night was a Travis County sheriff's deputy."

"It wasn't me. I was in civilian clothes," I reminded him.

"Yes. You said that before."

"Then you'll also remember how Moreno baited me into believing Cruz had the security tape that got leaked to the press the very next day. He knew I would go there. Anyone bother to ask Moreno where he went, what he did that night?"

David's eyes darkened to a deep black. "For the record, Deputy Moreno seems to believe you might be right about the killer discarding certain clothing on an unsuspecting Samuel White."

Prick was playing politics. The deputy chief was saying something about the material getting sent to forensics when I interrupted and asked, "Then why am I the focus of Vincent Cruz's investigation?"

"If you think you're the only one being looked at, stop."

That was welcoming news, even if I had a tough time believing it. "Regardless," I said, "I thought the Vincent Cruz murder was my case to solve."

"Not anymore. They found your fingerprints inside Cruz's house and, with the eyewitness's statement, I have no choice but to take you off the case."

CHAPTER EIGHTY-ONE

DETECTIVE TOM MORENO ENTERED THE BAR AND BEGAN looking around. A few faces turned to see who was standing near the front door, but no one paid him any attention. Dressed in blue jeans and a tan colored sport coat, he didn't have the appearance of a person looking for trouble.

He headed to the counter where the bartender greeted him and asked what his poison was. Moreno showed the man a picture and asked, "You recognize him?"

The bartender took a quick look and shook his head.

"Look again." Moreno held the picture higher. "Take your time."

After twenty seconds of staring, the bartender said, "Sorry. Never seen him."

"Are you sure?"

"Look," the bartender flipped a white towel over his left shoulder and pressed his right fist into his left hand. "You asked me to look twice. I did. You going to tell me who he is, and why I should care?"

"Forget about it."

Moreno exited the bar and knew he was running out of

options. There was a chill in the night air and the skies were clear. If he couldn't find this man soon, he feared what might come of him.

He debated his options as he walked to his truck. After an extensive search, Moreno was exactly where he had started. No one knew who this man was or where he might have gone. That was a problem Moreno couldn't accept.

He climbed into the front seat and checked the time, feeling the pressure to make something happen soon. If he didn't get to this man first, Jackson Payne surely would. Then what? Moreno knew there wasn't enough evidence to prove Jackson committed the murders himself. "But finding this mystery man could change that."

Moreno started the engine, switched on the dome light, and began reviewing his files.

Flipping between photographs, he knew there was a connection to be found somewhere in this tangled mess. Samuel White...the sheriff's jacket and the couple Samuel said sold it to him...Steve Eli and his stolen black Range Rover...and of course Whitney Voak's late-night visit to Jackson's. They all had one thing in common, but something wasn't adding up.

"It's up to you to make the equation work," he said to himself.

Then his cellphone dinged with a message.

FYI. Payne has left the nest.

Moreno cursed and tossed his phone on the seat next to him. He gripped the wheel with his right hand and squeezed. He had exhausted all his options except one. It was his last resort. At least the night was young.

CHAPTER EIGHTY-TWO

Twice, I was told to stay away, and not once had I said I would. I was on my own.

I left the deputy chief's office thinking about Moreno and his sudden change of heart. No doubt he was playing politics with the same people who kept deciding I wasn't fit to lead a new murder investigation. They'd lost trust in my ability to close a case. Since Frank's acquittal, I couldn't win with them.

As I passed the interrogation rooms, it surprised me to see Candy still sitting, looking lonely and scared. She was staring down at the table and didn't notice I was there when I peeked my head in and asked, "Need a ride?"

She snapped her head up. "That's it? We're done?"

"It appears so," I said.

"No deal?"

"Your lawyer will fill you in on the specifics."

"That would be nice, if he was here."

The way she had been left behind confused me, but I assumed it had something to do with Frank. That worried me. Candy had put herself out there and I let her down.

"I knew this was a mistake," she said. "When Frank finds

out where I've been—" She freaked out. "Where are the papers? I need the papers. Give me the papers."

"Candy, settle down."

She was on her feet when she shouted, "Give them back!"

"I'm sorry. They're not yours to keep," I said.

Her mouth opened, but nothing came out.

"How about I give you a lift to your car?" Candy was staring at herself in the mirror when I said, "Or there's always Uber."

She had sad eyes and something told me she finally realized she was on her own. Gathering her things from the table, she said to me, "And risk leaving a digital trace? I don't think so. I'd rather take my chances of being seen with you."

I led her through the same maze of hallways as when we had entered, and I listened to her high heels clack a gentle melody against the linoleum flooring. We exited the building together; I held the door open for her, then helped her climb into the front seat of my Cruiser. Once I was buckled into my seat, I offered her a cigarette. She cracked a window and together we smoked in silence as I drove her back to her car.

CHAPTER EIGHTY-THREE

TEN MINUTES LATER, I WAS PARKED, THE ENGINE OFF, behind Candy's pearl white Mazda Miata but she had no intention of leaving the safe confines of my car.

I didn't push her to leave, either. Instead, I leaned back and turned my body toward her, wondering what I could do to make her believe I cared. She was staring out the window with a twisted and painful look on her face.

Candy had a lot going for her. Her beauty was as fierce as her personality, but deep down I sensed she had a broken past that made her insecure enough to have to rely on Frank. For one reason or another he had a hold on her. As badly as I wanted to ask, I wasn't here to lecture her about what she should do with her life. I just wanted to understand who took my family away from me and move on.

"Can I ask you something?"

"Depends," she said into the window.

"Does Frank know who Steve Eli is?"

She laughed.

"Something funny?"

She turned her head and looked me in the eye, paraphrasing the same story Steve shared. "I shouldn't be laughing. It's awful. It really is. They hate each other with a passion, but it's so juvenile what Frank did."

I wondered if Frank hated him as much as he hated me. I asked, "Has Frank spoken to Steve since the trial?"

"I don't know. There are lots of things I don't know about Frank."

She was sincere with her words, and I saw for the first time I might have been wrong about her. "Did you ever see Steve at Frank's trial?"

Candy gave it some thought and couldn't recall. "Why do you ask?"

I didn't know if Steve was a victim or conspirator, but I was hoping Candy could offer more than she had. I showed her a picture of Mr. Aviators in the black Range Rover and asked if she recognized him.

"Kind of looks like Steve."

I turned the picture back to me and thought the same. Then I asked, "Does Frank ever buy you jewelry?"

"Frank loves me—"

"You certain about that?" I asked too soon and regretted it when I heard the words come out of my mouth.

Candy opened her door and turned to look me in the eye. She said, "I've said enough and got nothing to show for it, but if I end up dead, you'll know why."

CHAPTER EIGHTY-FOUR

RAYMOND FRANK MOVED SWIFTLY DOWN THE HALLWAY AND flicked on the light as he entered his study. One look at his enormous mahogany desk and Frank knew the contents inside the urgent manila envelope sent to him yesterday were gone.

Hanging onto his phone, he lunged forward and began a last ditch effort search. He didn't want to believe it was possible. He looked beneath papers and inside the desk drawers and still nothing.

His blood pressure spiked, his heart raced with sudden anger.

"You're right. It's not here," he said into the phone.

"This is a good thing," Frank's defense attorney said.

"A good thing?" Frank barked back. "That bitch went behind my back and gave the police a reason to search my home."

"That won't happen."

"Can you guarantee it?"

"Mr. Frank. Haven't I earned your confidence? Nothing to worry about. I have everything handled."

Frank balled his hand into a tight fist, thinking he should fire his lawyer for incompetence. He knew Jackson had gotten into Candy's head, but he never expected her to do this. At least the immunity deal hadn't been granted. Had it not been for Candy's perjury conviction, Frank was convinced he would be having a different conversation.

"Then explain it to me," Frank said.

"Jackson Payne took a key piece of evidence directly to his superiors—"

"Right, I understand that."

"But they and you are seeing two different views." Frank could hear his lawyer practically smiling through the phone line at his ability to paint a pretty picture. Frank kept his mouth shut and listened to see where his lawyer was going with this. His lawyer continued, "They now know what Jackson's wife was planning to take away from him."

"It makes *him* look like the guilty one."

"Atta boy."

Frank's chin raised at the revelation. Piecing the events together inside his head, he was starting to see the possibility. Perhaps the sun was rising after all. It was as if the skies had suddenly opened up, and between what the news was saying about Jackson and the citizen complaint Frank had filed against him, this could potentially be a lethal combination. But it still didn't explain how Frank had found himself in possession of Jackson's divorce papers.

"The husband is always the first—and most of the times the last—suspect to be cleared in the murder of a spouse," the lawyer said.

"Don't I know it," Frank responded.

"Like I said, don't worry about this, but let me know if he continues to harass you. I believe we can escalate matters further if push came to shove."

Frank smiled and ended the call. He sat in the leather

high-back chair and reached for the knife on top of his desk. Scraping the pad of his thumb over the razor-sharp blade, he needed to decide what to do about Candy. He might have escaped persecution this time around, but next time he might not be so lucky.

Then the front door opened. Candy was home. Frank stood and went to greet his disobedient firecracker of a girlfriend, making sure to take the knife with him.

CHAPTER EIGHTY-FIVE

I WAS ALREADY ON MY SECOND DRINK, AND THINKING about my third, by the time Tex arrived. He sat across from me and asked, "Why are you sitting in the dark? Anyone bothering you tonight?"

I kept my gaze down, twirling an unlit cigarette between my fingers. I shook my head no, but the question had me thinking about Samuel White.

"Well, that's good news," Tex said, leaning back. He slung his arm over the back of the booth and let his eyes wander around the room as he tried to break the ice by telling me a story about his new girlfriend, the brunette, and how badly she had him wrapped around her slim finger.

I nodded, but wasn't listening, and Tex knew it. Then he asked about the leak, and if the department was doing anything about it. I lifted my gaze and said, "The damage is already done."

Tex turned his head and stared at a couple of young women across the bar who kept stealing glances in our direction. Tex opened his mouth to say how we should do something about the two women, that it was our job to make them feel welcomed, but I beat him to the punch when I said, "I wanted to follow but couldn't."

Tex gave me a puzzled look.

I filled him in on the details and told him about Candy and how I feared for her safety. "If something happens to her, I don't know if I could live with myself."

He could see this investigation was wearing me down. Tex was the voice of reason, the friend who tried to lift me up without forgetting what I'd lost. But he surprised me when he said, "Jackson, this is a good sign. It means you're getting closer to proving Frank was inside your house."

I pinched my cigarette between my fingers, sipped my whiskey, then told Tex about my need to find Mr. Aviators. "He's the missing link. If I can find him, then I know who wants me dead."

Tex sighed. He knew I had my work cut out for me.

I said, "It gets worse."

"How could it possibly get worse?"

"They have my fingerprints inside Cruz's house."

"What did you tell them?"

"The truth. I was there. It's how I got the copy of my divorce papers."

Now Tex was the one looking like he needed a drink. I pushed my glass his way, but he pushed it back. The look he had stamped on his face was one of an attorney creating a defense strategy for his client. Then Tex dropped a bomb on me I wasn't ready for.

He said, "I know how Moreno knows about your Walker Colt."

I perked up. Tex's eyes glimmered. He produced a paper from his jacket pocket, unfolded it, and said, "My PI found the purchase history of supplies you bought for it."

I took the paper into my hand and checked it out for myself. All the purchases were mine. I even remembered the day and conversation I had with the clerk. I lifted my head and said, "The gun is worth a fortune if it still exists."

Tex's cellphone buzzed with a text message. He skimmed it, then told me it was from his new girlfriend. They were going out tonight, but he didn't say where. Then he asked, "You don't think the gun survived the fire?"

I didn't know how it could have. But it made sense why the Walker Colt was what Moreno was referring to when asking what I was hiding of high value that I didn't want my wife to have. The problem was, I didn't have the gun or know where it was. Then I asked, "Do you?"

Tex made it clear he had something different in mind. He raised both his eyebrows and said, "Or it survived, and it's waiting to be used."

CHAPTER EIGHTY-SIX

FRANK GRABBED CANDY BY THE ARM AND SPUN HER around.

"Ray!" she protested. "What are you doing?"

"We're going out."

"But I just got home."

"Then imagine you didn't."

He opened the big door with enough force to shake the walls and marched her straight to the garage where he pushed her into the back of his Royce. She whimpered and whined but didn't try to escape.

Frank climbed behind the wheel, backed out, and hit the gas. He drove across town, flitting his gaze between the road and rearview mirror. Candy stared out the window with fear lining her face. Soon, they stopped at a women's clothing boutique where Frank made a call. A minute later, a woman exited the store with a bag in hand. Frank powered down his window and said, "You're such a doll."

"Anything for you, Raymond."

Frank took the bag into the vehicle and passed a generous

tip to the woman. Keeping a hold on the woman's hand, he asked, "See you soon?"

"Hope so."

Frank drove some more, then found a quiet place to park. Candy hadn't spoken a word the entire drive, though Frank knew his silence was killing her. He needed her to know, without saying, that what she'd done tonight was wrong.

Candy touched her hair and he stared at her in the rearview mirror for a long pause. When she finally looked his way, he tossed the bag onto the backseat and said, "Take off your clothes and put on these."

Candy didn't move. She bounced her gaze between the bag and Frank.

"Go on," Frank said.

Candy shook her head and rolled her eyes as if it was the most ridiculous thing she'd ever heard.

Frank kicked his door open and got in the back seat with her. Candy quickly scooted to the far end of the bench and stared with wide eyes, unsure what Frank would do to her next. Her chest heaved with trepidation and Frank looked at his watch.

"Now, hurry up. I don't want to be late," he said.

"Where are we going, Frankie?"

Her voice was soft, catlike. Frank lit a cigarette and put the bag of clothes onto his lap. He peeked inside, liked what he saw. Candy slithered off her shirt and wiggled out of her pants. He could almost smell the police on her; he was so disgusted by what she'd done. When Candy reached for the bag, Frank pulled back, saying, "The underwear goes too, sweetheart."

Candy glared, but didn't argue. She pathetically obeyed, like a puppy who knew it had misbehaved. When she was finally completely naked, she hugged herself warmly and covered herself up.

"Can I have my clothes now?"

He grinned at her humility. Then he tossed her the bag of clothes. She caught it against her chest and clenched it tightly.

"Choose wisely," he said.

Candy unwrapped an arm, revealed a taut nipple, and peeked inside the bag. Then she gave him a disapproving look.

"Your hair is a mess; so is your makeup."

"Frankie—" She frowned.

At the sound of her moan, he snapped and lunged forward, grabbing her face with his powerful hand. Pinching her cheeks together, he put his face in front of hers and said, "I can't ever have you make me look bad again. Do you understand?"

Candy nodded with white, scared eyes, knowing she'd been caught.

"Now put your fucking clothes on and do it with a smile."

CHAPTER EIGHTY-SEVEN

"Get out."

"I can't."

"There's no other way. This has to be done."

She swallowed hard and he could see the stone get lodged in her throat. Without another moment to waste, he reached around her and opened the door for her. The cool night air rushed in and prickled her snow white skin.

"You can do this. Now go," Viper said, pointing.

With fear in her eyes, Viper's girlfriend swung her legs around and slid out of the vehicle in one fluid motion. She smoothed out her leather jacket and turned back to give him one last glance—one more plea for him to change his mind. Viper lowered his jaw, grinned and nodded, silently admitting she lacked the confidence she needed to pull this off.

The car door slammed shut and Viper let off the brakes as he watched her trot toward the entrance of the gentlemen's club. He turned right onto the street while sucking back the last of his cigarette before lighting another one.

For some reason, each time he flicked the ash, he thought of black powder and the Walker Colt he had stashed away.

Anticipation was high; the mood so tense the air crackled with electricity. The thought of another kill excited him, but tonight was about cleaning up loose ends.

It had to be done.

The last resort before his luck ran out.

He drove the speed limit and used his blinker when necessary. There was only one law he intended to break tonight and, even then, he planned to stay out of the spotlight.

Five minutes later he circled back around the building, listening to his tires crunch over stone and broken pavement. The street lights were sparse and useless. He slouched behind the steering wheel so his face wouldn't be seen and studied the vehicles he passed, noting where, and how, they were parked, instinctively memorizing plates.

This wasn't his first visit to the gentlemen's club, but it might as well be his last. The women were as mediocre as the security. Dimly lit, it was the perfect camouflage for an ambush predator like himself.

By the third rotation around the building, he got worried his girlfriend had bailed.

Where was she? What was taking so long?

Then the message came through, stating she was on her way out.

Viper acted quickly. He spun the wheel, whipped the vehicle around back, and parked beneath a big tree. He put on a cap before reaching for the plastic bag from the backseat.

Before exiting, he made sure it was clear. Then he left his vehicle and got into position.

He heard them before he saw them. Viper's girlfriend had the man guess where the black Range Rover was parked. He played along willingly, soaking up every second of her flirtatious smile.

They were getting closer.

Viper crouched lower.

Then, under the cover of darkness, Viper reached behind his back and pulled his knife—a Karambit with a hooked blade and ergonomic handle designed for precision and efficiency.

She had him so wrapped up in her smile, they hadn't even noticed Viper when they passed in front of him. Before they got too far, Viper jumped out of the shadows and said, "Hey asshole. Is that you who's double parked?"

The man turned, startled. Before he had time to answer, Viper tossed him the plastic bag and, as the man caught it, Viper lunged his hand forward and stabbed the man once in the side of his neck. His knees buckled. Before the man fell forward, Viper pulled the knife from the man's neck and slashed him again, making sure he hit the carotid artery for a second time.

The man fell forward onto his face, without making a sound, and quickly bled out.

Viper's girlfriend stepped closer and, when their eyes met, he knew she was into his world now, one-hundred percent. Never again would she disrespect him. Whether she wanted to be or not, they were both murderers.

CHAPTER EIGHTY-EIGHT

"DO YOU THINK HE'S DEAD?"

The older of the two boys shrugged and said, "He looks dead."

"What should we do?"

The boy stepped closer and tapped on the window. The man inside the SUV lay still, his lips parted and pointed up to the roof. Then the boy reached for the door handle and tugged the door open.

"What are you doing?" The younger boy nervously looked around.

Older boy stared at the man, flopped across the backseat, and whispered, "Maybe he has something I want."

Younger boy watched as his friend patted down the man's pockets. The man's face looked gray, his purplish fingers and arms dangled loosely at his sides. "Touch his skin. See if it's warm."

Older boy did. "It's cold."

A shiver moved up the younger boy's spine. Instinct told him to leave before something bad happened. He looked behind him. They were alone. It was too early in the morning and the sun couldn't come up soon enough. The night had been too cold to sleep, which was how they had found themselves here.

"What is it?"

Older boy said, "An iPhone and wallet."

"Any money inside?"

Older boy looked, and that's when Younger boy noticed the man had a gun.

"Shit. Dude. He's got a gun."

Older boy sprouted a smile, tossed the iPhone and wallet to his friend, then went in for the gun.

CHAPTER EIGHTY-NINE

As soon as I sensed it, I reacted on trained instinct. First, I grabbed the arm, then I pulled my pistol from its holster, all before I had my eyes open. The boy screamed like a girl. I latched onto his skinny wrist and he wiggled like a hooked fish. With sleep in my eyes and alcohol fogging my brain, I blinked and tried to remember where I was.

The kid screamed again, and said, "Let me go. Don't shoot me!"

A flash of movement had me sitting up. Through the front window I saw another kid sprint away.

"It was him. He robbed you," the boy pleaded.

I let go of the kid's arm, kicked the door open, and chased after his friend. He ran like someone who had a lifetime of experience running from cops.

"Stop! Police!" I yelled between coughs.

The boy cut a corner and ran faster. I yelled again. He glanced back and caught his toe on a crack in the sidewalk. He flung forward, flew through the air with his arms extended out in front of him, and landed hard on the concrete with a painful grunt.

"That will teach you," I said when I caught up to him.

He rolled around, wincing and grabbing at his knee. I couldn't believe how young he looked. Tattered clothes and a dirty face, he must have only been thirteen years old.

I pointed my gun at his face and asked, "What did you take from me?"

His eyes ballooned and he showed me his palms. "It wasn't my idea. Don't arrest me. Please. I swear, I didn't want to take it."

"Take what?"

He pushed his hand into his pocket at my command and handed me my wallet and cellphone. I opened up the wallet and checked to make sure everything was there, and then my cellphone started ringing.

I told the kid to get lost, and then answered the call. "Jackson."

"Jackson, it's Whitney."

I turned and looked back toward the Cruiser. The older boy was gone. "Everything okay?"

"Can we talk? It's important."

CHAPTER NINETY

Whitney was waiting for me at an AM Eatery downtown. She'd called shortly before seven o'clock. That alone made me suspect something was seriously wrong.

I saw her through the front window, sitting with a steaming cup of coffee at a center table. Her hair looked especially red today and was beautifully tied up in a messy knot on top of her head. She caught sight of me and waved, then followed me inside with her eyes.

I removed my hat as soon as I entered the restaurant and requested a coffee from the server on my way to the table. The mouth-watering smells of breakfast had me ready to soak up my hangover. As soon as I sat down, something about Whitney's look said that food might have to wait.

"I apologize for not looking my best," I said. "It was a frosty night."

An empathetic glimmer caught Whitney's eyes, but she didn't comment on the awful odor wafting from me. My coffee came, and she told me to get anything I wanted from the menu. Then she asked, "What's keeping you awake at night?"

There were lots of reasons I wasn't finding my rest, but I didn't dare embarrass myself further by admitting I had slept in my car last night. Instead, I responded with a question of my own. "What is it that couldn't wait?"

The look on her face changed. She leaned forward and stared into her coffee mug for a beat before saying, "Someone is watching me, Jackson."

"Who?"

"I don't know." We locked eyes, and she told me about a man watching her from his truck on the street last night. "I tried to ignore it, convince myself he was just parked there because he lived in the building, or had a friend nearby. But he stayed too long for me to believe it was for anything other than to monitor me."

It was a lot to take in. My head pounded and the coffee I drank offered little relief. Worse was Whitney knowing I was struggling to wake up, too.

"You think Frank knows I was at your house the other night?" she asked.

I scratched my head and sighed. "Well—"

"Jesus."

She leaned back in her chair and flitted her gaze around the room. A third of the tables were occupied, but more people were filing in. Soon there would be a line out the door and it would be time for me to leave.

I said, "You never said what you were doing, or where you were before letting yourself into my apartment."

"I'm sorry about that, Jackson. I really am. It was rude and presumptuous of me to enter without asking."

"So? What were you doing?"

"After work I attended my spin class, which I do three nights a week. Then dinner at home in front of the TV. Chicken parmesan with broccoli. That's when I saw the evening news and thought of you."

I stared, thinking how she had had twenty-four hours to plan an answer I could believe. I asked, "Would Frank know that schedule?"

"Is this about the piece of jewelry you found?"

I said, "It's not just any piece of jewelry. It was my daughter's birthstone."

Her mood changed. Suddenly she looked worried. I said, "It's at the crime lab getting tested for fingerprints." I looked for a reaction that might suggest she was guilty, but there wasn't one. "The results should come back soon."

Whitney touched the back of her head and said, "Nothing happened to me until I visited you."

I didn't have the energy to remind her it was she who came to me. Coincidence? Or was she just paying attention now?

"Why didn't you answer my call?" I asked. "I called the night you visited. Where did you go?"

There was a distant, strange look in her eye. Then her eyes came into focus when she said, "Jackson, I saw the same truck outside your apartment the night I left. If not for that, I wouldn't have thought anything of it."

CHAPTER NINETY-ONE

"You're telling me the man stalking you last night was also parked outside my apartment?"

Whitney said, "That's exactly what I'm saying."

The black Range Rover flashed across my mind, but Whitney wasn't the type of person to confuse her vehicles. I suspected she knew them well enough to know what she'd seen. I asked, "And you're certain the man who was stalking you was hiding out inside a truck?"

"Yes, Jackson."

"What kind of truck?"

Our conversation was getting louder and people were looking. I tossed down two twenties onto the table and took Whitney outside so we could discuss this in private. She squinted into the sunlight and said, "It was a Ford pickup truck."

"An F-150?"

"Is it one of Frank's? Does he have an F-150?"

Whitney seemed nervous. Something caught her eye. I glanced behind me and saw two men approaching. They were both wearing collared shirts, corporate warriors getting a late start on their day. Nothing to worry about. I ignored them and said, "I don't know."

"Oh my god, he's going to kill me. I know he is."

Finally, she was making the connection I didn't want to have to make for her. It was what I thought all along. But what worried me now was how she was losing trust in herself. It happened when paranoia overrode all other senses. Whitney couldn't keep eye contact and I knew I needed to get her someplace she felt safe.

I reached for her hand and said, "We don't know that's true."

"What are you doing today?" she asked me. "Can I come with you?"

"I have something else in mind," I said. Then I put her into her cherry red Camaro and told her to lead me to her place. "I need to see what you saw."

Whitney drove with a heavy foot and I struggled to keep up. I didn't think she was trying to intentionally lose me, but it certainly felt like she was attempting to shake her tail. She might have thought Frank was the one spying, but there was only one F-150 on my mind.

Moreno's.

Before I allowed my thoughts to get away from me, I needed to know I could fully trust everything she said.

We headed north and crossed over the Colorado River. She drove fast, sped through traffic lights, and barely used her blinker.

"Don't lose me," I mumbled, wanting to believe her intention was honest.

Though I believed it was, I couldn't take the chance of getting setup again. There was too much at stake to be fooled again. I wondered if she started the birthstone conspiracy so I would think Frank was behind it, so I could do the dirty work of killing Frank for her.

Soon, we were downtown and Whitney stopped in the middle of the street. She powered down her window and motioned for me to pull up alongside her. I leaned across the passenger seat and cranked down the window.

"Park on the street, there," she pointed to a space behind me. "And meet me in the garage."

After I parked, I met her at the elevator and it whisked us up to the second floor. She lived in a second story, two-bedroom condo with views of downtown. It was modern with gigantic windows and stainless steel appliances, all of which she owned.

"Mind if I look around?" I asked.

"I'd prefer you did."

As I inspected the locks and checked the doors and windows, it was easy for me to see the reason she felt vulnerable. The building had a concierge but no real security check. The windows were large enough to prevent any real privacy, even with the drapes drawn. I didn't see any signs I was being fooled, but wondered if she had a history with Moreno.

"Any other cops come talk to you?"

"About what?"

"This. That."

"No."

There were no signs Whitney was in a relationship. A single toothbrush in her single bath. Everything about the way she lived said she was a woman determined to make her own way. A career woman on the fast track to the top. I asked, "Can you point to where the truck was parked?"

Whitney stood next to me at the window and pointed to where my Cruiser sat. "There," she said. "He was parked right where I told you to park your car."

CHAPTER NINETY-TWO

"No cameras in the back."

"And nothing out front."

Detective Emily Sanchez stared up and into the slots where the cameras should have been mounted. "Then we get permission to review the security tape from inside. Perhaps we'll get lucky."

"Already on it."

"Then get to it."

The sheriff's deputy headed for the entrance to the gentlemen's club, and Sanchez took a moment to herself to piece together the little they knew about this morning's murder.

It was a club in northeast Austin, a favorite among those willing to keep the party going after all the other bars closed. That alone attracted a certain clientele—many of whom had a criminal history.

She found refuge beneath a tree and watched the techies comb over the scene, marking footprints and tire tracks, anything that could help explain why this mysterious John Doe had been murdered.

"What the hell has become of my city?" She sighed, the week of murders taking its toll.

Whatever the answer to her question was, she was certain it had something to do with the black Range Rover parked to her left.

When another news van arrived, Sanchez shifted her gaze to the two men who had discovered the body. They were in their early twenties and claimed they didn't see or know anything. Which meant no one knew anything.

She walked back to the body and the assistant medical examiner said, "I'm nearly finished, then he's all yours."

The victim was male and approximately forty years of age. No one knew who he was or why he was killed. There were no reported incidents according to the night manager, and yet the victim had been stabbed to death. Why?

"The carotid artery was hit at least twice. The victim didn't suffer. He bled out quickly," the ME said, unprompted.

Sanchez kneeled next to the doctor.

"It's a deep stab wound," the ME said, pointing to the neck. "I'm guessing it penetrated to the spine, but I won't know until I get him on the table."

Sanchez stared at the victim's neck, thinking of the incredible force behind his wound.

"Whoever did it is strong. Probably a male, and certainly an expert." The ME looked Sanchez in the eye. "They knew what they were doing."

A tactical kill, Sanchez thought.

"I won't know the official time of death until after the evaluation is complete," the ME said, "but I'd guess it happened early this morning. Sometime after midnight."

On one knee, Sanchez finally got the go-ahead to check inside the victim's pockets. She found a wallet full of cash, no drugs, a pair of sunglasses, and a gold watch on the man's wrist. According to his driver's license, the man's name was Eduardo Rodriguez.

"Where are your car keys, Mr. Rodriguez?" Sanchez asked the corpse.

With that in mind, Sanchez stood and looked around, hoping to see something she hadn't before. But it was the plastic bag full of mail carrier clothes next to Eduardo that was most puzzling.

"Detective," the deputy called from the entrance. "You're going to want to come see this."

CHAPTER NINETY-THREE

VIPER WOKE WHEN THE MATTRESS DIPPED. HIS GIRLFRIEND slid back into bed and stared up at the ceiling with a furrowed look that had him wondering what she was thinking, and where she just was.

Last night might have been too much for her innocent soul, but if Viper had to do it again, he wouldn't change a thing.

The maroon colored bed sheet lay loosely draped over her figure. A single bare breast was exposed and lay flat against her chest. She was as still as a log, like she was sleeping with her eyes opened, and he barely noticed her breathing.

"Have you been awake long?" he asked her.

She didn't respond. No blinking of the eyes, no adjusting of the head. Viper assumed she'd been awake for hours, with the dull glaze covering her pupils like an autumn morning haze. Your first murder would do that to you. Make you reflect on your own mortality.

He rolled onto his side, tucked his arm beneath his ear, and stared back. Her blue eyes came into focus, but not even a flirt of a smile threatened to tug at the corners of her lips.

Suddenly, he was worried about her. He was certain last night's activities were too much.

Viper wondered when the nightmares would come, how bad they would get. What worried him most was knowing she might eventually turn her torment on him.

Karma, he thought as he extended a hand and tucked her soft hair behind her ear.

"Everything okay?" he asked.

She was slow to respond, but eventually nodded her head. Her innocence of yesterday was gone. Like losing her virginity, it was something she'd never get back.

Viper kissed her forehead, then rolled over and took a cigarette from the pack off the nightstand. He struck the butane lighter and stared at the flickering flame with thoughts of Jackson Payne's wife and daughter flashing across the front of his mind. Their faces were as clear as day; two he'd never forget.

"We couldn't risk him identifying us if the police asked him questions," he said, blowing out a white cloud of smoke.

His girlfriend didn't respond. Her unfocused eyes drifted across the room and it was like she wasn't there at all.

Viper said, "It's just the two of us from now on. No more third parties. Everything that happens from here on out, we do ourselves."

He offered her a drag off his cigarette, but she didn't take him up on his offer.

Viper didn't want to go into detail about the work that still needed to be done; she didn't need to know the specifics. But this wouldn't stop. He couldn't stop. Not until it was finished.

Then she propped herself up on one elbow and surprised him when asking, "When can we do it again?"

CHAPTER NINETY-FOUR

Whitney backed away from the window and left a pleasant scent in her wake. I remained where I was, continuing to peer down at my old car. From where it was a parked, the driver would have a direct line of sight into Whitney's condo.

It was impossible for me not to clench my fist when thinking about what it was he was trying to prove by keeping tabs on both Whitney and me. But when I thought back to the conversation I had had with the deputy chief, I suspected Moreno was partly the reason I got pulled off both murder investigations.

It might have looked like I was covering up a crime, but Moreno's actions were nothing short of suspicious. Moreno had the knowledge to get away with murder—manipulate the evidence to make it look like something it wasn't. But if Whitney was right about what she saw here last night, I might have found my ticket back into the investigation. Now I just needed to catch him in the act.

Whitney was on the couch, hunched forward with her

elbows planted on her knees when I turned to her and said, "Please tell me you took a picture of the truck."

"And give myself away?" She shook her head. "I don't think so."

I couldn't fault her for not having the courage to reveal her hand to a suspected stalker. Her decision might have saved her life. Instead, I asked if the drapes were open or closed and had her walk me through her night.

"The drapes are on a timer. They close every evening at sunset," she said. Then she told me about a quiet night in front of the TV, replying to work emails until bed.

"You're sure you saw the same truck outside my place?" I asked.

"Maybe I'm not making myself clear," she said, squaring her shoulders.

I held up a hand, apologized. "It's important we get this right."

"Of course."

"Besides the truck, what else did you see that night?"

"There was a small gathering above your apartment. I heard a guitar playing. College kids laughing. They were grilling."

Whitney described what she remembered, but mentioned nothing about seeing a postman. Now I wondered if I was wrong about Frank. Was it possible Moreno had left me Selina's birthstone? If so, that might explain how the killer had thus far escaped capture. Then I asked if she had ever heard the name Steve Eli before.

"No. Who is he?"

The other person—besides you—who would like to see Raymond Frank dead, I thought, but couldn't say.

I gave her a quick history, told her who he was, why he was important to Frank. "His car was stolen two days before my house burned down, and he and Frank have an ugly history." Before she had time to respond, I asked, "Are you sure your sister never mentioned his name to you before?"

"When things got really bad between her and Frank, the less I knew, the safer I was." When Whitney paused, I watched doubt cross over her face. Then she said, "Or so I thought."

It was possible her sister was protecting her, but there was no way of knowing that now.

Whitney asked, "Is he who you think might be stalking me?"

"No," I said. "Steve is a victim of Frank's, just like us; but if we find who stole his car, we find who murdered my family."

CHAPTER NINETY-FIVE

I RECEIVED A CALL FROM SANCHEZ AND ANSWERED IT IN the kitchen. Sanchez said, "Jackson, we got another victim."

I asked where, and Sanchez told me the location. "Be there in ten."

"You're leaving me?" Whitney asked, hugging herself like she was cold.

"It's work. I have to go."

Whitney glanced toward the front wall of windows and stared through the glass, peering down at the street as if Moreno's truck was still parked below.

"Lock up after I leave. Don't let anyone inside while I'm gone. And if you see the vehicle again, get a picture if you can, then call me." Whitney didn't respond, and I touched her elbow, which only made her flinch. She pivoted before tipping her head back to look me in the eye. "Can you do that for me?" I asked.

"I don't know." Her eyes watered with obvious fear, pleading with me not to leave her alone.

"I have to go," I said, pulling my hand away. "If you have to leave the house, stay in a crowd. You'll be fine."

After she nodded her head in agreement, I let myself out. By the time I was climbing into my Cruiser, Whitney was at the window, still wrapped up in her arms with a look of betrayal stamped on her face. I hated to leave her, but I didn't have a choice. There was nothing I could do from here. Worse than that was how clearly I could see into her home from the street.

I raced north to the gentlemen's club on the outskirts of the city, needing to get there before the upper brass found a reason to pull me off this case, too.

Sanchez hadn't told me much about the murder over the phone, but as my mind raced with possibility, I began listing off all the different places I was last night, and who I was with, while maintaining hope that this had nothing to do with me. If not for the unease in my stomach, I might have thought it didn't. Something told me it did.

Nine minutes later, I arrived to the sight of news vans lined up along the street and their reporters loitering with their camera lenses all pointed at the club's entrance.

Without them noticing, I discreetly circled around them and checked in with a deputy who had opened the gates for me to park. As soon as I was on foot, I pulled my hat over my eyes and caught sight of what I was certain was Steve Eli's black Range Rover.

Two techies circled the vehicle like hawks. I instinctively flicked my gaze to the press corp. When their cameras were focused elsewhere, I made my move.

All four doors were opened, including the back hatch. Pictures were being taken, surfaces dusted for fingerprints. I asked one of the techs working, "Any gas in the cans?"

"Nearly empty," he said.

I stared at the welder's torch with thoughts of Ilene and Selina getting caught in a fire they couldn't escape. Inside the vehicle, I also saw several other items of interest. There was a roll of duct tape, a thirty-foot rope, a sheriff's cap, and a crumbled note with Vincent Cruz's home address attached to his picture. I took it all in but thought it was too easy for it to be believable.

"Never thought we'd see this car again," Sanchez said by way of greeting.

I blinked away the stars from the camera flashes and asked, "Who's the victim?"

Sanchez motioned for me to follow. She talked as we walked. "Victim is male. Stab wound to the neck. No witnesses. Just two men who discovered his body when leaving to go home after the club closed."

"What time was that?"

"Shortly after six a.m."

Steve Eli's face flashed like a neon sign in my mind, but once I got a visual on our victim I knew it was Aviators. Now I understood why Moreno was keeping an eye on both Whitney and me. While he knew I was busy at the station with Candy, he kept a close watch on Whitney to make sure he could pull this off. But if that was the case, that meant he was working with a partner.

Sanchez said, "His name is Eduardo Rodriguez."

The name didn't ring a bell. I gloved up and kneeled next to Mr. Rodriguez, silently asking myself if it was possible Moreno was cleaning up loose ends. I hadn't told anybody about what Cruz's editor-in-chief, Maxwell Sheldon, had provided of what Cruz had captured on camera that day in the park, yet it seemed someone else knew Eduardo's importance.

Sanchez asked, "Do you know him?"

My eyes drifted from Eduardo's neck to his chest. He even had his mirrored sunglasses tucked inside his jacket pocket. When I let my focus stop on his hand, I thought back to how he pretended to shoot Cruz and me with it.

"No," I said, though Eduardo cleared up any suspicions I might have had about Steve Eli. But was it Eduardo who stole Steve's SUV? With no other suspects, it seemed likely.

Sanchez said, "They executed him. Whoever killed him knew what they were doing."

I checked the wounds. "No fuss, is right. This was a quick, clean kill."

"Like he might have known something he shouldn't have."

Sanchez was alluding to a connection to Cruz's murder. As I processed the information myself, I looked inside the plastic bag to the left of Eduardo, and Sanchez saw me do it.

She said, "USPS uniform. We're thinking he could have been an employee, but I just don't know."

"USPS uniforms can be purchased online," I said.

"Then why bring it with him to a strip club?"

Aviators—Mr. Eduardo Rodriguez—otherwise known to me as another person with likely ties to Raymond Frank, was now dead. That didn't surprise me, but the uniform certainly did. My heart beat faster. After several minutes of assessment, I was certain the uniform was purposely placed so it would be easy for me to find.

"What if it wasn't his?" I asked.

"Are you saying someone planted it on him?"

I turned my head and gave Sanchez a knowing look. As I looked into her almond colored eyes, I debated how much information I felt comfortable sharing. Could I be right? Did Eduardo's murderer know I'd make the connection between the uniform and Selina's birthstone? It seemed likely, but nothing anybody would believe.

I turned back to face Eduardo and felt my brow tighten between my eyes. It felt like the killer was taunting me, sending the message that they couldn't be touched. Though it was only a hunch, why go through so much effort instead of bringing the fight straight to me?

When I stood, Sanchez asked, "Did you speak to Steve Eli?"

I nodded.

"And?"

"It's not him. He didn't do this."

"What aren't you saying, Jackson? Was Eduardo who you were looking for?"

She knew he was. "Possibly," I said. "Though Steve didn't have a criminal record, he had an interesting history with Raymond Frank."

Sanchez arched an eyebrow and said, "Interesting you say that. Frank was here last night."

CHAPTER NINETY-SIX

"FRANK WAS HERE LAST NIGHT?"

Sanchez raised her eyebrows and said, "For about two hours. We caught him on the security camera."

I wondered why she was just telling me this now.

I turned and faced the Range Rover, thinking about how I had initially assumed Eduardo was one of Frank's hired men. If that was true, it might explain why Eduardo was killed.

Until now, the only pattern to each of these murders was that I was one step behind. This time I hadn't just seen Eduardo like I did my family and Cruz, but I was certainly looking for him. Did Frank know that? How could he possibly?

Sanchez motioned for me to follow her inside. We entered through the front and stepped into a brightly lit room that did an outstanding job of highlighting the previous night's grime. Off to my left was a cleaning staff quarantined at the side, eager to not a miss a day's work. They watched as we weaved our way to the back and, as I took in the details, all I could think about was how much I hated places like this.

Gentlemen clubs were nothing but a front for criminal

activity. Whether it be drugs, prostitution, sex trafficking, or money laundering, I'd seen it all before. My first impression of this place told me it wasn't any different. But the greatest irony of all was how strip clubs lured men into pretending they held more power than their female counterparts who seduced them until they were broke. Why was Raymond Frank here? Coincidence? Not likely. And who came here first? Frank or Eduardo?

I followed Sanchez through an open door and stepped into a square office with a two-monitor computer stationed against the far wall. A deputy stood guard as Sanchez introduced me to the club manager. He was leaning back in his chair in the corner and had his feet up on the desk. He eyed me with crossed forearms and looked annoyed for having to work overtime.

Sanchez said, "This is Detective Jackson Payne."

I ignored the manager's droopy-eyed stare and asked to see the footage. The deputy played back what he'd already watched several times before.

"Our victim is here," the deputy said, pointing to the monitor. "And Raymond Frank is there."

I flicked my gaze between the monitors. Eduardo was seated stage left, drinking alone, pushing dollar bills to a topless woman dancing on stage before him. Frank was opposite him, but seated in a private booth in the back next to Candy. Neither Frank nor Eduardo seemed to recognize the other. And neither did Candy.

"This is where it happens," Sanchez said to me.

In that moment, I watched Eduardo check his phone as if he'd received a message, then stand and leave the building.

I said, "Check his phone records. Find out who messaged him and why." Then I asked, "Is that it? Where are the cameras outside?"

"There aren't any."

I turned my head and glared at the club manager. He turned his palms up and shrugged his shoulders. Of course there weren't any. Conveniently left out. It seemed the killer knew it, too.

"Was Raymond Frank a regular here?" I asked the manager.

"He was."

"What do you mean, he was?"

"I mean, he was. Used to come in same time, same day, every week. Then stopped when he was arrested for murder."

Either Frank was part of Eduardo's murder, or the killer knew Frank's pattern and hoped that now he was a free man, he'd continue the same routine. I said to play the tape back, but Sanchez told me to hang on. There was more.

"Watch what happens when Frank whispers something into Candy's ear," she said.

There was obvious tension between Frank and Candy, and I suspected it had something to do with Candy's secret plea for immunity. I didn't like how things were left when I had dropped her off last night, but at least I knew she was alive.

Frank took a call on his cellphone. Then he hung up and whispered something into Candy's ear. We watched her walk to the front of the club and exit the building. Five minutes later she returned, visibly shaken.

"What happened?" I asked the room. "Was that when Eduardo was murdered?"

"Possibly," Sanchez said. "We're working to locate both her and Frank as we speak."

Frustrated by the lack of security cameras, I asked Sanchez if that was all. She said it was and I headed for the exit, determined to find out where Frank's men were last night and what they were up to.

As soon as I exited the building, I caught sight of

Moreno. He was speaking to one of the men who had discovered the body. Of course he joined the party fashionably late.

I ignored his stare and turned toward Eduardo where I kneeled next to his head and asked, "Who told you to go outside?"

Then I searched him for his phone. I couldn't locate it. It wasn't here.

I paused and calculated what the chances were that the killer took it for themselves. It would have been a stupid move as we could easily trace its location, but I'd seen stupid before. What I didn't know yet was if Frank was cleaning up loose ends or if I had it all wrong and was being manipulated into believing someone else's narrative? Because I certainly didn't believe Frank would position him so close to someone he had ordered to have murdered. He was smarter than that. Even if he wanted to prove something to Candy.

"Do you know him?"

I stood and turned at the sound of Moreno's voice. I said, "Sounds like you might."

"Are you sure you've never seen him before?"

He had a look like he knew my secret—knew how I had been looking for Eduardo, hoping to connect him to Cruz's murder. I looked him in the eye and said, "I've seen him before, but I don't know him."

Moreno squinted his eyes, but never looked away. I wondered if he could see that I knew he had been watching Whitney and me. I hoped he did. If I found out he was behind any of this, I would kill him myself.

Then he shifted his gaze to the Rover and said, "Steve Eli will be happy we located his vehicle, but I'm not sure he'll like us implying he had anything to do with your house getting burned down."

Moreno was proving to me he was very much in tune with my train of thought. He'd done his homework. Of course I declined to respond. Instead, I watched him crouch next to Eduardo and think. After a silent minute of thought, he said to me, "Whoever murdered him knew what they were doing."

Moreno walked me through his theory, how he saw it go down inside the theater of his mind. It was a visual display, and he was quite animated when telling me.

"I'm guessing the killer used a Karambit," Moreno said, making a slicing motion across Eduardo's neck. Then he turned his head and asked me, "Jackson, you own a lot of weapons; you own one of those knives?"

"If you're asking me to give my professional opinion on what the weapon can do, you better ask an actual expert," I said. But he wasn't asking. Moreno was accusing me of committing the murder, yet again.

Moreno chuckled. "I thought you *were* the expert."

I said, "You have something you want to say, just say it."

"Okay then." He stood and got in my face. "Where were you last night between one and six a.m.?"

CHAPTER NINETY-SEVEN

A VISUAL OF ME PASSED OUT ON THE BACK SEAT OF MY Cruiser popped into my mind, quickly followed by the memory of almost getting robbed by a couple teenagers living on the streets. Moreno gave me a look that said he knew I hadn't been home—didn't have an alibi.

Catching him by surprise, I lunged forward without warning, and thrust my palms into the center of his chest, knocking him off his feet. He flew backward and landed on his ass, but he didn't stay down long. He scrambled to his feet and took a swing at me, but missed.

Two other deputies saw what happened and were sprinting toward us when I told Moreno, "You got anything else you want to say to me?"

"Jackson, stop!" I heard Sanchez yell from somewhere behind me.

Moreno reached for my shirt but I knocked his hand away. Sanchez skidded to a stop and put herself between us. "What the hell has gotten into you two?"

"You want to tell her, or should I?" I said to Moreno.

He glanced over his shoulder toward the loitering TV

reporters with a hopeful look in his eyes, that maybe our altercation had been captured on camera. Lucky for me, we weren't within view, but I wasn't going to stand for it. Moreno seemed hell bent on making my life miserable and it only made him look more suspicious than I already thought he was.

"C'mon, Jackson. Let's cool off in the shade," Sanchez said.

I gave Moreno one last look before turning my back to him.

Sanchez whispered, "I know you're going through a lot and the stress of these cases is more than any of us can handle alone, but don't let that asshole ruin your career."

"Simple question, Jackson," Moreno called out. "Where were you last night?"

I stopped walking and clenched my jaw. Sanchez grabbed my arm and said, "Ignore him, Jackson. He's only trying to get you to react."

I lowered my gaze and watched Sanchez's eyes drift down my neck as if suddenly taking in my haggard appearance, noticing I was wearing the same clothes as yesterday.

"Is that all it is?" I asked her.

Sanchez gave me a look that said don't go there. But I was already there, and I was done here, too. Before I told Sanchez goodbye, I looked around one last time before deciding where I'd go next. With Eduardo out of the picture, there were only a few options left.

I climbed into my Cruiser and sped off without looking back.

CHAPTER NINETY-EIGHT

MORENO KNEW EXACTLY WHAT HE WAS DOING, WHAT HE was asking. He had a game plan, a goal he wanted to achieve. I might not have understood what game he was playing, but I did understand Moreno was trying to get me to admit to something I didn't do.

Why?

There was a reason he was keeping tabs on me, and I thought I might know why. Either he thought I had committed these murders myself, or wanted to make sure I wasn't anywhere near where the murders happened. Neither of which I liked.

But there was something else, too. He knew I had been looking for Eduardo. How?

I thought about all these things as I headed across town. My window was cracked, and I listened to my Cruiser's wheels hum as they glided over the pavement.

Even now, the evidence found in the Rover seemed too easy. Especially the sheriff's cap. Was that part of Samuel White's disguise? Maybe, but was Eduardo really that stupid to drive around for nearly a week after the fire with the

evidence still in the back of a stolen vehicle? That, I didn't
know, but I planned to find out.

First, I needed to find Frank, clear him of Eduardo's
murder, and then turn my efforts back to learning what
Moreno was hoping to achieve by coming after me. It worried
me to think maybe Moreno wasn't acting alone.

I kept looking in my rearview mirror, expecting to find a
tail. None ever came and, though it was too early for Red
River nightclub to be open, I stopped and parked there
anyway. As I lit up a smoke, memories of fighting Mr. Big and
Smalls came to me without effort. I thought about the spec-
tators, wondered if anyone had caught it on film. I assumed if
they had, I would have heard about it by now. That I hadn't,
was just darn right lucky.

Soon, my thoughts circled back to Candy. I retrieved my
cellphone from my pocket and checked on her various social
media feeds. There was nothing new, which was odd for
Candy. The last post she made was yesterday morning, before
she had asked for her immunity deal. Why had she gone
quiet? I didn't like that.

I lifted my gaze with an uneasy feeling clenching my
stomach. I was worried about her. Maybe she was okay now,
but how long before Frank found out about her coming
to me?

Setting my phone on the dash, I thought back to the strip
club's security tape, wondering who might have called Frank
and what he had told Candy to get her to go outside. Those
were the questions that I needed answered. Without Candy
announcing her location, there was no telling where she
was now.

I felt the clock ticking, and I grew increasingly more
anxious.

I knew if I could find her, I could get her to talk, tell me
what she witnessed last night. But I was afraid of pushing

things too far with her, past the point of getting her killed. There had to be a different way. It wasn't like I could just roll up to Frank's house and knock on the door.

By the time I was finished with my cigarette, I had a strange feeling that Frank had been set up this time. I almost couldn't believe I was going down that road.

I made a couple phone calls. My first was to Candy, my second to Frank. Neither of them answered their phone, and I wasn't surprised, but I left a message with both. If I couldn't convince myself of the thoughts I was having, how could I convey them to Frank and have him believe I might actually think he was innocent?

I cursed and put another cigarette between my lips. Then, before I had it lit, I had an idea.

There was someone else who I could call who might know how Moreno had guessed I had been looking for Eduardo. I thumbed through my list of contacts and, when I found his number, I made the call.

CHAPTER NINETY-NINE

MAXWELL SHELDON WAS QUICK TO ANSWER MY CALL.

"Mr. Payne, what can I do for you?"

Talking over the sounds of the newsroom coming through his end of the line, I said, "I'm calling about Vincent Cruz's files."

"Not this again. First you, then your colleague."

"Excuse me?"

"Deputy Moreno." A quick pause before Sheldon continued. "He called here yesterday requesting access. Doesn't your office communicate?"

Sheldon's skepticism was evident. Not wanting him to lose hope in our ability to catch Cruz's killer, I said, "Our office has been busy."

"Yes, I heard about last night's murder."

He was hoping for an inside scoop, but I kept my mouth shut.

"Then answer this for me," he said. "Does it relate to Vincent's case?"

"If it does, you'll be the first to know."

I ended the call, satisfied I had confirmed my suspicions

about Moreno. It was why he was asking if I knew Eduardo. It was all coming together, but it pissed me off Sheldon had broken his promise and it only echoed my distrust for journalists.

I started the engine and headed home with plans to shower and change clothes.

I suspected Moreno knew Eduardo had seen me with Cruz that day in the park, but did he also know that was who I had been chasing when he pulled me over? He'd probably figured it out. But it was still up in the air whether he was protecting Eduardo or hiding something he didn't want to get found out about himself.

Ten minutes later I was in North University, circling the block, doing a quick recon around my apartment building to see what I might walk into—if anything. I couldn't take any chances. Not with Moreno on my ass, and certainly not with the media continuing to prey on my vulnerabilities. When I decided it was clear, I parked on the street and strode to my front door, when I saw Ronnie Gould step outside.

"Jackson, I'm so glad to see you," he said at the upstairs balcony rail.

I stopped to look up. "What is it, Ronnie?"

"Hang on," he said, indicating he was coming down.

I watched him bound down the steps and hurry to me, finishing his thought.

"There was someone here last night looking for you," he said.

"Who?"

"I don't know, I didn't catch his name, but we noted the vehicle he was driving." When I raised my eyebrows, he said, "A Ford Bronco Sport."

I filed through my mind without coming up with any hits.

"He was a big, mean looking dude," Ronnie said, describing my visitor. "Looked military."

"We?"

Ronnie had that same puzzled look he seemed to carry with him at all times.

"You said *we noted*—"

"Ah, right." Ronnie smiled. "Me and my girlfriend. The one you spoke to the other night. As soon as I heard the knock, we knew we had to see who it was. You know, in case someone was trying to break into your apartment again."

"It's not a big deal," I said. "Just a friend of mine visiting, is all."

"Good to know. You had us concerned something bigger might be going on."

I smiled and gave him a fist bump, reassuring Ronnie I wasn't a danger to our little community. "Thanks for looking out for me."

"Isn't that what neighbors are for?"

Ronnie was right, that was what neighbors were for, but once I stepped across the threshold into my apartment, I drew my gun and closed the door behind me. I stood with my back up against the wall, taking a moment to listen to the sounds creaking in the walls. It was quiet, and on my initial inspection I didn't see any sign anyone had been inside, while I was away.

Walking on tender feet, I swept the apartment and cleared it of any potential surprises.

The single bar of soap was dry, and my toothbrush was where I had left it. Same went for the cardboard box on my bedroom floor and the clothes that hung in the closet. Everything was exactly how I had left it. When I was satisfied I was alone, I holstered my gun and sat on the leather sofa in the living room.

Based on Ronnie's description of my visitor, I thought I might know who it was—and if I was right, I also might know why Alan Bolin had wanted to see me.

My cellphone buzzed with a text from Caroline. Instead of writing her back, I called.

"Hey Jackson," Caroline said when she answered. "I wasn't sure if you were busy."

"Caught me on my coffee break."

I caught her up to speed, said I was still working to figure out who might have started the fire. She said, "I arranged for the plots in the cemetery. I walked it myself. Nice mountain views. Good sunshine. They'll be together."

It sounded like a good place to rest for eternity. "Has a date for the funeral been made?" I asked.

"Not yet. We're waiting for you, Jackson."

I dropped my head into my hand and closed my eyes. The tears that fell burned like hell.

"Take your time. Clearing this case is what's most important now."

I appreciated Ilene's sister being so forthcoming. Immediately after my call with Caroline, I called Whitney to see how she was doing.

She said, "The fact you're calling has me worried."

It was good to hear her voice. "Nothing to worry about," I said. "I'm at my apartment and just got curious about where exactly you saw the pickup truck parked."

Whitney told me where and I made a mental note to myself to check it out on my way out the door. Then she said, "Thanks for checking in."

"Not a problem."

"Promise to do it again?"

Without thinking, I said, "I promise."

Then I was out the door to see if I could find a link between Tom Moreno and Eduardo Rodriguez so I could put this case to rest, once and for all.

CHAPTER ONE HUNDRED

STEVE ELI'S SPORTS CAR WAS PARKED IN THE DRIVE WHEN I arrived. I pulled my Cruiser behind it, blocked it in, then got out and inspected his fresh set of wheels.

It was a jet black Chevrolet Corvette C8 with cockpit style seats, a vehicle I wasn't aware he owned. It was fast, impressive, and way above what I could afford.

I whistled and walked to the house, thinking how my Cruiser looked like an ancient relic next to a modern marvel.

The garage doors were closed, as well as the front drapes. At the door, I rang the bell and heard it chime. Hoping Steve was home, I glanced toward the sun as a quick way to check the time, wondering if I'd caught him between conference calls again. A minute passed before the large wooden door finally opened.

"Detective?" Steve answered with a surprised look on his face. "Didn't expect to see you so soon."

"Have a minute?"

His dark eyebrows tightened. "Yeah, sure. Of course."

He stepped outside and closed the door behind him.

"New car?" I asked.

He crossed his forearms and beamed at his new ride. "The C8. First mid-engined Corvette in history," he said with a large, stretching smile. Then he told me about why it was a big deal, but I wasn't really interested. I wasn't a car guy. He read my expression perfectly and closed his story by saying, "It was on my list of things to get, and when my SUV was stolen, I decided no better time to pull the trigger than now."

I quirked a brow.

"Sorry. Poor analogy," he said, quickly changing the subject. "That your car? What year is it?"

I said, "We found your vehicle."

He gave me an incredulous look. "You did?"

I nodded.

"Where?"

"I'd prefer to do this at the station if you don't mind."

"Am I in some kind of trouble?"

"No, nothing like that." Steve didn't believe me. I said, "There were some items found in the car I think you might want back."

He scratched his head as if trying to recall the missed possessions.

"In order for us to release the chain of custody, I'll need you to fill out some paperwork. Shouldn't take too much of your day, and we'd really like to get it done today."

Steve squinted his eyes as if trying to recall what he might have left inside the vehicle. His cheeks never once flushed and he defended nothing I had said. If he was in any way guilty, he didn't show it.

The big door opened behind him and a gorgeous blonde wearing only his t-shirt, poked her head out. "Everything all right?" she asked.

She caught me assessing her slender tanned legs and young firm breasts. There was something in those eyes that made it hard to escape.

Steve told her to go back inside and added, "I'll be along shortly." When the door closed, he turned to me and said, "Give me an hour to shower?"

"Don't be late. I have lots I need to get done today," I said, heading toward my car.

CHAPTER ONE HUNDRED ONE

Viper found his girlfriend at the kitchen table, sitting down with a bowl of cereal. "How about I make you something with less sugar in it?" he asked.

"Trix are for kids." She smiled and plopped her spoon into her mouth.

Viper stared in bewilderment. The woman didn't know how to cook; cereal was all she ever ate. He said, "You keep eating like that and it will eventually catch up to you."

"What was that about?" she asked, motioning her head toward the front of the house.

"Don't worry about it."

"It seemed important."

"It's not. Just eat your cereal and we'll talk about it later."

He left the kitchen and went to the back of the house, wondering how much longer he could put up with her. Though he appreciated her naivete and tight skin, a part of him longed for a woman more his age. Someone he could talk to who would understand.

He stepped into the spare bedroom he'd converted into a

home office and sat down at the chair behind the desk where he took a moment to stare out the window and think.

They hadn't discussed more of his girlfriend's proposal. Her desire to want to murder again frankly surprised him. He hadn't expected that would be her reaction, and now Viper didn't know what to do about it. Fear and paranoia were gifts that would keep them from getting caught; being fearless could do just that the opposite—get them caught.

She had been a wild card from the beginning. Though she'd proved useful, now he thought he'd let her get too involved. If he didn't let her get her hands dirty soon, he might as well give himself up now.

Tipping forward, Viper gloved up and opened his desk drawer. He took the contents out and put both weapons on top of his desk. He laced his fingers below his chin and stared at both the box the Walker Colt was housed in, as well as the Karambit—last night's murder weapon—as he planned in his head what needed to be done to ensure he saw this to the finish. When he was sure of his plan, he loaded the items into a small duffel bag, then retrieved a few more guns from the safe. By the time he was finished packing, Viper had a complete arsenal on hand; ready for war.

After a quick shower and change of clothes, he was back in the kitchen, ready for the day.

His girlfriend was now sitting at the counter playing on her phone. She asked, "Did I say something wrong?"

Viper knew she was referring to the conversation they had had in bed this morning. "No. Of course not," he said, kissing her on the cheek.

She fisted his shirt and made him kiss her on the lips. She said, "I guess it's all the guns you've been teaching me to shoot that's gotten into my head."

He kissed her again, this time pressing his mouth harder

against her plump, moist lips that tasted like sugar. Maybe cereal wasn't so bad after all, he thought to himself.

"I have to go out," he said, stepping away.

"I hope not for long."

"Only a few hours."

This time she asked him directly. "Have you thought more about what we discussed earlier?"

He stared into her unwavering gaze. It was those same round eyes that drew him in initially. She was confident beyond her years, and Viper needed to use her God-given talent to his benefit. Hooking her chin with his finger, he said, "I'll have an answer for you by the time I get home."

She slid off the counter, stood, and pressed her hand flat against his chest. Dramatically gasping, she said, "You're making me wait?"

He laughed. "And I'll make you pay to play, too, if you're not careful."

CHAPTER ONE HUNDRED TWO

NINETY MINUTES AFTER MY VISIT TO STEVE'S HOUSE, I HAD him tucked away in the small windowless interview room commonly referred to around the station as The Box. He was impatiently waiting for the paperwork to arrive so he could get on with his day.

When I entered the room, I said, "You're late."

"I had a business call come in at the last minute that couldn't wait." Steve watched me settle into the seat across the table, set a paper bag down to the side, and place an envelope out in front of me. When our eyes met, he asked, "So? Can I see my car? They didn't trash it, did they?"

Steve was impeccably dressed in a gray tailored suit, freshly shaved, and reeked of expensive cologne that suffocated the entire box. He was rambling with nerves, so I got on with it.

"Do you recognize him?" I asked, showing him the picture of Eduardo Rodriguez I had pulled from our files.

Steve slid the picture closer to himself and stared at the bearded man he shared similar features with. He shook his head, no, then said, "Is he the reason you asked about my beard?"

"Are you sure you don't know him?"

His eyes moved back to the picture as if it was some kind of trick question. He said, "No." Then he looked me in the eye and asked, "Is he the one who stole my car?"

I reached for the photograph and put it back inside the folder. "We don't know yet," I said. "That's what we're trying to figure out. Preliminary evidence suggests maybe it was him."

Steve leaned back with a satisfactory look on his face. "I assume you took him into custody?"

"We have him contained."

"Contained? What the hell does that mean?"

"It means we found him murdered last night."

"Oh my God," Steve said, looking around the room, as if suddenly realizing the real reason I had asked him to come to the station.

I could guess what he was thinking; how the door behind me was latched shut and there was no way out. He suddenly gripped the table in a white knuckled squeeze and I watched his elbows lock.

"You can't possibly think I did it," he said.

"Tell me about your night."

"What? Last night?"

"Where you were, who you were with. Those types of things."

"Oh Jesus." He dropped his gaze to the table and whispered to himself. I watched him blink twice before telling me all about his very uneventful night. "My girlfriend can vouch for everything. She was with me the entire night. You saw her this morning. She was still wearing her gown."

"She was with you all night?"

"That's right."

"Who got up first?"

"She did."

I stared. He held my eyes and gave me his full attention.

"Before I can release certain contents found in your car, can you tell me what those might be?"

Steve listed off a few nonessentials and said, "Other than that, I can't recall leaving anything important inside."

"What about guns? Knives? You leave anything like that inside?"

Steve shook his head. "I own a couple handguns, but they rarely leave the house."

"Extra gasoline?"

He thought it was a joke and barked out a laugh. "I'm sorry," he said. "I don't even have extra gasoline at the house."

Then I showed him the sheriff's cap to little fanfare. "We found it inside your car."

His face told me everything. He knew what the TV news was suggesting about who killed Vincent Cruz. I asked him to tell me again about his history with Frank. "Start from the beginning and don't paraphrase," I said.

"I'm not getting my car back, am I?"

"Not until we clear this case."

"Okay," he said, "Just like I told you before..."

Over the next half-hour, Steve told me everything about his relationship with Raymond Frank. I looked for holes in his story, knowing that Steve was better off without Frank in the picture. By the time he was finished talking, my conclusion about him hadn't changed. Steve might have hated Frank as much, if not maybe more, than I did and wanted him gone just as much, but I didn't think he was guilty of last night's murder. I had no choice but to let him go.

CHAPTER ONE HUNDRED THREE

THERE WAS A MESSAGE WAITING FOR ME AT MY DESK. AFTER I listened to the voicemail, I responded to it by calling the crime lab.

"Detective Payne. I assume you got my message?"

I asked, "Were you able to pull any prints?"

"Clean as a whistle."

I leaned back in my chair and turned my head to stare at Moreno's empty desk chair across the way. I wasn't surprised the royal sapphire rose had been wiped clean, but it was worth a shot.

"Okay. Thanks," I said.

"Want me to enter it into evidence while I still have it?"

"No, that's all right," I said, saying I would stop by to pick it up later.

"Suit yourself."

I placed the phone back on its receiver, feeling completely defeated. Every time it felt like I was making a little headway, something else came up to knock me back one step. If it was Moreno who had left it for me to find, he was too clever to make a grave mistake such as leaving his prints behind. But why was he there that night? And why stalk me?

I spun around in my chair and glanced toward the lieutenant's office. I still hadn't heard a word on whether IA was planning to investigate Frank's complaint against me or not. Honestly, I didn't care. I pushed the thought to the side and began pouring over the facts inside my head.

I thought about how Moreno was on suspension the night of the house fire, and how Whitney claimed he was parked outside my house the night Selina's birthstone was found. Then, this morning he had asked me about owning a knife he suspected was used to murder Eduardo, without evidence to prove that was the actual murder weapon we didn't have. But he also alluded to knowing about me owning a Walker Colt. Again, I couldn't deny he wasn't up to something. The evidence was overwhelming and Tex might actually be right. I had a bad feeling that gun was going to come back to haunt me—and soon.

I worked the phone for the next hour, making several calls to gun dealers and pawn shops across the entire Austin area code. No one had an original Walker Colt, but all of them wanted one. Then, when I was finished, I went to work on my computer searching online auctions and several marketplaces on the web, when Sanchez snuck up behind me. "You're looking better."

"Cold showers will do that to a man."

"How did the interview go with Steve?"

"Fine."

Sanchez expected me to say more, but I had nothing else I wanted to share. She said, "I'm on my way to speak with Eduardo's sister. I'd like it if you came with me."

I closed up shop and said, "Anything to get out of here."

CHAPTER ONE HUNDRED FOUR

I WAS STARING OUT THE WINDOW, TAKING ADVANTAGE OF the silence and watching the world go by, when Sanchez turned to me and said, "Jackson, I can feel you closing up, but I need you to know that you can still trust me."

Wishing for a cigarette, I knew I'd recently asked a lot of her. Not once had Sanchez let me down. "I know that," I said. "There's just a lot on my mind."

When I felt her eyes move to me, I turned to look. She had both hands on the wheel as if it helped her to see over the dash. I could see there was more she wanted to say but didn't know how best to proceed.

"Something else on your mind?" I asked.

She firmed up her grip, but I watched the tension in her shoulders release. Sanchez asked me, "Why did Moreno ask if you knew Eduardo?"

"Because Eduardo is either our arsonist, or someone wants me to think he is."

"No," she said. "That wasn't it. There was another reason he was asking."

I kept my eyes on hers for a long beat before saying, "It's because I was looking for him."

She tossed me a surprised look, then I told her everything.

"It's why I was looking for the Rover. Eduardo came to the park the day I had met with Cruz—"

"To do what?"

"Not sure. But I'm certain someone told Eduardo where to find us, and to monitor either me or Cruz, perhaps both of us. We never could find out for sure, but we both thought maybe he was connected to Frank. Then Cruz gets whacked, and now Eduardo, too, and suddenly I'm the last man standing and the only one who looks remotely responsible for all four murders."

Sanchez took in a deep breath of air and had nothing else to add.

I asked, "Did the medical examiner make any predictions about what type of weapon was used to kill Eduardo?"

"Not that I heard, why?"

I told her what Moreno shared with me.

"I hope you're wrong," she said.

"Me too. But the fact I'm still standing must be driving whoever wants to frame me for these murders, insane."

"Let's assume Eduardo drove the Range Rover to the club. Why drive around with the evidence in the back of his car? It's been what, five days since the fire?"

"Makes little sense," I said. "None of it does. No one is smart enough to not get caught, but stupid enough to leave evidence of them committing the murders in their car. This was planted, and if Frank killed him, why do it where everyone knew he was?"

Sanchez had her own doubts, too.

I said, "I didn't tell Moreno where I was last night because I was passed out drunk in the back of the Cruiser."

She shot me another look. I wasn't sure if it was sympathy or disgust, maybe a bit of both, but she got the point. She said, "Which means you don't have an alibi."

I thought of the two teenagers who tried to rob me, when I said, "I wouldn't have had one if I was home." Then I asked her if she happened to see Moreno the night I told her to leave my apartment.

"No. Why do you ask?"

"Whitney Voak claims he was there."

"Why would Moreno be there?" Sanchez asked before remembering how I had found the birthstone. "But if Moreno left it there, how did he get it?"

"The night of the fire," I said, mentioning how I had sent it to the lab to be tested.

"Why wasn't I aware of this?"

"I had it done in a dummy case file. I got the results back today." She turned her head and looked me in the eye. I shook my head, no, and said, "Nothing."

"And what if it came back as Moreno's?"

"Then I would have known without a doubt, he killed my family."

CHAPTER ONE HUNDRED FIVE

EDUARDO'S SISTER WAS MARY RODRIGUEZ. MARY WAS A short, plump woman who lived in a single story, thousand square foot house with her mother and twin toddlers, whose father was no longer in the picture. Sanchez had filled me in on the details before we arrived and, as we stepped through the chain linked fence gate encasing the property, I made a note of the mostly dirt yard.

Mary answered the door quickly and Sanchez identified us as deputies with the Travis County Sheriff's Office. Mary knew immediately our visit was about her brother.

"He's not here," she said, sounding annoyed.

I assumed she was annoyed with him and not us, as I peeked over her shoulder and into the house.

Toys covered the floor and an animated children's film was playing on the television. One kid was on the floor, another on the couch snuggling a child's blanket, as if it was a lifeline into a safer world. Adjacent to him was an elderly woman, I assumed was Mary's mother. She rocked in her chair with a distant gaze in her eyes.

Mary asked, "What's this about, anyway?"

Sanchez said, "We found your brother murdered early this morning."

A hand flew over Mary's mouth, and she quickly glanced over her shoulder at her mother. Then she exited the house and shut the door behind her. "How was he killed?"

Sanchez shared enough detail to get the idea, and she told Mary where it happened. If it surprised her to hear her brother was at a strip club, she didn't show it.

"Eduardo had this house listed at his primary residence," I said.

"It's our mother's place, but Eddie hasn't lived here for several years now."

We asked about friends, who Eduardo hung out with, and who might have wanted him dead. The questions were too much for Mary and she started to cry. We gave her a chance to catch her breath. After a minute, she cleared her throat and said, "Eddie was a nice guy. Everyone but the cops loved him."

Then Sanchez asked what Eduardo had done for a living.

"Eddie made one mistake a long time ago, and it followed him everywhere he went."

"Grand theft auto."

Mary nodded.

"He couldn't get a job?"

Mary shook her head. "He was a felon. Few would hire him, and those that did never let him stick around for long."

Sanchez asked, "Was your brother still jacking cars?"

"I don't know. Eddie was good at telling me what he thought I wanted to hear."

"When was the last time you saw him?"

"Recently. Maybe a week ago. He looked good, said he had found a girl he liked. He seemed happy, and I was happy for him."

We asked what Eduardo's girlfriend's name was, but Mary didn't know.

My cellphone buzzed in my pocket and, after seeing who was calling, I excused myself to take it. "What can I do for you, Sergeant?"

"Frank is here at the office with his lawyer."

My ears perked up.

"He says he's ready to answer your questions."

I motioned to Sanchez and told her we needed to go. "Good," I said. "Don't let him out of your sight. I'll be there in fifteen."

CHAPTER ONE HUNDRED SIX

WITH A TOWEL AROUND HIS NECK, AND A WATER BOTTLE IN his hand, Viper circled the gym track for the ninth time in order to keep his attention focused on the slender woman who had just arrived and was now fiercely working the elliptical into a frenzy.

It didn't take her long to work up a sweat. She showed her intensity in the way her blonde hair swished across the back of her shoulders like a horse's tail. Her body was tightly wrapped in an aqua colored spandex suit that revealed a flattened midriff. It was an outfit designed to highlight the attributes few women actually had worth showing off, and Viper wasn't the only male who noticed her. She was easy on the eyes; the type to know it, too.

Finally, when the time was right, Viper stepped off the track and caught sight of himself in the big mirror. He hardly recognized himself. He'd grown a goatee and had changed the color of his eyes with colored contact lenses. He adjusted his cap and glanced to the diamond earring in his left ear, thinking the look suited him. When he turned around, the blonde was pushing herself even harder than before.

He could tell she was working off some steam. Without making it too obvious he was coming for her, he climbed aboard the empty machine next to her, dialed in his preferred settings, and went at it himself.

Music assaulted his ears and he found his groove. Nearly an hour passed before he stopped, turned to her, and said, "I don't know about you, but I hate this shit."

She laughed. "Couldn't tell, you look wonderful."

He made sure to smile when he said, "Only because I'm standing next to you."

"That doesn't actually work, does it?"

"What?" He arched an eyebrow.

"Is that how you pick up women? By giving them cliché one-liners you think are clever enough to get them to sleep with you?"

"Sleep with me?" Viper guffawed. "Who said anything about sleeping with me?"

She rolled her eyes but the smile remained.

He wiped the sweat off his brow with his towel and said, "Besides, you hit on me first."

Her eyes popped open. "Is that what we're doing?"

"Isn't it?"

She laughed and Viper introduced himself, giving her a bogus name she'd remember.

"Candy Scott," she said, extending her hand.

Viper took her hand and said, "Candy. How sweet."

She rolled her eyes again. Then she asked him, "So, if you hate working out so much, why do it? To blow off steam?"

"Oh, no," he said. "There are far better ways to blow off steam."

She gave him a sideways glance and said, "Now you're flirting."

He smiled. "And you like it."

Candy ducked away and said, "I have a boyfriend."

"I'm not talking about sex," Viper said. Candy's bright and curious eyes found their way back to him. "It's something far greater than sex."

"Then you're not having great sex," she said.

"Now you're the one teasing me," he said. "What do you say we hit the showers and meet in the parking lot in twenty? I'll show you what I'm talking about."

"You're not a stalker, are you?"

"Do I look like I'm a stalker?"

"I don't know. I guess not."

"What do you have to lose?"

Candy stared as if debating whether to trust him. Then she said, "Okay, you have a deal. But, just so you know, it takes a lot to impress a girl like me."

CHAPTER ONE HUNDRED SEVEN

WE PASSED FRANK'S ROYCE ON OUR WAY INTO THE station, and I asked Sanchez to slow down so I could get a look inside. Sitting in the front seats were Big and Smalls.

Big saw me first and flipped me the bird.

When I grinned, Sanchez asked, "What's that about?"

"Nothing," I said.

I couldn't believe Frank was here. I assumed he had heard what happened at the club and knew we'd want to ask him what he knew. This was a good thing. I just hoped I was right about him having nothing to do with Eduardo's murder.

When Sanchez parked, she asked, "What's your game plan."

"I need to do this alone."

"I understand."

"If I can clear Frank, then I can move on to Moreno."

"Tread lightly, Jackson," Sanchez warned. "You can't get this wrong."

We entered the building through the back door and worked our way toward the interview room, keeping an eye out for Moreno. Accusing him of murder was a heavy allegation to make, but I needed to follow my instinct on this one.

"Jackson," Sergeant Hart called as soon as he saw me. "What the hell is Frank doing here? I was told you called him in."

"I did," I said, asking for Moreno's location.

"What does that have to do with anything?" Hart asked.

"Is he here or not?"

"Not." Hart planted his hand on his hip and stared. "Now, about Frank, the district attorney's office isn't interested in having you orchestrate some sort of gimmick, and that's not something I'll sign off on, either."

I knew I was walking on thin ice with Frank. No one knew it better than me, but I needed to get them to see what I saw. I said, "You think it's coincidence Frank was at the same place as last night's murder? I don't. Of course, if you would rather I just assume he knows nothing and let him go—"

"Careful on this one." Sergeant Hart lifted a hand. "That's all I'm saying. Your career is already under the microscope."

"Quit worrying. I've got this," I said, slapping his shoulder.

I stepped into the box and felt the tension inside the room immediately. Frank sat to the right of his lawyer—the same man who came to represent Candy's quest for immunity. I let my gaze fall to the coffee tumbler and set of car keys on the table. Though both men were impeccably dressed in the same loud and arrogant kind of way, there were no disguises today.

"Good to see you got my message," I said after sitting down.

"Mr. Frank came here to cooperate because he's innocent of whatever bullshit you're making us step through today," his lawyer said, quickly establishing today's ground rules. "He doesn't have to be here and we can leave at any time."

"If that's true, this should be simple," I said, opening the file I had brought with me.

But Frank's lawyer stopped me when he said, "Ms. Scott failed to mention how she came to possess the document she presented to you yesterday."

"No. I don't think she did," I said, confused why we were speaking about her instead of Frank.

"My client would like to make it clear he received the papers in the mail from an unknown sender." Frank's lawyer produced an empty manila envelope with a stamp in the corner. There was no return address.

"Why would someone send you private information about me?" I asked Frank directly.

Frank looked at me with heavy eyelids and said, "If my wife was planning to take everything in the divorce, I'd have done what you did, too."

They were trying to turn the tables on me, but I wouldn't let them. As I inspected the envelope for clues, I thought about the USPS uniform we found with Eduardo and if there was a link between the two. Had Eduardo somehow got hold of my divorce papers and sent them to Frank? I wasn't sure, but Eduardo seemed to have been the middleman between me and the killer.

"Can I keep this?" I asked.

Frank said, "Sure. Why not? You kept what came inside it, didn't you?"

I set the envelope off to the side, pointed to his tumbler, and asked, "You like guns, Frank?"

Frank looked at his lawyer and his lawyer asked, "What's this have to do with anything?"

"Simple question." I continued to look Frank in the eye. "What guns do you own? Any old classics?"

Hot Shot Lawyer motioned for Frank not to answer.

Frank could afford to own a Walker Colt, but would he steal it to frame me? The look in his eye told me he didn't know what I was referring to. I pushed him some more, just to be sure.

"You know him?" I asked, sliding a picture of Eduardo across the table.

His lawyer nodded, and Frank answered, "No. Who is he?"

"The person murdered last night at a gentlemen's club." I told him the name of the club, and asked, "Isn't this why you're here? To clear your name?"

The lawyer held up his hand and spoke for Frank. "My client had nothing to do with this murder, or any others."

Frank said, "Just let it go, Jackson. You lost."

I mentioned the name of the establishment again, and Frank leaned back and stared.

"We know you were there. You were caught on security cameras. Did you see him or not?" I pushed the picture closer.

Frank didn't look at the picture again, but I was sure I saw a glimmer of recognition flash in his eyes. His lawyer leaned over and they discussed something in private. Then Frank shook his head, no.

"We also found Steve Eli's stolen vehicle at the same club. It was stolen a week ago, and we found some very interesting items inside it. Know anything about that?"

"My client knows nothing about the murder or stolen vehicle. Unless you are going to charge him with a crime, we're done here."

We all stood. Before I allowed either of them to go, I said to Frank, "You might not have done this one, but you may know who did."

CHAPTER ONE HUNDRED EIGHT

I WATCHED FRANK LEAVE THE BUILDING, CONVINCED I HAD given him plenty to think over, but it worried me that he'd figured out what Candy had done. I still didn't know what happened to her last night and wondered if I ever would.

Hart came up behind me and said, "You might be onto something."

He was referring to the link between Steve Eli's stolen vehicle and Frank. I said, "Frank didn't kill Eduardo, but someone wants us to think he did." Hart gave me a funny look, and I continued, "Frank might even like me if I can pull this off."

"Do I want to know what you're planning?"

"I don't know, do you?"

I circled back to my desk with my thoughts bouncing around my head. I didn't expect Frank to rat out who he thought murdered Eduardo, but maybe he would. Though both Whitney and Steve benefited from Frank's absence, it seemed like Moreno was most likely to do it. I just didn't know if he'd actually go through with something like murder, or how I could prove that was what was even happening. However, whoever had wanted to set me up for murder was now trying to do the same to Frank.

As soon as I sat down, I picked up the phone and tried calling Candy again. When she didn't answer, I left her a message asking her to just let me know she was okay. Then I hung up and reviewed the strip club security tape hoping to see something we had missed before.

I spent the next ninety minutes playing the video tape back, occasionally stopping to jot down something I deemed important. I found nothing new. Eduardo was there, but never with Frank. It was like they didn't know how closely their paths crossed. They both divided their attention between their phones and the dancers, paying little attention to other men in the club. People came, then went. Then I noticed a pattern.

There was a single woman opposite Eduardo, sitting alone with her back up against the far wall. The lights obscured her face, but her hands and phone were clear enough for me to see her thumbs busily work the screen. She'd send a text message, then Eduardo would receive one. Back and forth it went for about ten minutes; then I watched them both leave the club, one at a time. Neither Frank nor Candy realized Eduardo was gone.

I paused the tape and stared at my computer screen. My heart beat faster. I was certain this woman knew what had happened to Eduardo, perhaps killed him herself. But who was she? And how could I figure that out without having a clear picture of her face?

I picked up the envelope from Frank and leaned back in my chair. Then I flipped it around, asking myself if someone had sent it to Frank or if he had sent it to himself.

Frank didn't seem concerned about the implications of having it; in fact he seemed happy to get it off his mind. But there was something here only known to a select few. It wasn't a mistake we found Eduardo with a bag full of mail carrier clothes, but figuring out where the envelope had been sent from would be nearly impossible. There were twenty-one different post offices in Austin alone. But why send my divorce papers to Frank in the first place? Someone knew about my beef with Frank and wanted to get him involved.

"What's that?" Sanchez asked over my shoulder. I caught her up to speed. Then she said, "Hart is concerned about what you're up to."

"He shouldn't be."

"That's what I told him," she said. "I did some digging of my own. Look at this." She handed me a file, and I opened it to scan the reports inside. "Seems our victim had a history with deputy Moreno."

I lifted my head and locked eyes with Sanchez. "News to me."

"News to me, too."

I continued to leaf through the papers and couldn't believe what I was reading. Three years ago, Moreno and Bolin arrested Eduardo for his alleged connection to the murder of a nineteen-year-old Latina woman. Moreno put the pressure on Eduardo hard, but he couldn't break him. Eduardo maintained his innocence throughout it all, and Moreno had no choice but to eventually let him free. Then the case went cold.

When I set the papers down on my desk, Sanchez said, "There wasn't ever any evidence Eduardo was anywhere near where the murder took place."

"And now we know why his sister said he hated cops."

But was this the reason Eduardo was killed? Maybe. Either way, I knew Moreno was hiding something. Could this have been it?

"Perhaps I should have been the one to ask him if he

knew who Eduardo was," I said, tugging on my collar, thinking about how Bolin broke up the fight outside Red River nightclub. Moreno would never answer to his history with Eduardo, but Bolin would. I just hoped I could find him in time.

CHAPTER ONE HUNDRED NINE

VIPER LEFT THE SHOWERS FIRST AND WAITED JUST OUTSIDE the front door to the gym. He sat on the concrete planters, but his knee wouldn't stop bouncing. Candy pretended to play hardball, but beneath the façade, she was an easy egg to crack. Though he had promised himself to not let it get personal, she was easy to like and that had him feeling nervous.

He kept looking for her through the glass, wondering if she'd come. He doubted himself. A minute passed. Then another. Finally, he saw her coming.

Viper's knee stopped bouncing and he stared through the glass to marvel at her stride. She was a total bombshell walking on two legs. Everything about her was perfect—from her heeled boots to the way she held her head up high—he couldn't believe what money could buy. Flawless teeth and physical features that highlighted every aspect of her femininity, were just a few of her attributes that were making him crazy. She even had the confidence to back it up.

Candy saw him and smiled. Viper smiled back, stood, and

opened the door for her. She touched his arm and said, "Thank you. You're such a doll."

"And I was about to leave."

"You wouldn't."

"I would."

They sang their call and response, picking up where they had left off before. Candy reached over and touched his arm again. They both stopped and Viper tried to play it cool, like he hadn't noticed her touches increasing. Then she asked, "Will what I'm wearing work for you?"

Viper took a step back, stroked his chin, as he raked over her body with his eyes, and took advantage of the question. She was wearing skin-tight jeans with holes in the thighs, knee high leather boots, and an angel white V-neck t-shirt beneath a zipped up leather jacket. He felt the heat inside him spread. "It's perfect," he said.

"Excellent." She flipped her hair and started walking. "I'm excited to see what could be greater than sex. Perhaps we'll have to compare the two, just to be sure?"

When she turned around and winked, with her blonde hair blowing in her face, Viper knew he was in love. Where did this woman come from and how had he not met her before?

He walked her to his rental, talking and laughing the entire way. Once they were close, he popped the trunk with the push of a button. He said to her, "Go ahead. Peek inside."

Candy gave him a look and he nudged her closer. She cautiously stepped forward, giggling with excitement, as she peeked over the ledge, looking into the deep, cavernous trunk.

Viper studied her reaction as she stared at his trunk full of guns. First, Candy seemed hesitant, and he was afraid he had completely misread the situation. Then he saw a sparkle of curiosity catch her eye, chased by a thick shot of adrenaline.

"Blow off steam. Of course," she said.

"Want to hold one?"

"I've shot a gun before."

"Not my guns."

"How are yours any different?"

Viper stepped forward, bent at the waist, and flipped back the blanket that covered his mini arsenal. Then he opened the lid on the revolver case and stepped back.

Candy quirked an eyebrow and crossed her arms. She wasn't impressed.

"I like assault rifles, machine guns. Those are the guns that get a girl wet."

"Go ahead. Pick it up."

She eyed him first, then she reached into the box and wrapped her slender fingers around the pistol handle.

"With a fifteen pound trigger, there's no need for a safety," Viper said. "You shoot that, and its kick will make you feel on top of the world."

"What if I already feel like I'm at the top?"

"You are hard to impress."

She smiled and lifted the pistol higher in the air.

"Whoa, there. Keep it down. We're not at the range yet."

"But I want to shoot it. See if what you say is true."

"It's true, honey."

With a sparkle in her eye, she lowered the pistol. "Then prove it to me."

CHAPTER ONE HUNDRED TEN

I LEFT SANCHEZ AT HER DESK TO TRACK DOWN MORENO and climbed into my Cruiser intending to find Bolin as quickly as possible. The problem was, his records weren't up to date and I didn't know where he lived. His shift at Creek House wouldn't begin until at least four or five at the earliest. That gave me at least an hour to kill between now and then. Luckily, I had something else that needed to get taken care of before then.

The logo to a gun range on Frank's coffee tumbler gave me a clue to what he might have been up to recently, and just the sight of it had me thinking about my Walker Colt. Not that I was changing my mind about him, but I needed to be absolutely sure he was as innocent as I thought.

It was a fifty-two-thousand square foot facility south of the city, just off the highway. I was aware of the range, had driven past it thousands of times before, but I hadn't been there myself.

I parked near the entrance and entered through the double-glass doors. A middle-aged woman with braids worked the front desk and greeted me with a smile.

"Welcome to the range," she said.

I nodded, smiled, and looked around the room. There was a wall of windows behind her, and through them I counted at least a dozen shooting bays for both pistols and rifles. There was a room to my left with display cases full of a variety of different styles of guns, including full-autos, that could be rented for in-house use. They had something for everyone, but I doubted they had what I came here to find.

I introduced myself, flashed her my badge, and showed her a picture of Raymond Frank. "Have you seen this man here recently?"

"Mr. Frank. You bet I have. Mostly he comes alone and shoots for an hour or two." She lifted her eyes and asked, "He's not in trouble again, is he?"

"When's the last time he was here?"

"Two days ago."

"Alone?"

"He was with a friend that day. The friend was only interested in watching Frank shoot."

"What did his friend look like?"

She gave a quick description of Smalls, and said, "He came after Frank and handed him some kind of yellow envelope. I don't know what was inside but, after that, Frank let his AR-15 rip, if you know what I mean?"

"How so?"

"Let's just say I wouldn't have wanted to get in his field of fire that day." She chuckled.

Frank's story was checking out, just as I hoped it would. But there was one more question I needed to ask before leaving. "What was he shooting?"

"Shot off hundreds of rounds, all guns he had brought with him." She rattled off a few different makes and models.

"Any of them a Walker Colt?"

"Like the 1847 Colt?"

"Exactly like the 1847."

"No. But if he had, I'd have asked to shoot it myself."

CHAPTER ONE HUNDRED ELEVEN

VIPER SAID, "GUNS ARE A RELIGION IN AMERICA."

Candy rolled up her sleeves and said, "The right to bear arms." They both laughed. Then she asked, "What was your first time like?"

"Quick." He gave her a sly grin that had her slapping his right thigh. "Oh, you mean my first time shooting guns?"

"Yeah," she laughed, "tell me about it."

Viper was having a great time. Pop music blasted through the speakers and Candy hung on his words, like she did his arm. They were an instant couple, a real Bonnie and Clyde.

Viper said, "It wasn't my first time shooting, but certainly one of my first memorable experiences with a gun—"

He glanced in her direction. Candy leaned back with her knee to her chest, looking sexy and relaxed. He'd promised to take her shooting but what he really wanted was to book a room, get her clothes off, and shoot her between the legs; see if she was as good as she claimed to be in the sack. He almost did it, too, but he was on a more fulfilling mission. He couldn't allow a simple willingness to spread her legs distract him from his end goal.

"—I was visiting my Mom's uncle on his ranch—West Texas. I must have been twelve or thirteen at the time, when Uncle Joe handed me his twenty-two rifle and told me to *shoot at anything that moves.*"

Candy turned her head, put her other boot on the floor, and angled her body to face him. Looking him directly in the eye, she waited with bated breath.

"I shot at a turtle," he said.

Candy gasped. "Did you hit it?"

"You kidding?" He laughed. "Too far to the left. The moment the bullet hit the water, the turtle went under and swam to safety."

Candy burst out laughing. She thought it was the funniest thing in the world. Viper asked, "What about you?"

"My story isn't as exciting as yours."

"Try me," he said.

"Well, my boyfriend, he's the one that got me shooting lots of guns..."

Her words trailed off and Candy started fidgeting with her fingers. It was their first awkward pause and Candy recognized it, too.

"I'm sorry," she said. "My boyfriend can be such a jerk sometimes."

"Is that why you ran off with me today?"

"Maybe," she admitted. "But I did something I shouldn't have."

"Want to talk about it?"

"It's complicated."

"Nothing comes easy."

"I had no choice. I just wish he would listen to me. I have ideas. Good ones."

He reached for her hand. "No doubt you do, sweetheart."

When their eyes locked, Candy pulled her hand away and suddenly got excited. "This is going to be a smashing hit for me. Is that where we're going?" she asked, pointing her finger toward the gun range.

Viper furrowed his brow and turned into the gun range's parking lot. He saw Candy had pulled her phone from her purse. He realized what was happening and quickly put it to a stop. He said, "Let's stay focused on hitting our marks before putting it on film."

Candy agreed. Then Viper lifted his gaze and slammed on the brakes. Candy's head flung forward. "What the hell?"

"Was that my phone I heard?" Viper said, pointing at the glove-box while trying to keep what he'd just seen, discreet.

His heart beat as fast as a rabbit's. The collision between worlds was sudden. First, Candy was familiar with the gun range, probably knew the people who worked there, too; now Viper saw Jackson Payne exit the shop.

Candy rubbed the back of her neck and winced. "What?"

"In the glove box. I heard my phone." Viper snapped his fingers impatiently. "Will you get it for me?"

Candy leaned forward and dug for his cellphone. While he had her occupied, he jerked the wheel hard to the left and kept Jackson Payne in his rearview mirror, hoping Jackson hadn't seen him, too.

Viper watched carefully as Jackson stared out over the sea of cars. He instinctively reached for his pistol. His hand was sweaty on the handle. What was Jackson doing here? Waiting for him to arrive? He could only assume so.

Candy popped her head up and said, "Your phone, your royal highness."

Viper took his phone without a hint of amusement on his face and kept driving. With Jackson Payne on his trail, he knew the party was over.

CHAPTER ONE HUNDRED TWELVE

EMILY SANCHEZ KNEW SHE WAS ONTO SOMETHING, BUT SHE was also nervous to speak to Moreno alone. She'd never trusted the guy. Didn't like him, either. But she couldn't have Jackson approach him. It was up to her to follow through on proving Jackson was right about Moreno all along.

"This is so messed up," she muttered to herself.

Jackson had suspected Moreno from the get-go, and now Moreno was out for some kind of revenge. Blaming Jackson for Eduardo's murder couldn't be a coincidence. Those were fighting words, and the records she discovered today proved Moreno had had it out to make Eduardo's life miserable. But who else's? Jackson's? Hers, too, if he discovered her suspicion? The possibilities seemed infinite.

After several reluctant minutes, she picked up the phone's receiver and dialed Moreno's cellphone. The line rang several times before clicking over to voicemail. She cleared her throat and left a brief message asking him to call her back. Then she added an incentive. "We might have caught a break," she said.

Since coming back from his suspension, Moreno hadn't

been the same. He'd put up walls and had a vendetta against Jackson that anyone with two eyes could see. Though most in the office ignored it, Sanchez couldn't entirely blame Moreno for his actions—she'd have done the same—but things were getting past the point of repair and she was afraid of what might happen next, if not stopped now.

Bringing her elbows to her desk, she picked up the report on Moreno's interview with Eduardo, and shook her head as she read it again. Maybe Jackson was right when suspecting Moreno was hiding something. But was this it?

She closed the file and picked up the phone again, this time calling Eduardo's sister, Mary. After a quick update into her brother's murder, Sanchez asked, "Did you know your brother was questioned for murder three years ago?"

"He didn't do it. There was a deputy hellbent on making Eddie's life miserable."

"Do you remember that deputy's name?"

"Tom Moreno," Mary said as if she'd never forget. "Asshole terrorized my brother endlessly."

"There was more than one time?"

"It got so bad, Eddie couldn't go anywhere without having to look over his shoulder."

Sanchez heard a couple suits approaching and, when she lifted her gaze, she saw the deputy chief walking with the two IA investigators assigned to look into Frank's complaint against Jackson.

Mary shared more stories from Eddie's life and, when she was finished, Mary asked, "Did a cop kill my brother?"

Sanchez's heart leaped into her throat. She wasn't sure she knew. Then she caught Sergeant Hart heading straight for her. "Thanks for your time," she said, hanging up. Turning to Hart, she said, "These cases are getting more bizarre by the day."

Hart asked, "Do you trust Jackson?"

"What kind of question is that?"

Hart frowned and stuffed his hands deeper into his pants pockets. There seemed to be something on his mind but, whatever it was, Sanchez couldn't read it.

"He'll be back to his usual self after we solve his family's murder," she said.

Hart nodded as if he agreed. Then he said, "Let me know if Jackson does anything strange."

Sanchez squinted her eyes a fraction and wondered what his definition of strange was. She said, "You know I will."

Hart nodded and left. As soon as he did, Sanchez's desk phone rang. Thinking it might be Moreno, she answered quickly. "Deputy Sanchez."

The line was open but quiet.

"Hello?"

A heavy whispered voice said, "I know who killed Eduardo Rodriguez."

Sanchez perked up and reached for a pen. "Can I get that name again?"

"You know who he is."

"And how do you know this?"

"Because I saw one of your deputies chasing him."

"Do you know the name of the deputy you think did this?"

"Jackson Payne. And I don't think. I know. It happened right after I saw him talking to that reporter who was also killed."

Sanchez asked for more details and jotted down the information as it came in. Then she asked for the caller's name. "And your name is?"

The line clicked, and the caller was gone.

"Shit." Sanchez tossed her pen onto the desk. Just when things couldn't get worse, Jackson had another connection to the most recent murder.

CHAPTER ONE HUNDRED THIRTEEN

MORENO KILLED THE CALL, LOCKED HIS PHONE'S SCREEN, and dropped the cellphone into his back pocket. A lot was on his mind as he stared through the wall of windows toward where his truck was parked out front. He took a moment to process all that he had just seen. It was all starting to click, and he was feeling like he was getting a clear picture of what was happening. With a clear head, he turned back to the clerk and said, "Sorry about that."

The woman with braids behind the counter, smiled. "Not a problem. You were asking?"

"Fees."

"Ah yes. Inquiring about classes."

She handed him some brochures and started explaining the price structure and different types of classes the gun range had on offer. That was when Moreno noticed Jackson's business card next to the register. Pointing to it, he said, "The cops just can't leave Raymond Frank alone."

The woman lifted her eyes and looked puzzled. She struggled to keep eye contact and kept shifting her weight to her opposite leg. "Are you interested in shooting today?" She tried to change the subject.

"I know he shoots here."

The woman cast her gaze down to the counter.

"Hell, I see what's being said on the news. That's why the sheriff was just here, isn't it?" Moreno kept up the pressure.

"I really shouldn't say," the woman said.

"I'm a friend of Mr. Frank." He smiled. "It's who referred me to the range."

That got her attention. Her eyes were back on his, only this time they were softer than before. She leaned forward, with a glint in her eye. Then she asked, "Did he do it? You know—"

Moreno leaned closer and dropped his voice down to a whisper. "What do you think?"

Her eyes rounded and he was certain she was holding her breath.

"Don't worry. I won't tell him." He winked.

She swallowed. "Between you and me, I think he killed his wife."

Moreno pulled back and said, "We might never know."

"That's not all the deputy was inquiring about, you know."

"No?"

She shook her head. "Wanted to know if Mr. Frank owned a Walker Colt."

"A Walker Colt?"

"And not just a replica, either. But a real one. Can you imagine? I've had my privileges over the years, but it's been a while." She smiled. "It's not a pistol you own, is it?"

"Unfortunately not." Moreno frowned. *But I know someone who does.*

CHAPTER ONE HUNDRED FOURTEEN

AFTER VIPER DROPPED CANDY OFF AT HER CAR, HE SPED away, realizing just how close he had been to getting caught. The difference of a few seconds and he might not be going home tonight. The thought was sobering—if not also unsettling.

A minute earlier and Jackson would have seen him with Candy. He'd have put it together. Had the final evidence he needed to make his case. Viper had gotten lucky, but now he was wondering if he'd have to make sure Candy wouldn't talk.

As his speedometer increased with his speed, he angled the rearview mirror on his face and stared into his disguise. He always enjoyed having blue eyes. The color fit him, and soon he was convinced that today hadn't been a complete bust.

Candy had revealed enough about Raymond Frank to buy him some time. But Viper would need to act quickly. The pieces on the chessboard were falling; soon it would be checkmate.

With one hand on the steering wheel and the other

holding his cellphone, he called his girlfriend to check in. "Hey babe. What're you up to?"

"Watching a movie," she mumbled. "I'm bored. When you coming home?"

"I don't know. It depends."

"Depends on what?"

"What you're wearing." He smiled.

"If you get home soon, I won't be wearing anything."

"Tempting," Viper growled and adjusted his crotch.

Candy had left him feeling more than hot and bothered. He couldn't get her out of his head and needed to work it out of his system, before it clouded his judgement. Perhaps his girlfriend would have to cure that ache; at least for the time being.

A few minutes later, he turned into an apartment complex in North Austin and circled the building before parking near the unit number he was after. Acutely aware Jackson might come here next, he put on his cap and quickly got to work.

Viper rummaged around in his trunk and loaded up everything he needed before entering the building and taking the elevator up to the third floor. The hall was empty when he exited the car. As he walked down the hallway, he gloved up and took out the key at the door. It slid into the lock and the door opened easily.

Viper was in and out in less than ten minutes, only carrying what he didn't purposely leave behind. Then as he drove away, he began peeling away his disguise, one layer at a time, until he was back to his normal appearance. By the time his contacts were tossed out the window, Viper had convinced himself that his plan would work.

Thirty minutes later, he was home and sitting down on the couch with his fully clothed girlfriend. She leaned into him and he asked, "What happened to being naked?"

She tipped her chin back and looked him in the eye. "You were late."

He wiggled himself free, stood, and walked away. Sensing something was wrong, she followed him to the bedroom. "You're mad at me," she said.

"No. I'm not mad."

"Then what is it? Did something happen?"

"I just have a lot on my mind."

"If it's something I said—"

He turned his head and they locked eyes. "No. Of course not. I told you I would have an answer for you when I returned."

"If you think I'm not ready..."

He walked over to her and put his hands on her shoulders. "You like cops?" he asked.

"Hate 'em."

He laughed. "Well, I need you to pretend to like them."

"Them? I have to like all of them?"

"Just one cop in particular."

Her eyes lit up. "We're going to kill a cop?"

"Shhh..." He pressed his finger to her lips and asked, "Does that excite you?"

"Are you kidding? Of course it excites me."

Then he told her his plan. "You think you can do that?"

"I'm good at making men fall in love with me."

He hooked her chin with his finger, bent down, and kissed her hard, murmuring against her lips, "Yes you are."

CHAPTER ONE HUNDRED FIFTEEN

NINETY MINUTES AFTER MY STOP AT THE GUN RANGE, I received a call from Sanchez.

"Did you find him?" I asked.

"Where are you, Jackson?"

The moment I heard her voice, I knew that something was wrong. "Creek House," I said. "About to meet with Tex. Why? What's going on? Did you talk to Moreno?"

"I just received a call from someone claiming they saw you chasing Eduardo from the same park, where you met with Cruz. Is it true, Jackson? Did that happen?"

Everything inside me froze. I cursed—couldn't believe the late connection to Eduardo's murder. As much as I wanted to let it go, I couldn't. I asked, "Did the caller give their name?"

"No."

Of course not. Though there was no way to prove it, I had a feeling it was Moreno. My gut was saying we were getting close to unveiling our culprit, and I assumed they could feel it too. But I could also hear the doubt creeping into Sanchez's voice, and that bothered me. She was losing trust at the exact moment I needed her to believe in me most.

I asked Sanchez, "Where is Moreno? Have you talked to him?"

"I don't know where he is and I can't seem to reach his cell." Then Sanchez told me about her conversation with Mary.

I leaned back and stared off to my left. Everything I had assumed about Moreno earlier seemed to ring true. I didn't like the feeling I had in my stomach. A fight was coming and someone was about to die.

How could he possibly know we were onto him, and where did he run off to?

My mind raced.

I thought about contacting the upper brass to alert them to what I was uncovering, but I didn't feel like I had their full trust, either. That gave me no choice but to keep this a secret and continue on the path until we were proven wrong—or killed ourselves. Why no one else had picked up on this was beyond me, but it also had me thinking about Whitney.

"Find Moreno," I said to Sanchez, "and let me know when you do."

I sat for a few minutes, thinking things through. Then I called Whitney.

"Everything still okay?" I asked when she answered.

"Fine here."

"You haven't seen him, have you?"

"No. I've been looking, too." Neither of us said anything for a long pause, then Whitney requested I stop by later. I considered it and didn't see a reason I shouldn't.

"Please, Jackson," she asked kindly. "It would make me feel better if you did."

"I'll be there as soon as I finish up work."

I gave her an estimated time of when that might be, and then got out of the Cruiser to marvel at the setting sun. It hung low in the sky and the grill at the restaurant was just getting started. My stomach rumbled with hunger and I realized I had gone most of the day without eating.

Once inside, I ordered a drink at the bar and was half-finished with it when I caught sight of Bolin coming in from the back. As if knowing I was here to speak with him, he came straight for me. "I've been looking for you." We shook hands. "There's something I needed to talk you about," he whispered into my ear.

It sounded serious and I couldn't wait to hear it.

"Take a seat at a back table," he said, "and I'll bring us some food."

I found my way to an empty table and couldn't keep still. He had me curious to know what couldn't wait. Fifteen minutes later, Bolin strode to the table with two plates of hamburgers and fries. He set one plate in front of me and said, "I hope you like yours medium rare."

"I do."

"Then it's on the house."

After taking my first bite, I said, "I heard you stopped by my place."

"You have quite the neighborhood watch program." He lifted his gaze and my thoughts skipped to Ronnie. "That place is a dump. What are you doing living over there?"

When I mentioned my divorce, Bolin realized his mistake.

"I'm sorry. I forgot."

"Don't worry about it."

"Have you caught the person who did it?"

"No," I said. "What is it you needed to tell me?"

Bolin lowered his burger away from his mouth and looked at me from beneath his brow. "They captured the fight you had the other night on about a half-dozen cellphones," he said, correcting course.

"Hope I looked good for the cameras," I said.

Bolin wasn't amused. "I took them down for you."

I stopped chewing. "You did?"

"Would you have preferred I didn't?" He quirked an eyebrow. "I didn't think so. What are you thinking, fighting Raymond Frank's guys?"

"Long story," I said, sipping my beer.

Bolin knew what it meant to lose better than most of us, and I knew how it looked, but it wasn't about that. Or maybe it was. I really didn't know anymore. I just wanted to make things right for Ilene and Selina.

"Do you recall the name Eduardo Rodriguez?" I asked.

Bolin's spine straightened. He squinted his knowing eyes and nodded.

"You and Moreno questioned him for murder three years ago."

"And we cleared him of any involvement."

"But the case was never solved."

"Why are you asking? You think he might have killed your family?"

"They found Eduardo murdered early this morning."

He leaned back, inhaled a deep breath of air, gripped the table and stared. Then Bolin said, "Remember I warned you about Moreno's grudge?"

I nodded.

"Well, Eduardo was the reason."

"What do you mean?"

"I mean, once Moreno learned about Eduardo jacking cars, he wouldn't let the kid get out of his sights. It seemed every time he saw Eduardo, he'd find a reason to pull him over on some bogus suspicion he made up in his head." Bolin looked me in the eye and said, "Eduardo wasn't perfect, but he also wasn't the man Moreno thought he was."

"I'm not sure I follow."

"This one time, Moreno and I were drinking off duty. Just

a couple drinks after work. Must have been a tough week. Anyway, we called it a night and after I hit the head, I found Moreno outside pointing his service weapon at Eduardo's heart."

"What the hell for?"

"Moreno claimed Eduardo was breaking into a car."

"Was he?"

"We later learned the car was Eduardo's. He had locked his keys into his own car."

"Christ."

"The incident seemed to embarrass Moreno because, after that, he found any excuse to pull Eduardo over, as if to remind him who controlled his freedom."

"And all this happened before they questioned Eduardo for the murder of the young teen?"

"Exactly." Bolin nodded. "Moreno knew before we arrested him that Eduardo was innocent, but Moreno wanted to scare the shit out of him again, as if Eduardo was challenging his manhood or something."

It was a lot to hear, but, after a moment of thought, I asked, "Do you think Moreno has it in him to kill?"

Bolin raised both his eyebrows and said, "I don't have to tell you, because I think you already know the answer yourself."

CHAPTER ONE HUNDRED SIXTEEN

I HUNG AROUND THE BAR FOR ANOTHER HOUR TOSSING darts, thinking through Bolin's story and waiting for Tex to finish up with work. As surprising as Bolin's story was, I wondered why I hadn't heard it before. It seemed like a story that would have gotten out. Regardless, it explained everything I had already been thinking about Moreno. Once again, I was feeling sorry for Bolin. He played by the book, did everything right, but when it was all said and done, he learned how unfair the world really was, reduced to having to work security detail for minimum wage.

When I didn't hear from Tex, I called to see what was up. He answered his phone and I asked, "You still up for that drink?"

"Oh, shit. I'm sorry, Jackson. I lost track of time. It seems like I'm up to my eyeballs with paperwork tonight." He must have known I had something I needed to ask, because he said, "Why don't you stop by my place instead?"

I said I'd be there shortly and pointed toward Bolin on my way out the door as a way of saying goodbye, let's do this again sometime soon. I was on my way to the Cruiser when I

spotted a Ford F-150 speeding away. I stopped in my tracks
and stared in its direction, certain it was Moreno. Unfortunately, there was no way to be sure as it was too dark to see
clearly. It didn't make me feel good that he could have been
here.

I thought about warning Bolin, but then thought twice
about it. Bolin was no longer in the game and I didn't see him
being in any real danger—at least nothing he couldn't handle
himself.

I arrived at Tex's house fifteen minutes later and let
myself in. "Don't shoot," I said, announcing my arrival. "It's
only me."

"In the kitchen," Tex called out.

Tex's house was beautiful. A large four bedroom he had all
to himself. I walked through the living room, past the deer
and elk and African antelope hunting trophies he'd taken over
the years, and found him with his head down at the kitchen
table.

"Can I get you a drink?" Tex asked without ever lifting his
gaze. He pointed at the bottle of bourbon on the table. I
thought better of repeating last night's mistake.

"Not tonight," I said.

Tex lifted his eyes and stared as if he couldn't believe I'd
say no to whiskey.

"I just wanted you to know it wasn't Frank who left me
Selina's birthstone."

Tex leaned back and took off his reading glasses. I imagined I had a similar face when coming to the same conclusion. Tex asked, "Did you find that guy you were looking for?"

"I did. He was murdered last night."

Tex sighed and reached for his tumbler. "Is it connected
to the other murders?"

"I don't have any evidence to prove it, but yeah, I
think so."

I caught him up to speed, said how I believed Eduardo's murder was made to look like Frank did it. I told him about the unknown Jane Doe at the strip club and my desire to find her. Tex crossed his forearms, then stroked his chin. He kept shaking his head like he couldn't believe what was happening —wondering if it would ever stop.

"If it wasn't Frank who left Selina's birthstone, then who was it?" Tex asked.

"You might be right about the killer having my Walker Colt," I said. "Deputy Moreno was seen outside my apartment the night I found Selina's birthstone, and he was also recently spotted spying on Whitney Voak, and I can't shake the feeling that he's the only one who mentioned anything about that particular pistol."

"Why spy on Whitney?" Tex asked. "What does she have to do with any of this?"

"She was with me the other night," I said. "She saw Moreno at my apartment—"

"And he must have seen her there." A witness.

Tex understood the implications of being in the wrong place at the right time, but he also made the next prediction for me.

"If you're right about this, Moreno is going to use your gun to kill Frank and frame you for it."

A chill moved down my neck. I was afraid Tex might be right. I said, "Then it's up to me to stop it."

CHAPTER ONE HUNDRED SEVENTEEN

THE MOMENT RAYMOND FRANK STEPPED INTO THE kitchen, Candy knew he wasn't happy.

"Where the hell have you been?" Frank asked.

"Nowhere," Candy said.

"Bullshit. Don't give me lip. I've been looking all over for you and you weren't answering your phone."

"I needed some space." Candy closed the fridge door and took her juice into the living room where she plopped down on the couch and turned on the TV.

Frank followed her with a suspicion that she wasn't telling him the complete truth. He wondered what it was this time, if she was speaking to the cops without him knowing again. It could be anything with her. After all they had been through, he found it hard to accept she'd decided to give him up now.

Standing over her, Frank asked, "You were with that cop again, weren't you?"

"I was at the gym." Candy barely glanced in his direction. "I needed to blow off some steam."

The word steam had Candy thinking about her day with Mr. Flirt. It was going so well. Then something happened that made him change his mind. She didn't know what it was exactly, but thought she had said something she shouldn't have. He left her with a false promise to do it again sometime soon, but she knew it would never happen and that disappointed her.

Candy said to Frank, "You can't keep me cooped up inside all day like a caged animal. I'm a free bird who needs to fly."

"Don't get smart with me," Frank snapped, just as the house intercom rang.

Frank motioned to Smalls and told him to answer the call. Smalls slid off the stool and lumbered across the room, pounding his finger into the box on the wall. A voice rang out and said, "An officer of the law is here to see, Mr. Frank."

Frank gritted his teeth and glared at Candy.

"It wasn't me," she said. "I didn't bring him here."

Frank hurried into the den, opened the cabinet door, and checked the video monitors to see which officer wanted to visit. Stupid gate rent-a-cop was getting smart, too, Frank thought, losing patience with everyone around him.

"It's my goddamn lawyer," he said, buzzing him up. Then he motioned at Big to get the door. "Freshen up or get lost," he told Candy. "We have company."

"You're such an asshole," Candy said, turning off the TV and prancing to her bedroom.

A minute later, Frank's lawyer walked through the front door. He set his briefcase on the counter, took off his coat, and made himself at home. "I did some digging," he said to Frank, "and it wasn't Steve Eli."

"You're certain?"

Lawyer nodded. "I had my investigators check him out. The story about his vehicle getting stolen is legit. The police weren't lying."

"And the man murdered last night?"

"Eduardo Rodriguez. Convicted of grand theft auto,

served nine months in prison. No telling if he also stole Steve's Range Rover. The investigation is ongoing, and public relations hasn't doled out any information on it."

"Regardless," Frank said, "it's no coincidence Steve's vehicle was at the same nightclub I was at."

"Agreed."

Frank still had no clue who had sent him the envelope, but it was clear it was from someone who knew about his beef with Jackson. Now he understood why Jackson had been riding his ass all week, and it had nothing to do with his acquittal.

"They're going to blame me for last night's murder," Frank said.

"They don't have anything."

"We don't know what they have."

His lawyer sighed.

"If it's not Jackson or Steve trying to set me up, then who could it be?"

"There is one other name I had in mind."

"Who?"

The man looked Frank in the eye, and said, "Whitney Voak."

CHAPTER ONE HUNDRED EIGHTEEN

As soon as I left Tex's house, I called Whitney. The line rang in my ear as I climbed into my Cruiser and fired up the engine. I tried not to worry when she didn't answer, but I did. It was ten minutes before ten o'clock; late enough to convince myself she had called it a night and gone to bed.

That was what I hoped had happened.

I drove faster than I should have and didn't take the most direct route. Most of my focus was behind me instead of the road ahead. I saw nothing to suggest I was being followed, but seeing Moreno speed away from Creek House tonight had me concerned with what he had planned next. The last thing I wanted was to lead him straight to Whitney's and have him see us together again.

Before I knew it, I was on Whitney's block and quickly approaching her condo. I spotted Frank's Royce parked in the exact spot Whitney swore Moreno had been parked, only twenty-four hours ago.

I tapped the brakes and felt my heart pound.

There was a great deal of fear bubbling up inside of me that had me thinking I was too late.

Turning the wheel to the right, I zipped up the adjacent street and parked. Then I was on foot, trying to figure out who might be sitting in Frank's car. I couldn't risk ruining the element of surprise, and I hurried back a block questioning everything, including if I was wrong to think Frank might be innocent.

When I came up behind Frank's Royce, I crouched low to the ground, stayed in the shadows, and pulled my sidearm. With both hands gripping my pistol, I snuck up to the back windows and peeked inside. The tint made it near impossible to see through, but I was fairly certain the car was empty. Then I checked the front seats before holstering my weapon.

Whitney's condo lights were on and, though the drapes were drawn, I could see movement behind them. I counted three people inside, but planned on there being at least four. Regardless of Frank's reason for being here, I got excited just thinking about my chance to pound my fist into both Big and Smalls again.

I entered the building through the front and passed the empty concierge desk before skipping the bank of elevators in favor of the stairs—which I took two at a time. At the second floor landing, I drew my SIG, cracked the door an inch, and peeked down the empty hallway. The floor was silent, when I slid out into the open. I shut the door quietly behind me before moving quickly down the hallway, only stopping at Whitney's front door. Once there, I could hear the soft murmur of conversation inside.

Certain they didn't know I was here, I held my hand over the peephole and knocked.

CHAPTER ONE HUNDRED NINETEEN

As soon as I heard the door open, I side-stepped to my left, squared my shoulders, and kicked the heel of my boot dead center into the wood grain. The door held, but hit whoever was behind it square in the nose. I dropped my left shoulder and burst inside to screams and shouts, quickly shutting the door behind me.

Big made a move like he was going to charge me. Acting on the sound of his grunt, I aimed the P320 at his fat head and said, "Take another step and you're dead."

He stopped, growled, and tossed up his hands in a show of surrender.

Just below me, Smalls lay on his back holding his bleeding nose. "You broke my nose," he cried, though no one paid him any attention.

Frank remained seated at the kitchen table and just stared like he'd seen it all before. His hands were empty and his shoulders had a slight slouch to them. Though nothing about him was threatening, I kept my aim on Big and flicked my gaze over to Whitney.

Her big green eyes were round and watery and it killed me

to see how scared she was. This was probably her first face-to-face encounter with the person she had testified against—the same man she claimed held the murder weapon that had killed her sister.

I asked her, "You okay?"

Whitney nodded, but kept her arms tightly wrapped around her slim body. Judging by what she was wearing, it looked like they had caught her by surprise; a silk bathrobe with nothing underneath. Her red hair was pulled into a ponytail, and I regretted taking that extra hour at Creek House when waiting around for Tex.

"Jackson, put your gun away," Frank said.

I moved my eyes to his. "Not until you tell me why you're here."

Frank clasped his hands on the table and shared a quick glance with Whitney. Then he sent Big and Smalls outside. Big helped Smalls to his feet; I stepped to the side to let them pass. As soon as the door closed behind me, Frank said, "I thought about what you said to me earlier."

"And?"

"You were right."

"Care to elaborate, or are you going to make me guess?"

"I didn't murder Mr. Rodriquez, but I think I might know who did."

Whitney glared at Frank and said, "I told you I didn't do it."

Frank chuckled and shook his head.

"What the hell is going on?" I asked, still holding my gun on Frank.

Frank said, "You had me curious to know who would want to frame me for murder. So, after my visit to the office earlier, I had a nice discussion with my lawyer about how I was certain you'd get me for last night's murder."

Whitney kept bouncing her gaze between Frank and me.

She seemed calm enough to let this ride out. I suspected where this was going, but I kept my mouth shut to see if I was right.

"But something about it didn't seem right—" Frank said, putting his eyes back on Whitney. "—that is, until her name was mentioned."

Interrupting, I asked, "Have you been followed?"

His eyebrows pinched and he stared at me with squinted, untrusting eyes. He had every right to not believe me, but I had to sell him on the theory Tex and I had worked out.

"It's important you tell me," I said. "Were you followed here tonight?"

"No," he said, but his eyes told me he didn't know if that was true or not.

Not caring, I said, "You're in danger, Frank."

"Until you put your gun away, I'm not going to argue with you on that." He chuckled.

Whitney silently pleaded with me not to follow his suggestion. But I had no choice. As soon as I tucked it away, Whitney closed her eyes and shook her head as if it was all over now.

It was a strange group to have come together, but I needed to believe it was meant for a reason. A glimmer of curiosity caught Frank's eye, and I watched his spine straighten with renewed confidence. He kept glancing from Whitney to me, wondering if this was part of some elaborate plan of ours.

"It's not us you should be concerned about," I said.

"Then who should I be watching?"

"The person who sent you my divorce papers."

"And who is that?"

I knew he was thinking it was Candy I was referring to, but I enlightened him when I said, "I think it might be a cop."

"A cop?"

I nodded. "Who's intending to murder you with my gun."

Frank shifted his gaze to Whitney and pointed his index finger at me. "Is that a threat?"

"It would be a lot easier if it was," I said, quickly explaining how I came to the conclusion. Frank kept swiping a hand over his face, and Whitney looked as skeptical as he did. Then, when I was finished explaining things, I said, "I know it sounds crazy, but you have to agree it makes sense."

Frank was quiet for a long pause and, for a moment, I thought he had actually believed me. Then he got up from behind the table and brushed past me. "If I get killed by a gun you own, how could I not think you had something to do with it?"

When Frank left Whitney's condo without another word, I wondered if I'd ever see him alive again.

CHAPTER ONE HUNDRED TWENTY

WHITNEY HURRIED TO LOCK THE FRONT DOOR AND THEN scurried across the floor to the living room windows. I stood beside her and, together, we watched Frank climb into the back of his Royce. A moment later, the headlights flicked on and I saw Smalls look up at the condo from the front passenger seat. Our eyes met and something told me he wouldn't forget who had broken his nose.

After we watched them drive away, Whitney asked, "What is going to happen now?"

"Either Frank believes me or he doesn't."

Whitney released the drape, moved to the couch. She dropped her head into her hand and looked smaller than she actually was. I heard her stifle the tears and joined her on the couch, where I put my arm around her. She leaned into me and I felt her entire body tremble.

After a minute of silence, she said, "I thought they were going to kill me."

"You're safe now."

Whitney lifted her gaze, brushed the hair out of her eyes,

and looked at me for some kind of reassurance. "You're going to kill him, aren't you?"

My chest tightened around my heart at the sudden impact of her words. Her beautiful green eyes made it impossible to look away. There wasn't anything I could say to convince anyone any differently. She believed what Frank had, too.

As much as I wanted to kill Frank for the evil he'd done, I couldn't. Who I wanted, was Moreno. Even I struggled to understand how I suddenly wanted to protect the monster, who only a week ago, I couldn't wait to see put in prison.

I took her face into my hand and stroked her soft cheek with my thumb. "Not unless I have to," I said.

She told me with her eyes to find a way, then she wrapped her arms around my waist and refused to let go. It felt good to be held. We clung to each other and got lost in the rhythm of our breaths, letting our thoughts drift this way and that. When I closed my eyes, I held onto something warm and genuine.

Whitney made me believe we were meant to be together. It made sense. We'd both lost the people we cared about most, and were brought together because of it.

Soon, we were on our feet, rocking back and forth, forgetting about Frank's visit entirely. Then, slowly, her fingers crawled up the center of my chest before clasping behind my head. There was a crackling in the air and, when I opened my eyes, she stood on tiptoes and pressed her moist lips against mine.

My entire body lit on fire.

What started slowly, quickly grew into something more passionate—something I hadn't had in my life in a very long time. I forgot what it felt like, how great it was, and though I didn't care to understand how she did it, I was suddenly falling backwards onto her bed.

All my worries disappeared. I didn't fight what I was feeling—what was happening. I wanted it as bad—if not more —than she did. Then she ripped off my clothes, dropped her robe to the floor, and was on top of me, taking me to the moon and back.

CHAPTER ONE HUNDRED TWENTY-ONE

VIPER CLOSED HIS EYES, STILLED HIS HEART, AND ACCEPTED he was out of time.

He went through his plan again inside his head, anticipating every scenario he could drum up so that he'd know exactly how to react and what to do when it happened. Tonight, there couldn't be any mistakes. This was it. His chance to seal his legacy and make his mark on the world that thought so little of him.

"Game, set, match," he muttered as he opened his eyes.

A sly victorious grin tugged at his lips. Though all the pieces were in place to ensure he'd succeed with his mission, there was one variable he couldn't control that could destroy it all.

A vehicle came; another went. He was tucked behind the steering wheel of his Ford, discreetly parked between two SUVs, having gone unnoticed for the last hour. He sat in the dark and, each time anxiety crept up his chest, he pushed it back down by inhaling a deep breath of air.

Viper was counting on his girlfriend to come through. Though he'd trained her well, a rookie was a rookie, and rookies made mistakes. But even that was part of Viper's plan.

Palming his cellphone, he messaged his girlfriend. *Ready?*

Viper checked his mirrors. The line waiting to get into the nightclub was growing and the big bouncer was slow to allow more through. A minute passed without a response and he worried she'd fallen asleep or, worse, could not leave.

Then his phone dinged with a response. *Born ready.*

Be outside in ten.

Viper started the engine, left the parking lot, and headed across town to pick up his girlfriend. Ten minutes later, he was parked in the back. The night was pitch black and even the house lights were turned off. A second later, he spotted his girlfriend hurrying to the car through the shadows with hair bouncing off her rolled back shoulders. Viper liked the confidence he saw and knew without a doubt she was ready to assist him with his next murder.

She opened the door and dropped her bottom onto the seat. Viper flipped on the dome light, leaned over and kissed her on the cheek. He said, "You smell like sex."

She smiled and touched his face. "Just playing my part."

Viper latched onto her wrist, leaned over and kissed her again. Though he felt guilty for doubting her abilities before, in this moment she was absolutely incredible.

"A role you play well," he said. "Now, shall we get on with it?"

"We shall, darling. We shall."

CHAPTER ONE HUNDRED TWENTY-TWO

I AWOKE THE FOLLOWING MORNING AND FOUND MYSELF alone in bed. It took me a moment to come to, and when I did, I remembered where I was and who was supposed to be next to me.

Wondering how long Whitney had been gone, I reached my hand beneath the covers to her side of the mattress and splayed my hand flat on the bed. The sheets were cold to the touch; she'd been gone for a long time.

I lifted my head off the pillow, perked an ear, and listened. The condo was quiet. I looked to the bathroom. The door was open and the lights off. Nothing came from the kitchen, either, and I was certain I was alone.

Feeling uneasy about the situation, I swung my feet to the floor and slipped on my boxer shorts before reaching for my piece neatly tucked beneath my pillow. Then I checked my phone with my free hand.

There were no messages or calls, and nothing from Whitney.

Feeling like something was off, I tightened my grip on my pistol and padded lightly into the kitchen. Again, everything was dry and cold to the touch. At the window, the drapes were already open, and I peeked outside to the street below.

Taking a deep breath, I convinced myself not to worry, figuring she hadn't gone far and wasn't in any kind of trouble. But I was feeling the morning-after regret and, as great as the sex had been last night, it put me into a deep slumber that made me lose all sense of awareness.

In the bedroom, I dressed and started snooping around. Her silk robe hung on the bathroom door and her toothbrush was damp. It was the first sign of life I had come across, and it settled at least some of my worries. But it also got me curious to find more.

I opened drawers, peeked into her closet, and poked around in the bathroom. Snooping into Whitney's private life wasn't something I was comfortable with, considering our complicated history, but I needed answers. Whitney was an enigma who was hard to define. There was a lot I didn't know about her, but the more I looked around, the more I understood her story.

She was a career woman with a deep moral compass. A daughter. A sister. And a woman who had lost everything the moment her sister was murdered. I couldn't decide if Whitney slept with men regularly or if last night was just a fluke.

Nothing suggested Whitney was the type of woman who picked up men at bars. Last night was completely unexpected for both of us; not something either of us had planned. But there was still something I couldn't get out of my head. Whitney had come to my house uninvited the night Sanchez discovered Selina's birthstone, and she convinced me it was nothing more than coincidence. Then my mind jumped to last night and how Frank seemed to have connected with Whitney, too.

I turned my head and stared at the queen sized bed.

Was Whitney trying to get Frank charged for new crimes by killing Eduardo? Did Frank figure that out before me? It had crossed my mind once before that Whitney was something more than what she appeared to be, but until now I refused to believe it was possible that she had it inside her to manipulate and murder. Now I wasn't so sure. Just because she didn't seem like the type to do it, she was certainly smart enough to pull it off.

Then, when I thought about what Moreno might be planning, I doubted myself entirely. Was I getting played? Had Whitney actually seen Moreno parked outside my apartment, or was he there to make sure nothing happened to her? But why tell me about it if they were working together?

I didn't know what was happening, but I knew I needed to figure it out soon.

CHAPTER ONE HUNDRED TWENTY-THREE

WHITNEY WASN'T ANSWERING MY CALLS, AND I WASN'T feeling any better about her leaving without saying goodbye. I was genuinely concerned for her safety and, when feelings of betrayal kept creeping up, I had to remind myself of the fear I saw in her eyes when sitting across from Frank. That was real, and so was the way she held onto me as we made love. At the time, nothing about it felt fake, yet here I was questioning its authenticity.

As I drove around looking for her and her red Camaro, I kept wondering if I had let my guard down, when I shouldn't have.

The week of murders was wearing me down, but there was something about Whitney I couldn't let go. Perhaps it was because everyone I got close to had been murdered and I was afraid she might be next. Or maybe it was because I wasn't one to easily forgive. Whatever it was, the rational side of me told me to stop calling a woman, whose trust I was now putting into question.

Finally, I tossed my phone onto the seat next to me and punched the dash.

I couldn't allow anger and grief to take control of my life. I'd suppressed my emotions for nearly a week now, but I felt the shell I'd been hiding inside, crack. I didn't like what was about to hatch. If I wasn't careful, my insides would begin pouring out and I might as well kiss this investigation goodbye.

I kept up the search for Whitney. After looking everywhere I thought she might be, I finally called it quits. Truth was, I didn't know her well enough to know where she might be, and soon I was running in circles. But there was one last place I thought to look; it was the one option I really didn't want to explore but knew I had to at least take a look.

I jerked the wheel hard to the left, flipped the car around, and sped toward Moreno's house, feeling like there was no time to lose.

CHAPTER ONE HUNDRED TWENTY-FOUR

Viper had lost his sense of direction when his girlfriend lazily asked him, "Where are you taking me?"

He realized he hadn't told her, and now he was certainly going to keep it a surprise. They'd been driving for nearly an hour before Viper turned onto a gravel road. The tires crunched over the stone—*snap, crackle, pop*—and he was happy to have exchanged the city skyline for views of rolling prairie and brush. Out here he could breathe, relax, let his guard down.

"I thought you said we wouldn't be gone long?"

"Why? What's the rush?" Viper asked, turning his head to look her in the eye. "Someone going to miss you while you're gone?"

She stopped twirling her strand of hair around her finger and glared at him. "I just wasn't aware we'd be going so far from home," she said.

"Does that worry you?"

"Should I be worried?"

They shared a quick glance. Neither of them had humor in their eyes.

They hadn't discussed what had happened last night, and Viper wasn't sure they should. He could see she was fine with what they had done, and it was better to let it go into the wind than rehash what might cause problems in the future. Besides, the world would soon learn about their actions. Before that could happen, Viper needed to prepare her for one last stand.

A mile further, Viper parked. He opened the car door and stepped into a warm breeze. There was a mild humidity in the air and the sky was overcast gray. He made his way to the back and popped the trunk.

"You coming or what?" he called to his girlfriend.

Once out of the car, she stood and stretched, squinted across the distant horizon. "There's nothing out here. How did you find this place?"

"A friend of a friend," he said, digging through his bags.

His girlfriend kept brushing hair out of her eyes as she lazily made her way to the back of the car. "You're not going to bury me out here, are you?"

Viper dove into the trunk and wrapped his hands around a fat, cold melon. He swiveled toward her and dropped it into her hands.

"What's this for?" she asked.

Viper said, "See that rock outcropping over there?" He jerked his head to the right. "Set it on top. We're going to practice your long distance shooting."

She stared across the way. "Long distance shooting?"

"It's your turn to pull the trigger next."

Her eyes lit up, and he told her to hurry and place the melon.

As she trotted off, he got the rifle ready. When she was back, Viper said, "This is a Remington Model 700 CDL 30-06 Springfield Bolt-Action Rifle. It has an effective firing range of one thousand yards." His girlfriend reached for the rifle stock but Viper pulled it back and continued, "There is a flip up rear leaf sight for ranges exceeding two-thousand-five-hundred yards, but point-blank range for standing, man-sized targets is a measly five-hundred yards."

"Who am I going to be killing?" she asked. "I didn't know there was anybody left."

"There are over seven billion people on this earth. Trust me when I say, there are plenty of people deserving of punishment."

"Okay, you won't tell me who, then how far away do you expect me to hit my target?"

"You'll be shooting from one-hundred yards out." Viper chambered a bullet, handed her ear and eye protection, and led her to a clear spot in the dirt. "You'll be lying on your stomach when you shoot."

She dropped to her knees, then lowered herself flat onto the ground. Viper laid next to her and set up the rifle to her right. They got into position and he told her to take aim at the melon.

"Line it up like I taught you and, when you're ready, pull the trigger."

A still second passed before she fired. The bullet exploded out of the muzzle and the melon detonated into the air.

"Fuck me," she said, lifting her eyes above the scope.

Viper laughed. "Do it again?"

"Oh, hell yeah."

This time they lined up three melons and two milk jugs and she hit them all. Each one exploded with vigorous energy.

"You're a natural," he said.

"I have an excellent teacher."

Viper reached behind his back and dove his hand into his back pocket. He showed the picture to his girlfriend and said, "Now imagine putting a bullet between his eyes."

She studied the picture. When her head snapped up, her

eyes said it all. She couldn't believe he was asking her to kill *him*.

Viper smiled. "It's what you asked for, isn't it?"

She swallowed and nodded.

"Then what are we waiting for?"

"What now?"

"If you don't do it, I will."

CHAPTER ONE HUNDRED TWENTY-FIVE

MORENO LIVED IN A SINGLE-STORY HOUSE IN A MIDDLE-class suburb where nothing exciting ever happened. I had never visited, but it was one of those things everyone just knew.

I parked a block away and just sat and watched.

I was still coming to terms with the idea that Whitney wasn't who she said she was. Though there was no sign of either Moreno or Whitney, I waited for over an hour before losing patience and deciding I'd better inspect inside.

As I walked casually to Moreno's house, I stuffed my hands into my jacket pockets and kept an eye and ear out for anything suspicious. Instead of going to the front door, I headed to the back.

The house needed repair. The paint was chipping and it needed a new roof. At the back door, I opened up my swiss army knife, jammed the blade into the keyhole, and twisted it hard until I heard the lock release.

With my gloved hand on the doorknob, I glanced behind me, put my knife back into my pocket, and entered the house with my M17 drawn.

I stayed at the door for a long minute, listening to the house sounds. Enough outside light filtered inside for me to see clearly. I was certain Moreno wasn't home, but I cleared the house, anyway. First the kitchen, then the living room, the bath, and hallway closet, then the spare bedroom, finishing at the master. I paid little attention to detail, other than making sure I wasn't about to be ambushed, but I did notice a woman's underwear on the bed that had me thinking about Whitney.

Moreno had pictures of himself on the hallway walls and I stopped to study the progression of his career. First the Army, then him in his sheriff's uniform. He was a proud patriot and defender of the second amendment; a man who took his job seriously. But it was at his gun safe in the spare bedroom, where I asked myself if this was where he kept my Walker Colt.

Knowing it would be impossible to break into, I turned to face the corkboard wall behind me. On it was an impressive and thorough display highlighting his own investigation with me at the center.

It wasn't just me he had pictures of, either. There were also those of my family, Vincent Cruz, Eduardo Rodriquez, Raymond Frank, Whitney Voak, and Alan Bolin. I studied it quickly, following his lines back and forth, but it wasn't until I saw the mention of a Karambit knife with a Walker Colt that my heart beat faster.

Now I was certain it had been Moreno, who I saw speeding away from Creek House last night. When I remembered the story Bolin had told, I had a bad feeling that Bolin wasn't as safe as I thought he might be.

CHAPTER ONE HUNDRED TWENTY-SIX

I took a picture of Moreno's investigation board with my cellphone, before leaving through the same back door I had entered. Now I was racing toward Creek House, hoping to find Bolin, so I could warn him about what might be heading his way.

"C'mon, answer me."

Bolin's phone went straight to voicemail and I left him an urgent message telling him to call me back. Five minutes later, I slammed on my brakes, parked near the entrance of the bar and grill, and ran inside to see what I could find.

They had just opened their doors for the day and it took me a couple minutes to find someone who could answer my questions. "Alan Bolin—is he here?" I asked the first person I saw.

A man behind the counter said, "If he's working, he'll be here later."

"Later won't work. What about his house? Do you know where he lives?"

"Sorry, man. I don't."

Running out of options, I headed back to the door when

the woman at the front stopped me. "I heard you're looking for Alan?"

"Yeah. You know where he lives?"

She squinted her college-aged eyes at me for a quick second before she smiled. "That's right. You were with him last night."

"That's right, I was."

"I thought I recognized you."

"So you know where he lives?"

"What's it about, anyway?"

"Forget about it." I made for the door and she stopped me.

"Don't tell him I told you. He's only taken me there once before and he doesn't like visitors, but I can see you have something important to tell him."

She handed me a small note with his address scribbled on the back. I glanced at it and said, "Thanks," just as my phone buzzed in my pocket. When I saw who was calling, I answered. "You're alive."

"Have you seen Frank?" Candy softly asked.

I had so many questions I needed to ask her, but felt like I should ease into the conversation before asking why Frank took her to a strip club the other night, or what she knew about Eduardo's murder, and if she recognized the mystery woman texting with him that night. Instead, I said, "No. I thought he was with you?"

A long pause of silence followed. Then, finally, she said, "He's not, and no one has seen him since last night. He's not answering his phone, Jackson, and I'm worried about him."

My thoughts jumped to last night and how I had warned Frank he was in danger. Now I was certain that Tex and I were right about Moreno.

"I don't know what I should do," Candy said.

"Do you know where he was last night?" I asked.

"Nightclub on Red River."

"I'm sure his friends wouldn't let anything happen to him."

"You'd be right, except Frank was alone. The club wouldn't let anyone but him inside."

I assumed it was because of our fight the other night, but why did Frank go there after Whitney's? Did he consider it a safe place, or had he met someone there? And if he did, who could that be? I was asking myself all these questions, but it was the next thing Candy said that knocked me sideways.

"There's talk you had something to do with it," Candy said, in a non-threatening tone.

My thoughts did a U-turn in my head and, once again, I was thinking about Whitney. The paranoid side of me had me asking if this was some kind of setup. Had Frank fooled us all? Was he really the killer I thought he was all along? Did he see his chance to get away before getting caught?

"Where are you?" I asked.

"At Frank's."

"Anyone know you called?"

"No."

"Stay put. Pretend this conversation never happened." I didn't think she actually would, especially not if she also believed I had something to do with Frank's disappearance, but it was worth a try.

Candy raised her voice and asked, "Do you know where he is or not?"

"I'll look into it."

"Please tell me I didn't get him arrested."

My mouth opened, but no words came out. It wasn't until then that I realized Candy thought Frank was still alive. Now that she mentioned it, a small part of me hoped he was too.

CHAPTER ONE HUNDRED TWENTY-SEVEN

I LEFT THE BAR, CLIMBED INTO THE CRUISER, AND CALLED Sanchez. She answered after the second ring. "I still don't know Moreno's location," she said into my ear. "Something weird is going on, Jackson. It feels like I'm being excluded from the investigations. Is that even possible? Would they do that to me?"

I said, "Candy called. Said Frank is missing."

"What do you mean, missing?"

"He wasn't arrested, was he?"

Keyboard keys clacked and then Sanchez said, "He's not in the system. It's quiet around here. What the hell is going on?"

I turned my gaze out the window and thought about everything I needed to say. "Not over the phone," I said. "Can you meet me?"

"Of course. Where?"

"My house."

"I'm leaving now."

Ten minutes later, I rolled up to the apartment complex, painfully aware of it being an easy place to strike. My nerves were tense and I thoroughly vetted the entire two-block radius before parking my car on the side street.

A warm breeze swirled around my ankles as I walked toward my door. I kept looking around, taking notice of every parked car. I made mental notes of license plates and if the vehicles were occupied or not. Then I slipped into my apartment without being noticed, closed the door, and looked for any fresh surprises that might catch me off guard.

CHAPTER ONE HUNDRED TWENTY-EIGHT

VIPER PARKED NEXT TO A MIDNIGHT BLUE TOYOTA SEQUOIA and killed the engine. Neither he nor his girlfriend had spoken during the drive back into the city. After a minute of sitting in silence, Viper turned to his girlfriend and said, "Do exactly as I taught you and you'll do fine."

Her head was turned away, but she nodded in response. Viper thought her face looked pale, but didn't mention it to her.

"If you miss the shot—"

"I won't." She turned her head and looked Viper in the eye.

Viper grinned at the confidence in her voice. "But if you do," he continued, "chamber the next round and try again."

"Realistically, how many chances do I have?"

"Two."

"Then I'll make it in one."

Viper looked at the clock, said, "The delivery truck should have arrived by now."

"I'm ready."

They opened their doors at the same time and met

behind the vehicle. Viper unlocked the Sequoia with the key fob and took the rifle case from the back of his Ford, loading it onto the backseat of the Toyota.

"When did you do this?" The girlfriend asked about the custom platform in the back of the Toyota.

"When you weren't looking." He smiled, jerked his head, and motioned for them to both climb inside. Once the doors were shut, he prepared the rifle, and said, "You'll be able to shoot from the platform without being seen." He powered down the rear hatch window to show her how. Then he continued, "Once you've taken out your target, immediately power up the window and sit still. Don't move. Don't drive away. Just wait. No one will be able to see you inside, and that will be the most difficult challenge you'll face all day."

"Okay. Just wait. Got it."

"Only drive away when you're absolutely certain you're a ghost." Viper angled toward her, put his hands on her shoulders, and said, "I won't be too far behind. If it doesn't go as planned, I'll be there to pick up the load, but you should be fine as long as you get yourself set up exactly where I showed you."

She nodded, blew out another breath.

He gripped her hands and felt her pulse ticking in the tips of her fingers.

"How long will I have to wait until he shows?"

"Shouldn't be too long, but longer than you think. Don't watch the clock, and if, for whatever reason, he doesn't show, you'll hear it first from me."

"Okay." She ducked her head and swiped at her blowing hair.

"Now, remember, you'll be one hundred yards out, but as long as you have a clear shot, take it."

Another nod of the head.

"Oh, and I nearly forgot." He reached into his pocket and revealed a black velvet box. "I got you a gift."

Her eyes sparkled when she looked into his. Then she gasped after she opened it up. "It's beautiful," she said.

Viper spun her around, clasped the 18K gold chain around her neck, then kissed her goodbye, knowing it would be the last time he'd see her alive.

CHAPTER ONE HUNDRED TWENTY-NINE

JONATHAN THOMAS PACED IN FRONT OF HIS WHOLESALE lighting shop and couldn't stop glancing at his wristwatch. It had been nearly five minutes since he had called the police and he was growing impatient.

"What do you want us to do?" the delivery driver asked Jonathon.

"Nothing. When I can open my doors, I'll let you know."

"Suit yourself." The delivery driver shrugged. "We get paid regardless."

Jonathan cursed under his breath. He glanced at the wreaker off to the left, then swung his eyes to the right where he caught sight of the first APD black and white heading his way. Their bar lights were flashing, but they didn't appear to be in too much of a hurry.

"For chrisake, hurry up," Jonathan said, jumping into the street, waving both his arms over his head. The police cruiser stopped in the middle of the street and parked near the tow truck. As soon as the officers exited the vehicle, Jonathan said, "About time you guys arrived."

"What seems to be the problem?" one of the officers asked.

"That car." Jonathan pointed toward the Rolls Royce. "It's blocking my delivery bay."

"Uh-huh."

"I open at eleven. Each minute they're here is a minute I have to pay for." Jonathan jerked his head over his right shoulder to get the two police officers to follow along.

They shifted their eyes toward the delivery truck driver who was smoking a cigarette and tugging on his belt in an attempt to keep his pants from falling down.

"Why can't you just have it towed?" an officer asked.

"That's just it. We were about to do that, but the driver noticed what he said was blood on the outside, and thought maybe he shouldn't touch it."

The officers shared a skeptical look with one another. "Do you know whose vehicle it is?"

"I would have told you if I did."

"All right. Easy. We'll take a look."

"Considering the price tag of the vehicle, I'm guessing it's someone well-known. That car runs over $300K. I looked it up."

The smaller of the two officers called to the tow truck driver. "You were the one to find the blood?"

"That's right." The driver hurried over. "On the back bumper. Not really droplets; more like a smear." He pointed.

The second officer was on the radio talking with dispatch. "Pearl white Rolls-Royce Cullinan."

First officer crouched down near the bumper to have a closer look at the supposed blood. Then he put his hand to his brow and peered inside the vehicle.

"I tried that myself," the shop owner said. "It's like peering into the night, the tint is so dark."

First officer pulled away from the back window and shook

his head at the second officer. "Have you tried opening it?" he asked Jonathan.

"You kidding? What if there's a body inside?"

Second officer opened the hatch and, as soon as the lid lifted, an intense smell billowed out into the air.

"Jesus Mother Mary," Jonathan said, jumping backward, cupping a hand over his nose and mouth. "He's missing half his head."

CHAPTER ONE HUNDRED THIRTY

I WAS OUT OF THE SHOWER BY THE TIME SANCHEZ WAS knocking at my door. I let her inside and said, "I made coffee."

"That would be great. You must have a lot to tell me."

I looked over my shoulder and caught her staring at my couch as if wondering where I had slept last night. Before she could ask, I put a black coffee on the counter and said, "The anonymous caller who said they saw me chasing Eduardo—"

"Yeah. What about them?"

"Is it possible it was Moreno?"

Sanchez slid onto the bar stool and wrapped her hands around her mug. "I think I would have recognized his voice."

"But can you be sure it wasn't?"

"What are you getting at, Jackson? And how does this relate to Frank? He's the reason you invited me here, isn't it?"

"Frank visited Whitney last night."

Sanchez's eyebrow twitched with surprise. "Is she all right?"

"She was last night, but now I don't know," I said, filling in the gaps. "Whitney swore she saw Moreno staked outside her condo the other night."

"Wait, you mean to tell me Moreno is stalking you both?"

I nodded, summed up the reason I was at Whitney's. "But the reason Frank was at Whitney's was because he thought she was the one who sent him my divorce papers."

"The papers Candy brought to the station?"

"Exactly."

"Did she?"

"I don't see how she could have, but we never established it either, because I had something I needed to share with Frank."

"Which was what?"

"I think he's in danger."

"What kind of danger?"

I shared the theory Tex and I had put together about Moreno and my missing Walker Colt. "Everyone knows I want Frank gone, and what a perfect way to frame me for the murder. Don't you think?"

Sanchez stared into her full mug, pondering everything I'd just said. "Are you sure you're not getting played? I mean, you said it yourself, no one knows where Frank and Whitney are right now."

"Possibly," I said. "But take a look at this."

I opened my cellphone and showed her what I had found inside Moreno's house.

Sanchez gripped my device with both hands, and, after a quick look, she asked, "How did you get this?"

"It's better I don't tell you."

Sanchez sighed. "Jesus, Jackson. You know what will happen if the deputy chief learns about this?"

My face said to study the board, and she did. A minute later, Sanchez put it together. "If I'm reading this correctly, he's already got to him."

"I don't think Candy would have called if he hadn't." We locked eyes, and I said, "And he'll go after Bolin next."

"That's what I don't understand. Why Alan Bolin? What's he have to do with any of this?"

I rehashed the conversation I had with Bolin at Creek House and told her the story of Moreno's grudge with Eduardo Rodriguez. "Moreno was there last night at the bar. I saw him speeding away just as I was leaving. He knows Bolin is helping me piece it all together."

Sanchez was on her feet, pushing her fingers through her dark hair. I could see how it was all coming together for her, but it was the call she received from Central Command that changed everything.

CHAPTER ONE HUNDRED THIRTY-ONE

SANCHEZ TOOK THE CALL IN THE KITCHEN. I PRETENDED not to listen.

"Uh-huh. I see. Understood," Sanchez said.

It was a quick conversation. Then the call ended.

"Austin Police found Frank," she said.

"Where?"

She told me where, then added, "Murdered in the back of his Royce."

My temperature spiked. I knew it was happening. "How was he murdered?"

"I don't know. They've asked me to come down to confirm his identity."

"What? Why?"

"I didn't ask."

My heart was pounding faster, and I knew this was it. But there was something they weren't telling Sanchez, and I couldn't figure out what it was.

She said, "I suppose it's because they knew our office had a recent history with him."

"Maybe, but still—"

"It's okay. This gives me a chance to see how he was killed."

"My guess is it will be from my missing Walker Colt. If it is, then Moreno will have it stashed somewhere and he'll miraculously find it, to become the local hero he's always wanted to be."

"You really have it all figured out, don't you?"

My eyes lifted and fell on Sanchez.

"What is it now?" she asked after seeing my face.

I looked her in the eye and said, "Unless they're taking you away to clear the path to get to me."

Sanchez's eyes went wide. "Jackson, you mean to tell me you think they're coming after you?"

"That's exactly what I mean. Which also means they might already know you're here."

I told Sanchez to go before it was too late. She gathered her things off the counter and said, "But what about Bolin?"

"No time to discuss," I said. "If Moreno is behind this, like I think he is, he'll make his next move and head straight for Bolin while everyone's sights are set on me. You let me worry about him and text me if you can. If Frank was murdered with anything other than my gun, I need to know about it."

"Okay. I will."

She hugged me goodbye and told me to be careful. Then I pushed her out the door, intending to leave soon after.

CHAPTER ONE HUNDRED THIRTY-TWO

THINGS WERE HAPPENING MUCH FASTER THAN I EXPECTED.

Through the front window, I watched Sanchez drive away and then I hurried to get ready—to prepare for the inevitable war heading my way. The clock was ticking. I didn't know when they'd come or from what angle, but I expected to see them soon.

In the bedroom, I dumped the cardboard box out onto the floor and rummaged through the contents, reaching for my vest. I slid the Kevlar vest over my head and secured the straps around my chest, then attached my Fairbairn-Syke's tactical knife to the inside of my boot.

On my way out, I tore a jacket off the hanger in the closet and headed to the front of the apartment. Before opening the door, I looked up and down the block. I didn't have the greatest view, but things seemed quiet enough. Then, on my next breath, I opened the door, dipped out the front, and edged my way around the building before hurrying to my Cruiser, where I climbed inside and sped away just as the first sheriff's vehicle arrived.

CHAPTER ONE HUNDRED THIRTY-THREE

SANCHEZ TRIED CALLING MORENO'S CELLPHONE WHILE SHE drove, but he didn't answer. Jackson had her thinking. She knew Moreno was up to something, but could it be what Jackson was suggesting? She didn't want to believe it, but Moreno had been working secretively nearly the entire week. He certainly seemed set on getting back at Jackson for something.

She arrived to the crime scene a few minutes later and was welcomed by a large fleet of emergency vehicles and EMS vans. After parking, she checked in with the recording officer and made her way to the lead detective.

"Deputy Sanchez," he said when he saw her. "I'm Detective Theodore."

"This is city jurisdiction," Sanchez said, getting straight to it. "Why get the sheriff's office involved?"

Theodore held still for a beat, then said, "Follow me and you'll see why."

A chopper flew overhead and Sanchez shot a quick look at the news vans circling on the far perimeter. A crowd had grown, as if everyone knew it was Raymond Frank who had been murdered. Even with the canvas wall put up to block the view, news had spread.

"The owner of the building called it in," Theodore said. "At first he was going to have the car towed, but then the tow truck driver noticed blood smeared on the back." Theodore stopped at the back of the Royce. "Officers arrived, and well...found this."

Sanchez rounded the back bumper and looked inside. She'd seen a lot over the years, but nothing like this. Raymond Frank lay in a fetal position with half his skull blown off.

"Murder weapon?" she asked.

"Location unknown."

The ME working on Frank turned to Sanchez, said, "Victim was shot in the back of the head and exited below the left eye."

Sanchez didn't need an explanation. She could see it for herself. It looked like a canon had split his noodle in two.

"Definitely high caliber. Very close range." The ME pointed to burn marks on the head. "Executed sometime early this morning, but not here. Whoever did this drove the car here with the body in it, then left the scene."

Techs were busy dusting for fingerprints, collecting fibers and hairs, anything they could pick up inside the vehicle.

"Why dump the car here?" Sanchez asked.

"Could be random. Maybe they knew we would find it at a certain time. Hard to say," Theodore said.

"Okay, so I'm familiar with the victim, but I still don't understand why I was called to assist. Seems like you have everything under control."

Detective Theodore dove his hand into his coat pocket and produced an evidence bag. He showed it to Sanchez. She peered through the clear plastic and read what was written on a napkin in ink.

IF FOUND MURDERED, JACKSON PAYNE DID IT.

Theodore said, "We found it inside the victim's pocket."

Sanchez glared. Everything inside her wanted to lash out and smack Theodore across the face. But if Jackson was right about this, what else was he right about? And why did it seem like she was the only one to believe him?

"Don't hate me. I'm only the messenger," Theodore said, taking back the evidence. "Apparently they didn't trust you wouldn't try to protect your partner."

CHAPTER ONE HUNDRED THIRTY-FOUR

MY EYES WERE GLUED TO THE VIEW BEHIND ME. MY thoughts as well. Focused on the rearview mirror, I dug out the note I had received earlier from the attractive woman at Creek House and refreshed my memory of Bolin's house address. It wasn't far, but it would take me longer than normal because I had to stay off the major streets and avoid being seen.

Something told me that if I got caught, Bolin would die. It was up to me to save him.

My phone was quiet in my pocket, but I didn't need Sanchez to tell me what I already knew. The sheriff's office told me Frank had been murdered the moment they came to arrest me.

I stopped at stop signs, rolled inconspicuously down side streets, while keeping a close eye on my surroundings, knowing full well that every deputy and officer in the city of Austin were now looking for me.

I couldn't get to Bolin's soon enough.

It took every ounce of strength to drive within the speed limits. To pass the time, I let my thoughts drift over to

Moreno. I needed to think like him. What would he do, where would he go, how would he attack? I had to think like a murderer. After the week I had, it came far too easily. Though it was impossible to plan an exact counter attack, since I didn't know the layout of Bolin's neighborhood and house, I tried anyway.

By the time I got to his block, I was fully expecting to see Whitney's red Camaro parked near his house. Instead, Bolin's short driveway was empty. I rolled past, making note of everything I saw. His garage was closed and there weren't any signs he was actually home.

On my second pass around, I pulled to the curb and parked. A new vehicle had arrived in the short time I was gone. That was when I knew this was really happening.

CHAPTER ONE HUNDRED THIRTY-FIVE

MORENO SAT IN HIS TRUCK FOR A LONG TIME. EVEN through the binoculars, I couldn't tell exactly what he was doing. I wondered if he'd followed me or was just fulfilling the prophecy he'd laid out on his private investigation board. I was suspicious of his timing and considered myself lucky to have circled the block a second time.

I was parked behind a Suburban, but not completely out of sight. At any minute, I could be seen. Perhaps that was what he was waiting for? Backup.

Feeling like I couldn't wait for him to make his next move, I reached for my SIG, chambered a round, and gave myself seventeen shots to get the job done.

I hoped it would be enough.

To my surprise, Moreno opened his door first. I watched him step out beneath the mid afternoon sun and look around. If he knew I was here, he didn't show it. Nothing changed my mind. I still assumed he was here to murder Bolin.

Moreno headed toward the house. I liked that he was out in the open. He didn't hide his presence; even the way he walked seemed overly confident. A strut that said he'd gotten away with murdering five times before, so why not make it six?

I quietly opened my car door and slid out, without him noticing. I was certain he wasn't expecting anyone to be watching what he was doing. He'd created the perfect diversion, as they redirected resources to searching for me, while also dealing with Frank.

As if he'd caught a sudden scent in the breeze, Moreno stopped and turned on a heel.

I quickly crouched low to the ground and watched him draw his sidearm. His eyes darted from side to side and I could tell he was on edge. He had that same tense look on his face, as when learning he might be suspended. Then, when he turned his attention back to the house, I sprang into action.

Hurrying between thick tree trunks, hedges, and parked cars, I soon took cover behind his truck. Moreno hadn't heard me and I watched through the car windows as he checked to see if the house door was locked. It was. Then, on swift, tender feet, I snuck up behind him and pointed my M17 at the center of his back.

"Put down you weapon, Moreno. It's over."

CHAPTER ONE HUNDRED THIRTY-SIX

MORENO HELD STILL. HIS HAND WAS STEADY ON HIS PISTOL, but he never raised it above his waist.

With his back to me, he said, "What are you going to do, Jackson, shoot me, too?"

"I'd love to. Give me the chance and I'd do it in a heartbeat," I said.

He angled his head just enough to get a visual through the reflection in the house window. I stepped to his right and took away his line of sight. Keeping my muzzle pointed at his heart, I said, "I figured you out. You're finished."

"Figured me out?" He raised his arms out to his sides and slowly turned to face me. "Oh, you mean how you think I had something to do with this past week's crime spree?"

The moment our eyes locked, my memory jostled through the files that led us to this point. A visual display played out in my mind. I saw my murdered family, remembered the leaked surveillance video and Selina's birthstone, his rousing me into believing he had my Walker Colt.

"I know it was you," I said.

Moreno laughed. "Not this again," he said. "How many

times do I have to tell you, it wasn't me who killed your family?"

"I know about your hatred for Eduardo Rodriguez."

"When will you realize we're on the same team?"

"That's why you're here, isn't it? To silence another witness?"

"You have quite the imagination," Moreno said. "But this time, your creativity isn't doing you any favors."

"Then why were you at Creek House last night? And why have you been stalking Whitney?"

"Is that what this is about? Did you fall in love, Jackson? You don't have to worry about her—"

"Where is she?!"

"I don't know."

"Bullshit!"

"Believe what you want, but Bolin—"

It happened in less than three seconds. A loud buzzing sound flew above my head, and a second later my cheek burned from the shattered window that exploded behind Moreno's shoulders. His head detonated right in front of me and split like a melon. Then the air cracked behind me, in what sounded like a shot from a single hunting rifle.

I hit the deck to take cover and began my search for the shooter.

CHAPTER ONE HUNDRED THIRTY-SEVEN

I MEASURED TIME BY COUNTING THE BEATS OF MY HEART. Twenty seconds passed, then thirty. I waited for the next bullet to arrive, but it never came.

One shot. One kill. Then complete silence.

I was trying to wrap my head around that as I lay flat on my stomach, busily bouncing my eyes between structures, inside parked cars, through house windows. Nothing moved; not a sound was made. With Moreno gone, it felt like I was alone. Just me and the undisclosed shooter that had murdered him.

Feeling like a sitting duck, I needed to move— fast. Next second, I commando crawled to the side of the house where I took position. A shot was never fired, and though I assumed there was only one shooter, I didn't know.

My skin burned with shrapnel and I clawed at my face, taking out shards of glass. Blood dripped, but nothing serious. When I looked at Moreno, I knew he was gone. But who had killed him? And why?

I leaned back against the house and closed my eyes. Then I replayed everything that just had happened inside my head.

I did the calculations and estimated the bullet's trajectory, dividing it by the time Moreno was hit, to the sound that followed after. The shot had to have been taken about seventy-five to one-hundred yards out and done by a skilled marksman.

With that in mind, I turned the corner and looked up the street to the north.

There were a couple possibilities, but it was the single Toyota Sequoia I had my eye on. I recalled seeing it there on my first pass through the neighborhood, and it was definitely there on the second. At the time, I thought nothing of it, but whoever was inside saw everything. Which meant they didn't want to kill me, but were aiming for Moreno.

On my next breath, I stood and began my march to the vehicle, hoping I was right.

CHAPTER ONE HUNDRED THIRTY-EIGHT

MY HEART BEAT FASTER WITH EACH STEP THAT DREW ME closer to the blue Toyota. The windows were tinted a deep shade of black. Though I couldn't see inside, I could feel I was being watched.

I kept my grip firmly secured around my SIG, my finger on the trigger. I pointed it at the back corner of the SUV, ready to be raised at a moment's notice.

I was tense but ready to strike. Then, without warning, the engine cranked and the taillights glowed red. As soon as it sped off the line, I popped off a couple of shots at the back tires but missed. Then I sprinted back to my Cruiser, climbed inside, and hurried to speed after it.

It didn't take me long to find it speeding through the neighborhood. There were really only two ways out, and I was familiar with both. Whoever was driving must have seen me coming, because they went even faster.

My engine revved and then I watched the Toyota nearly tip onto its side when it took a right-hand turn too hard. The tires slammed back onto the pavement and kicked up a white smoke. Once all four wheels were spinning, the SUV went even faster, weaving between traffic.

Somehow, I freed my cellphone and call Sanchez.

"You were right," she said by way of greeting.

"Moreno is down," I yelled into the phone.

"What? Where?"

"I'm chasing the suspect now." I gave her the description of the vehicle, then told her where to find Moreno. "The driver is going for I-35. I need air support. We're going Southbound at about seventy on the frontage road—"

Then the most extraordinary thing happened. Not believing my eyes, I watched the Sequoia lose control and crash into a parked eighteen wheeler on the side of the road. Slamming on my brakes, Sanchez listened to me skid to a stop. I dropped my phone onto the seat and jumped out of the Cruiser with my P320 in my hand.

The Sequoia's engine hissed and spewed a thick white smoke. The driver wasn't moving and appeared unconscious. Cautiously, I opened the driver's door and discovered a woman, alone.

Her head was bleeding badly, and her legs had been crushed. I glanced to the back and saw a Remington bolt-action rifle attached to some kind of platform. Then I checked for a pulse. It was faint—she was still holding on— but I didn't think for too much longer. Though I didn't recognize her face, I was familiar with the necklace she was wearing. No doubt in my mind it was Ilene's.

Something popped, then the semi caught fire.

As the flames grew larger, I worked the woman free, dragging her to safety. It was too late. While we waited for help to arrive, I took the necklace from her neck and watched her die.

CHAPTER ONE HUNDRED THIRTY-NINE

THERE WAS NOTHING I COULD DO TO SAVE HER. HER injuries were too severe.

Eventually, I moved away from the body and sat on the side of the road, clutching Ilene's diamond necklace inside the palm of my hand. I wanted to know who this woman was, why she had killed Moreno, and if she was the murderer behind this week's ongoing massacre.

The fire continued to blaze out of control, traffic stopped in both directions. The air overhead blackened with smoke and people shouted for me to get further away, but I didn't respond. I felt numb, confused, but mostly just sad and tired.

Soon, every cop and emergency vehicle in a five-mile radius was working the scene, and I still didn't know who this person was or how she fit inside the puzzle. Inside, I knew she was the woman caught on tape, messaging Eduardo the night he was murdered outside the strip joint.

"Jackson Payne?"

I looked up.

A uniformed Austin Police Officer stared down and said, "They have tasked me to take you into custody."

"Am I under arrest?"

He and another officer helped me to my feet, took away my gun and knife, and cuffed my hands behind my back. I was put into the back of a squad car and, once seated, leaned my head against the glass to stare at the scene unfolding before me. I watched the firefighters work to put out the blaze, as Austin police prepared to search the Toyota.

I was taken away and, though the ride to the station didn't take long, I closed my eyes and didn't open them until I heard the engine stop. They had taken me to the Central Command office. I was never booked, but they put me inside an inter-view room and told me to wait.

"I'd like to call my lawyer," I said.

The rookie said, "A detective will be with you shortly."

"Did you hear me? I'm requesting counsel."

The door closed. They had denied my request. They were delaying the inevitable, and I couldn't figure out why.

Nothing happened for the longest time. An hour passed. Then two. When the minutes were closing in on hour number three, the door finally opened.

Sergeant Hart entered the room, and my spirits lifted, along with my head. "What the hell am I doing here?" I asked him.

Hart sat across from me and said, "They didn't tell you?"

"I didn't kill Frank," I whispered.

"I believe you—"

"But do they?" I asked, pointing my finger at the two-way mirror on the wall.

"You left us a big mess to clean up today, Jackson."

"Who was she?"

"You don't know?"

"Besides the person who shot Moreno, no."

"Is that why you were chasing her?"

I inhaled a deep breath and Hart saw I wasn't going to get

roped into answering his questions. He said, "Give a little, take a little. You know how this works."

"Am I under arrest?"

"No. Not yet."

I leaned back in my chair and nodded my head. "Yes. It was. I saw everything. Now tell me, who was she?"

Hart's eyes squinted at the corners. "We'll get there. First, I need you to tell me where you were last night."

"Not until you tell me why you think I'm responsible for Frank's murder?" I knew they had something on me, but I couldn't figure out what. Maybe Moreno had the Walker Colt closer than I thought he did.

"Were you with anyone?"

I stared into his eyes and it was clear he was only asking because he already knew the answer. It crossed my mind that maybe they had Whitney in custody. It would explain her sudden disappearance. I asked, "Is she okay?"

"Is who okay?"

The games Hart was playing were driving me nuts. I still didn't know if Whitney was who I thought she was, or if she had played a role in Frank's murder. Finally, I said, "Whitney Voak. Is she okay?"

Hart's eyes told me my answer surprised him. "Is that who you were with?"

"I slept at her place."

Hart looked toward the glass and something told me Sanchez was listening to the conversation, learning about my affair. But I still didn't know exactly when Whitney dipped out or where she was now, and my alibi was only as good as my word, until she backed it up.

I watched Hart stand and leave the box without saying another word. None of today made any sense, and neither did his quiet departure. My head was pounding with a thick headache and, a minute later, Hart entered the room and dropped a picture of my Walker Colt onto the table in front of me.

I didn't know where he found it, but I knew what he was suggesting.

"I want my lawyer," I said. "Wyatt Blackwell. I don't say another word until he's here."

CHAPTER ONE HUNDRED FORTY

A HALF-HOUR LATER, SANCHEZ OPENED THE DOOR AND KEPT it open.

"Can you believe this shit?" I asked. "I told you this would happen."

"Her name was Allison Joslin."

I jerked my head back. "Was that who was messaging Eduardo?"

"We believe so."

"What about my gun? Where was that found?"

"Inside the Toyota she was driving."

I leaned back, pushing a heavy hand through my hair. Now I understood what was happening. I said to Sanchez, "I didn't plant it, if that's what everyone is thinking."

"We know."

"You know?"

"She's the one, Jackson."

"What do you mean, the one?"

"She killed your family."

"It can't be." I narrowed my eyes and angled my head. "It doesn't make sense."

"It didn't to us at first, either. After we identified her, we searched her apartment. Inside, we found an overwhelming amount of evidence, all of which suggests she's the person we've been looking for."

I dropped my gaze to the left. Sanchez continued giving me specifics to help convince me Allison Joslin was our killer. "The evidence is still coming in as we speak, but we believe she was pretending to be Eduardo's girlfriend. We found a set of keys to the Range Rover, and the Karambit knife used to kill him."

"What about Samuel White? Where did he get the uniform?"

"Her. It was all there, Jackson."

I kept shaking my head. "How did she get a sheriff's jacket?"

Sanchez shook her head. "Still a mystery."

A quiet beat passed before I asked, "Was Frank murdered with the Walker Colt?"

"Almost definitely." Then she told me about the note found in his pocket. "Do you know why he would have written that?"

I told her the complete story of how I had found Frank at Whitney's and what I said to him. After, I brought my elbows to the table, looked Sanchez in the eye, and leaned forward. "This Allison, she's a nobody. Don't tell me she went on a murdering spree for no apparent reason."

"Life doesn't have to make sense, Jackson."

I slammed my fist onto the table. Sanchez's pen went airborne. "Then how do you explain Moreno following me? Watching Whitney? Huh? How can you explain that?"

Deputy Chief David walked into the room and said, "I assigned Deputy Moreno to keep an eye on you. First, out of precaution, then to build a case against you. As you can imagine, we were extremely concerned about your mental state, after losing your family."

"If you were so concerned about me, why not just take my shield until I cooled off?"

"Because we knew we'd lose you."

"You're a skilled detective," Sanchez said. "You almost had this right."

Though I was furious, they were maybe right. I would have walked away, probably forever. But almost, wasn't good enough.

I sat for a long time thinking about Allison, and everyone just stared. It still wasn't adding up for me. She didn't fit the profile, and I'd never seen her before in my life. I asked the questions and the conversation soon circled back. There wasn't anything I could say to convince them otherwise, but if Moreno was building a case against me, why did I find him at Bolin's? With that thought in mind, I stood and made my way to the door. No one tried to stop me, or tell me I couldn't leave.

On my way out, I said, "But you lost me anyway."

CHAPTER ONE HUNDRED FORTY-ONE

I SLEPT AT THE APARTMENT ON MY COUCH AND WOKE EARLY the next morning, to figure out who exactly Allison Joslin was. I needed to see the evidence for myself. Have a peek into her life. Know without a shadow of a doubt, she was the person Sanchez said she was. Allison might have had the evidence to convince a jury she was guilty of the murders, but not me.

The hours passed quickly as I retraced Allison's footprints. First, I stopped at her one-bedroom apartment in North Austin and looked around. All the evidence Sanchez said they had found was gone and, with it, my chance to see it with my own eyes.

I wrote my resignation letter at lunch, then stopped at Allison's last known place of employment. It was a strip joint on the east side, where I learned Allison had quit dancing three months ago.

"Why?" I asked the manager.

"Never gave a reason. None of the other girls knew why, either. It seemed the decision was made completely out of the blue."

"You don't seem bothered by it."

"Her loss was someone else's opportunity."

I asked, "Did Allison ever exhibit any violent tendencies?"

"She could pretend to be tough, but deep down she had a kind heart. I never asked, but I didn't think she was cut out for this kind of work. Men can be dawgs and women love to get their claws out. But Allison was quick to learn and seemed determined to make it work. That's what I'll always remember about her. She was extremely curious and highly impressionable."

I explained this past week's crime spree and the club manager was aware of what had happened. But he seemed shocked when I suggested Allison had anything to do with it.

"Look," he said, "Allison was smart, but if she did what you're suggesting, I don't think she would have done it alone."

Before leaving, I asked about past boyfriends, clients Allison might have been dating. The manager wasn't aware of any names but also admitted to not wanting to know, either.

Again, I was left with only the speculation swirling in my gut. The case was far more complicated than what it appeared to be on the surface.

My next stop on the circuit was Bolin's house. When I arrived, I found him loading up his Ford Bronco with boxes.

The scene had since been released, but crime tape still hung on the far reaches of the property. As I approached the house, I watched Bolin traveling back and forth between his garage and vehicle, walking over the stain of blood that marked the place where Moreno had died.

"Going somewhere?" I asked by way of greeting.

Bolin turned and didn't look surprised to see me. "I don't know where, but I can't stay here," he said.

"What are you going to do with it?" I asked about the house.

"I suppose I'll fix it up and put it on the market. Though I don't expect anyone to be interested in purchasing a home where..." His words trailed off. Bolin had a look that said he couldn't believe what had happened.

I said, "I get it."

"I never thought he'd actually come for me."

I opened my cellphone and showed him a picture of Allison Joslin on the screen. "Do you recognize her?"

Bolin took my phone into his hand and stared at Allison's picture. A moment later, he said, "I heard it was a woman who had shot him. Is that her?"

I nodded. "Her name is Allison Joslin."

Bolin handed back my phone, and asked, "Who else did she kill?"

"They are saying she's responsible for it all."

"They? I thought you were one of them?"

"Not for much longer," I admitted for the first time out loud.

Bolin said, "Some days I don't miss being a cop." His eyes met with mine, and he asked, "What's next for you?"

I looked away, shook my head. My thoughts were on Montana and giving myself time to grieve. I said, "I haven't decided."

"You're better than I could have ever been. Still, you don't look satisfied."

My cellphone buzzed. I flicked my eyebrows and said, "I'm not."

I left Bolin to finish packing and I answered the call on my way to the Cruiser.

"Hi, Jackson."

"Whitney."

"I've been meaning to call—"

"Yeah."

"I'm sorry. I should have left you a note."

"It would have made things less awkward for me." An uncomfortable pause followed, and I waited for her to say something. When she didn't, I asked, "Where did you go?"

"I don't regret what we did," she said, "but you scare me, Jackson."

Her words knocked me backward. I knew I shouldn't have been surprised, but I was.

"Bad things follow you," she said. "I mean, look around and you'll see how many people around you were getting hurt. I didn't want to be the next."

I didn't know what to say, so I told her the truth. "It's over," I said. "We caught the suspect who's responsible."

"That's good. I'm happy for you."

I said, "I'd like to see you again."

"It's too late, Jackson. I've decided I'm leaving Texas."

"Leaving Texas?"

"I have cousins in Florida. I need to be around family. You understand that, don't you?"

I did.

I wished her the best, said my last goodbye, and thought how I could use a fresh start myself.

CHAPTER ONE HUNDRED FORTY-TWO

A WEEK PASSED, AND I STILL HADN'T LEFT TEXAS. I'D SINCE resigned from the Travis County Sheriff's Office, but I was dragging my feet on leaving the state. Deep in my heart, I knew it was because I wanted to delay having to say goodbye.

My family deserved better, and the death of Allison Joslin wasn't the closure I wanted.

Internal Affairs dismissed Frank's complaint, and I never received an apology from the local journalists who had accused me of murdering my family. They moved on to the next story like nothing had ever happened, without concern or care that they destroyed my reputation. As difficult as it was, I was learning to let some things go.

Caroline was expecting me in Montana in two days and, though I knew my departure was inevitable, I felt like I was leaving prematurely.

No matter what I did to convince myself that it was over, I couldn't. I still struggled with the idea that a random person I had never met, did all this. Tex helped me through it, said he would do anything I asked of him. Except there wasn't anywhere to go or anything for him to do.

Allison Joslin had a mountain of evidence in her apartment, but never gave a reason for her actions. There was no letter of intent, no manifesto, just a presumed vendetta to publicly humiliate me, sprinkled with an affection for mean men who did bad things.

I kept wondering, how did she know where Bolin lived? Was her manager right in thinking she couldn't have done this alone? How did she know Moreno would go for Bolin on that day, at that exact moment?

I didn't have answers to any of those questions, but I kept coming back to Moreno's private investigation board, and that was when it all came to me.

What if Moreno wasn't there to kill Bolin, but had suspected Bolin was behind the attacks? I thought back to that day and remembered watching Moreno sit inside his truck. The more I thought about it, the more certain I was that Moreno was only there to check out his theory that Bolin was behind the attacks, and somehow Bolin knew Moreno was coming. Bolin then covered his tracks, by making himself look like a possible target.

My heart beat faster. I was about to call Tex when there was a knock on my door.

I reached for my SIG on the counter, tucked it behind my waist, and went to see who was there.

The man stood close to the door, sideways, and his downward facing head had his face covered by the brim of his cap. I smiled, opened the door, and said, "Tex, you sonofabitch."

In a single split second, he lifted his head, raised his back arm, and shot me at point blank range.

CHAPTER ONE HUNDRED FORTY-THREE

THE SLUG HIT ME HARD AND FAST. THE PAIN WASN'T instant, but the impact was. It tore through my right shoulder and spun me completely around. I landed on my ass and bit my tongue. My left hand pressed against the wound and I fought to catch my breath. Then the pain hit.

I lifted my eyes and watched Bolin lock us inside. He stepped around me as the blood spilled between my fingers and I listened as he cleared the apartment to make sure we were alone.

As much as it hurt, I reached my hand to the back of my waist, searching for my pistol, but it was gone. I was looking for it when Bolin came back into the room.

"I thought about letting it go," he said, "and let Alli take the fall; but then I thought what a waste, after all this? Your family would have died for nothing."

"You'll never get away with this," I said through clenched teeth.

Bolin kneeled in front of me and stared at my wound. The fact I was still breathing had me guessing it was a clean shot —the bullet went straight through, hitting only muscle.

"I know it was harsh of me to kill your family," Bolin said. "But I needed to get your attention somehow. Did it work? Were you mad? Confused? I bet you were."

I glared from beneath a heavy brow.

"Want to know what they were doing before I killed them?"

"I know what they were doing."

"Ah, right. You were there yourself." Bolin grinned. "Did your wife wake for you? No? Not for me, either. But your daughter, Selina, looked as innocent as could be that night." He paused for effect, and I waited for my chance to kick him in the teeth. "The way her soft hair fell between the tips of my fingers—" Bolin laughed as he stood and moved away, as if feeling what I was about to do.

My legs were splayed out in front of me and I felt light-headed, I assumed because of the loss of blood. Bolin kept rambling on while I searched for my lost gun. I was thinking he had picked it up.

"I never imagined I'd like it so much," he said. "Turns out I had a knack for killing the innocent."

"What did anyone ever do to you?" I asked, coughing.

"Nothing like what you did to me." Bolin opened the fridge and I heard him crack a beer.

He was quiet for a long while before he said, "I knew they would acquit Frank. The DA's strategy was shit. I would even say they set you up to fail on purpose. Would you agree with that assessment, Jackson?"

I spit some blood onto the floor next to me.

"Manipulating Frank was easier than I had thought it would be. You two really hated each other. I must thank you for that." He howled. "Fools. All of you, fools."

I needed him to get close to me, to have a chance at surviving this. Bolin kept his distance and his muzzle trained on me. With each minute that passed, I grew weaker than the second before. He must have seen me losing strength because he kept talking about how great his week of killing was for him.

"One by one, I took them down." He listed off his many victims, telling me his reasons for killing each of them. "Cruz hesitated to tell the story I needed him to tell. Hesitated like I did when taking that shot."

"It wasn't—"

"Dead!" Bolin screamed loud enough for Ronnie upstairs to hear. "There is no room in this world for the weak. That's what I learned when the sheriff's office dismissed me."

"Is that why you killed Eduardo? Because you thought he was weak?"

"Eduardo was only a pawn to make you believe Moreno was the bad guy. He was onto me and something needed to be done to stop him. Too bad he was a hothead, because he was actually a good cop."

"Probably why he wasn't canned after the excessive force incident," I said. "But then that would mean the upper brass thought you were a bad cop, they could afford to let go." I was razzing him, pushing him closer to the edge to see how far he'd go before he broke. "Bye bye," I said.

He was red in the face, but quick to shake it off. He told me it was easy to kill Frank; he didn't need to explain his reasons because they were the same reasons I would have used to justify his murder, if I had done it myself. But I was curious about Allison.

I said, "And Allison was your fallback."

He shifted his eyes over to mine. "I had the entire city fearing I'd come for them next."

"You felt powerful."

"After I saw you kill that man, I could never look at you the same again. That's why you're respected by your peers,

Jackson. It's not because you're a great man, who does great things. No, that's not it at all. It is because they fear you."

Bolin exited the kitchen and crouched in front of me. He looked me in the eye when he said it, but all I could hear was Whitney telling me something similar.

"And you wanted that for yourself?" I asked.

"I was going to kill myself. It wasn't like I had anything left to lose after you took away my career."

"It wasn't me. I didn't do that to you."

"Yes, you did! You don't see it, do you? I loved being a cop. It was all I ever wanted to be, all I had. If not for you and your happy trigger finger, I would still work the job I love."

"They should have never let you go."

Bolin's watery eyes drifted to the floor. "Though you were first to shoot that day, I always knew I would be the one taking the last shot."

Bolin scooted forward and pawed my head with one hand while pressing the muzzle of his pistol to my temple with the other.

I calmly closed my eyes and turned inward. Working my senses, I relied entirely on instinct. I listened to Bolin breathe, the way his breaths whistled softly through his nose, and when I heard the faint sound of his trigger finger flex, I sprung backward a split second before he fired.

The bullet exploded into the opposite wall.

My head slammed hard on the floor and my ears rang, but it was the pain in my shoulder I felt most. Then I rolled to my right, brought my right knee to my chest and kicked Bolin in the mouth.

He flew backward and landed on his sacrum. I must have hit him just right, because he dropped his gun and cried out in pain. Seeing my opportunity, I scrambled on all fours and picked up his piece.

"Go ahead, do it," Bolin said as he lay on his back like a dog, his palms face-out.

I stood over him, thinking it was too easy. Bolin didn't deserve a quick death. That was the easy way out. Instead, I tucked the gun behind my waist and jammed the heel of my boot straight into his nose. Then I pulverized his face with my foot, kicking and stomping him repeatedly until he stopped moving. By the time I was finished working out all my pent up aggression, I spit on his face.

I did it for each of his victims, but mostly I did it for my family.

They died because he couldn't accept a decision outside of his control.

"An eye for an eye," I thought when I sat on a stool at the kitchen counter, finishing the beer Bolin had started and lighting myself a smoke.

I smoked my cigarette, conjured up a plan to patch up my shoulder, and stared at the piece of shit dying on my floor, asking myself what I should do with him now. By the time I was finished with my first cigarette, I lit another and dragged Bolin near the sofa where I carefully placed my smoke on the armrest. As the ember burned into the couch, I flipped Bolin onto his stomach and stepped back.

Soon, the couch caught fire. The flames flickered and licked up the walls. It jumped to the floor and spread like spilled water where it then caught Bolin's pants. I watched the fire get bigger—watched his skin blister and boil—and didn't leave until the fire got too hot.

With the apartment going up in flames behind me, I pulled the fire alarm and casually strode to my Cruiser, climbed inside, and started my journey north.

. . .

I hope you enjoyed the story. If you'd like to see more Jackson Payne thrillers, please consider leaving me a quick book review.

Never miss a new release. Sign up for Jeremy Waldron's New Releases Newsletter at JeremyWaldron.com

A WORD FROM JEREMY

Thank you for reading FIELD OF FIRE. **If you like the stories I'm writing, don't forget to rate, review, and follow. It really helps my books get in front of new readers.**

ALSO BY JEREMY WALDRON

The Samantha Bell Mystery Series

Dead and Gone to Bell

Bell Hath No Fury

Bloody Bell

Bell to Pay

Burn in Bell

Mad as Bell

All Bell Breaks Loose

To Bell and Back

Never miss a new release. Sign up for Jeremy Waldron's New
Releases Newsletter at JeremyWaldron.com

AFTERWORD

A special thanks to my editor and brilliant proofreaders for cleaning up the errors I missed. I couldn't do it without you.

One of the things I love best about writing these mystery thrillers is the opportunity to connect with my readers. It means the world to me that you read my book, but hearing from you is second to none. Your words inspire me to keep creating memorable stories you can't wait to tell your friends about. No matter how you choose to reach out - whether through email, on Facebook, or through a review - I thank you for taking the time to help spread the word about my books. I couldn't do this without YOU. So, please, keep sending me notes of encouragement and words of wisdom and, in return, I'll continue giving you the best stories I can tell. Thank you for giving me an opportunity of a lifetime.

Never miss a new release. Sign up for Jeremy Waldron's New Releases Newsletter at JeremyWaldron.com

ABOUT THE AUTHOR

Waldron lives in Vermont with his wife and two children.

Receive updates, exclusive content, and new book release announcements by signing up to his newsletter at: www.JeremyWaldron.com

Follow him @jeremywaldronauthor

- facebook.com/jeremywaldronauthor
- bookbub.com/profile/83284054
- amazon.com/Jeremy-Waldron/e/B07MJCG5QR

Made in the USA
Las Vegas, NV
06 March 2023